ICE

To Claire
(Shaftesbury Fringe 2017)

ICE

A TALE OF HORROR

FRANK PICKERING

Frank Pickering

evertype
2017

Published by Evertype, 73 Woodgrove, Portlaoise, R32 ENP6, Ireland. *www.evertype.com*.

First edition January 2017.

A catalogue record for this book is available from the British Library.

ISBN-10 1-78201-199-4
ISBN-13 978-1-78201-199-6

Typeset in Minion Pro and **Franklin Gothic** by Michael Everson.

Cover design by Michael Everson. "Ice Blue Photo" © Marina Scurupii, Mara008 | Dreamstime.com.

Printed and bound by LightningSource.

❋ CHAPTER ONE ❋

The valley cleared its throat and waited. Beneath a hissing T-bar six giddy teenagers heard without comprehending. "Shit! Thunder! Great! Triffic!"

Four boys and two girls sprawled in heavy snow. Like discarded sweet wrappers, they made a tiny patch of colour against the white mountain. Their laughter was swallowed by snow-heavy conifers. Rainbow clothing faded slowly to grey as the west-facing valleys gulped the closing light.

"That was your fault, Dean! Wanker," crowed Becky, her sharp features radiating venomous spite. "Thought you could ski."

"Fuck off, dog's breath. You didn't have to run into me. You got me in the bollocks with them ski-poles."

"Didn't know you had any."

"I haven't. Now."

Sniggers filtered through the darkening pines. They had squabbled and giggled from the moment Dean's legs had parted company on the drag lift, bringing him down and causing the others to bomb into him with the doomed inevitability of kamikaze pilots. Marco, brilliant in instructor's scarlet, had steered casually around the spiky tangle as he brought up the rear. "We finish now," he had called as he glided past. "You go down," and he had disappeared over the next rise. No-one followed him on the drag. Becky stared hungrily at his receding figure.

"God, he's so horny. Do you think he'll take us to his disco tonight, Lis?"

"No chance, you skinny cow," called Dean, fighting to remove his skis.

"I wasn't bloody talking to you, if you don't mind," said Becky. "Don't you fancy him, Lis?"

"Miss wouldn't let us," said Lisa.

"True. Bitch."

"Guppy? What you doin'?" Dean shouted at a leggy figure who had blundered to his feet and was wading like a zombie towards the trees.

"Goin' for a slash."

"Hey, Guppy's having a slash! Don't eat the yellow snow! Don't eat the yellow snow!"

Simon and Matthew, the two other boys, laughed and flung snowballs at Guppy.

"Just fuck off, will you!" he shouted over his shoulder, pulling up his collar with one hand whilst aiming with the other.

"Who wants a swig?" Dean asked.

"Whatcha got?"

"Beer. It's dead cheap. Me and Matty got smashed last night, didn't we, Matt?"

"Miss'll do you if she finds out," said Lisa. "It says in the booklet you get sent home for booze. Anyway, you're not supposed to carry bottles when you're skiing."

"Bollocks. Anyway, she won't find out."

"Gi's a swig, then," said Becky. The bottle circulated, emptied and was thrown into the trees.

"Anyone know the way down?" asked Guppy, fiddling with zips.

"Why don't we just walk down the T-bar?" suggested Lisa.

"It's bleedin' miles!" said Becky.

"Why's it gone quiet?" asked Simon.

They stopped talking and listened. An unregarded clock had ceased its tick. Wind hushed in the trees.

"The T-bar's stopped."

Above them, black crosses swayed from side to side, no longer ascending. They noticed the gloom and the gathering mist.

"What's the time, Matt?" asked Simon.

"Five past four."

"Don't they close the lifts at four?"

"Shit."

"We'd better get a shift on. We're supposed to meet old fart-face at four. She'll go mental."

Simon and Matthew struggled to their feet. Still clipped into their skis they began laboriously side-stepping up the slope. The others had removed theirs and were trudging upwards. Either way was exhausting.

Anita Shepherd stood conspicuously by the ski-waxing sign at the prearranged meeting point. Her bilious yellow hat with its oversized pom-pom was her prize for committing yesterday's "boob of the day"—walking into a window display at the hotel instead of out of the door. She had made sure the other staff voted for her to show the youngsters how to accept a joke against yourself graciously. She was a good teacher. The hat, she realized on this murky afternoon with snow falling and wind rising, was a useful beacon for the ski classes as they clattered up to be checked.

"Miss! Miss! Did you see me on the jumps? I went miles!"

"Yes, Gary, I saw you. I also saw you land. That is what is known as a 'head-plant'. Candidate for 'boob of the day' I think?"

"Ah, you wouldn't, would you, miss?"

"What's it worth, Gary?"

"I can tell you some worse ones, miss."

"OK. Save them for dinner-time." She turned to one of her colleagues. "How's it going, Paul?"

"All except Marco's group. Again."

"I shall have to have a word with him. It's not good enough. Would you and the other staff get this lot onto the cable-car and into the bus? I'll wait and bring the rest down."

"Yep. No problem."

She turned her gaze towards the pistes which converged here. The mountain was emptying rapidly. Nursery groups plodded in from their safe meadow, ski-schools trailed noisily down and independent skiers hurtled to spectacular, snow spraying stops. The temperature was plummeting and clouds of breath and cigarette smoke hung over the crowds as they queued to be winched down into the valley. Anita pushed her way through the crush towards the ski-school hut, searching for a string of fifteen year olds behind their red-clad leader. She was tugged from behind.

"Miss! It's bin great! Marco took us right to the top! I can nearly do a parallel turn now! He says we can try snowboarding later!"

"Thank God you're back, Julie! I was beginning to get worried. Where are the rest?"

"They're just comin', Miss, except for them what fell off the T-bar."

"What?"

"Dean and that lot."

"You didn't ski down on your own?"

"No, Miss."

"Has Marco gone back up?"

"No, Miss, he's gone 'ome."

By now more youngsters were gathered, bubbling with excitement.

"I'n't it great! I'm comin' back next year, can I , Miss?"

"Miss, what we doin' tonight, miss?"

Anita felt a twist of fear in her stomach. She asked herself, not for the first time, what she was doing here, away from Tom, looking after other people's children during her own half-term. Was it worth it for the two or three runs she managed each day, to be on duty for the rest of the twenty-four hours? She was a skilled, experienced skier but spent most of her time counting youngsters out and in, organizing every evening's activities, being first out of and last into bed, dealing with alcohol-induced quarrelling and vomiting, comforting the home-sick, medicating the bruised, the sprained, the ill. And worrying.

The ski-school hut, with its unhelpful, indecipherable notices, was shut and deserted. The cable-car had arrived and would soon be filling. She raised her voice.

"Shush, shush, shush, you lot, and let me think! Julie, which T-bar did they fall off?"

"That one, Miss," she said, pointing. "They were right near the top."

It was closed.

"Miss, the chair-lift goes to the same place. That's still running."

"You're right. Thanks, David. Now what I want you all to do is to go to the cable-car where you can see Mr Williams and Mrs Thompson. Tell them what's happened and that I'm going up to collect them. Then you go down and wait in the bus for me, OK?"

The chair-lift was disgorging but no-one was ascending. Those being helped off, muffled to the eyes, looked pinched and stiff. They were dusted with snow. The air was thick and freezing, making it difficult to breathe. Anita stepped into her ski-bindings and slid along the empty channels to the turnstile. As she operated her ski-pass she heard a guttural voice calling something unintelligible. The ancient lift-attendant, leathery face hidden deep within a black hood, was looking in her direction. He spoke again and she shrugged. He pointed to a clock face pinned to the wall. Anita smiled grimly, nodded and skied into position for the next chair. As it scooped her up and she pulled down the safety bar she could feel eyes watching her.

The chair swung out into swirling whiteness, the rumble of the winch motor suddenly fading. She knew it to be hopeless but her eyes still tried to pierce the opacity. The chair bumped and jogged over the guide-wheels and she gripped her poles tighter. The down cable was weighted with holidaymakers looking forward to a drink, thinking of dinner. She felt very alone. Numbered pylons loomed and passed, loomed and passed. Cold stung her face like acid.

"What do we do now, Dean, smart-arse?" demanded Becky.

They were at the top of the T-bar. The wooden hut was locked and empty and there appeared to be three different tracks leading down. Dean had assured them that they would be able to see the piste or there would be someone to call for help. Lisa had gone white and quiet.

"Let's sit down and have a fag. I'm knackered," said the irrepressible Dean, pulling off his glove. "P'raps not," he continued, hastily pulling his glove back on. "Shit, that's cold!"

"Can't we just stay here and wait for someone to come and get us?" whined Lisa.

"Don't be such a girlie. Anyway, we'll freeze to death if we don't move. What do you think, Matt?" Dean glanced at Matthew who was flicking snow off the end of his skis all over Simon.

"What? Yeah, let's go."

"Which way, dickhead?"

"I dunno. Does it matter? They all go down."

"I don't like it steep," said Lisa.

"Oh, yeah, we know. The snowplough queen," sneered Guppy as he practised kick-turns.

"Piss off, you. Leave her alone," said Becky. She pointed. "That way looks easiest."

The ground dropped away gently in front of them and there were ski tracks just visible although everything was being quickly covered by new snow. The other routes looked steep.

"Right then. This one it is," said Dean. "Follow me."

"Not too fast!" wailed Lisa.

"Look, you ski right behind me, then you won't get lost. Becks, you next, then Matt and Si, and Guppy, you at the back."

Simon spoke sepulchrally. "Oooh, they always get the one at the back."

"Bloody good riddance,"said Becky.

Slowly snowploughing, bowed into the wind, the frail caterpillar felt its way down. The slope was slight and Dean sensed that it was narrow. He could feel an emptiness on each side. Ice particles drove upwards as if blasted against a wall. Lisa slid her arrowed skis behind Dean's and locked in, clutching his jacket, trembling. Dean, reassured by tracks that were still faintly visible, looked over his shoulder and gave her a grin.

"Someone's been this way. Bet there's a pub down here."

But the slope flattened out and they came to a stop. Ski tracks still beckoned forwards but were now mingled with the marks of heavy pole-plants and bootprints. The ground began to rise. As they huddled like penguins, looking to Dean for a decision, there came another rumble like a tipper-lorry unloading. Vulnerability announced itself quietly. Lisa whimpered.

"What we gonna do, Dean?" Faces serious. No joking now. Dean felt the pressure of command.

"How should I know? Why haven't you lot got any bloody ideas? It's not my fault."

"Yes it is," snapped Becky instantly. "If you hadn't fallen off the fucking drag-lift we'd be back in the hotel by now."

"Well if you hadn't laid right across the piste, you clumsy cow, and wouldn't bloody shift, you wouldn't have brought the rest of us down, would you, so you can shut the fuck up," said Guppy with venom.

"I'm scared," sobbed Lisa.

"You're always scared," mocked Simon.

"I think we should just follow these tracks," said Matthew quietly. "Somebody came this way for a reason. I think we're on a walker's route or one of those whatchumacallums, lang-something trails. They have huts for shelter with firewood, matches, blankets and things. I saw it on telly. Hey, they might send out the helicopters for us. Ace!"

"Wow, yeah!" picked up Dean. "Wicked!"

Their mood swung giddily upwards again. With skis shouldered they began the climb towards Matthew's imagined hut which they could all see clearly, the crackling fire, cosy candlelight and a bulging food store. The ground rose inexorably, the walking warmed them and they began bickering familiarly again. They were above the tree line and entering a steeply rising gulley. Again, they sensed rather than saw the presence of the valley sides, hollow exposure giving way to enclosure.

"Can you smell something?" said Simon.

Distinct against the scoured alpine purity came the sweet/sour smell of machine oil. Oil meant engines, meant people. They hurried forward until they could see three large, blurred shapes, pistie-beasties parked at the side of the trail, looking as if they had been there a long time, caterpillar tracks hidden under snow, tarpaulins roped over their engines and large padlocks securing the cabins. Scattered around were indications of old working—stacks of galvanized steel girders, drums of cable, piles of heavy, sawn timber. All were covered by tarpaulins, snow heaped high over them.

"Building something," observed Simon.

"Not for a long time," said Matthew.

"Is this it? Is this as far as it goes?" Becky was querulous again.

"No, look. The tracks still go up," said Matthew.

Dean was disappointed. He would have liked to have a go at Matthew and restore his own position.

"What I reckon we do is this. We keep going up to see if we can find this hut of Matthew's and if not, we come back here and use the tarpaulins for shelter. Someone'll come for us. Or oi could start one of these 'ere traactors, loike on the faarm and we'll droive down!"

"Don't be a fucking plonker, Dean," said Becky.

Climbing steadily once more, faint footprints now their only guide, they felt the altitude burning in their nostrils. Eyebrows crystallized and faces flayed. Something also was happening to the landscape. The reassuring valley walls were gone. The wind, which had been funnelled into their faces, now howled across them. They sensed an edge nearby.

"Let's go back!" shouted Lisa into Dean's face. "I don't like this."

Dean had come to the same conclusion and was about to agree when he saw something ahead.

"No!" he bellowed back, and pointed. "Look!"

A block of darkness was visible ahead, rising squarely out of the snow. The youngsters cheered and whooped and floundered through the soft snow towards it until they saw what it was—a huge rock, roughly squared and pitted with scratches and gouges, louring down over them. Black, cracked and glistening, it commanded the mountain. Behind glittered the glacial gleam of eternal ice. The children felt cold hostility and backed away, except for Dean who seemed drawn towards it. He took off a glove, his hand instantly red raw with cold, and laid it flat against the icy stone.

"What the fuck are you doing, Dean?" screamed Becky.

"It's all right," he called back. "I'm just—"

He felt his way around the side and disappeared, only to reappear instantly, stumbling backwards in his hurry to get away.

"Jesus!"

"What?"

"Get away, for Christ's sake!"

"What's going on?"

"Just fucking run! Go on!"

Dean's face was enough to infect them all with a deadly fear. They hurled their skis down and turned to flee. At the same time, the overhang on which they had been standing, a thin ridge of frozen snow, a few feet of ice crystals curled like a breaking wave over the abyss, broke without warning. Their impudent tiptoe on the edge of eternity was over. Without even time to scream, they were gone, hurtling downward a thousand feet. Arms and legs flailed until the first crunching blow against rock, then six rag dolls smeared a scarlet warning against the indifferent mountain. Above, in the blackness, a yellow eye blinked.

The chair carrying Anita jogged past the sign which warned passengers to raise the safety bar. She scanned ahead anxiously. She had conjured up a faint hope that the youngsters had skied from the top of the T-bar to the chair and taken it down, imagining their familiar voices from the descending seats calling across to her, "Miss! Miss! It's us! See you at the bottom!" and the rush of relief that would follow. She checked every chair. Strangers. Empty. Perhaps they would be waiting at the top, sheltering by the wheel-house. She pushed herself off the seat as the icy ground rose to meet her skis. There was no-one. No-one queuing to descend and worse, the T-bar was invisible from here. Would they have known where the chair-lift was? Dismay flooded through her and her knees buckled. She was caught by the lift-attendant who grabbed her arm and hauled her upright. He pointed to his watch and Anita nodded. The unthinkable began to stir but she suppressed it for the moment. She must call for help.

"Ich bin, er, teacher? Lecteur—no—professor, you understand? Mein kinder, sie sind—da?" She pointed.

The attendant creased his brows. "Ja, ja," he nodded, and smiled.

"No, er… nein. Ich need er (oh, damn) help. Help! Sie sind lost! Gone! Oh God. Er. Hilfe!" The word surfaced from beneath her desperation. Her urgency conveyed itself and the attendant nodded.

"Ja, ja, Ich verstehe." He entered his hut and spoke rapidly into the telephone. Anita was setting off along the track to the T-bar when he emerged.

"Nein! Nein! Warten sie!"

Anita ignored him, driven by appalling responsibility and the need to do something. In her pocket was a piste-map and she had a clear mental picture of the mountain. This was not her first visit. New snow creaked as she skate-stepped along the short route to the T-bar. Visibility was so bad that each thin wooden pole marking the way was hidden from the next. The T-bar was deserted and silent, wheels still and furred with driven snow. She could see where her pupils had scrambled up the slope and then there was a confusion of footprints and ski tracks. She looked at the three runs that led from here down to the cable-car station. They dropped away steeply but Anita knew that once off the ridge they flattened out into gentle blue runs through the trees. Dean's group could have managed it easily, but the runs were covered with undisturbed new snow. The only ski marks visible were straight ahead. Anita knew all the runs in the valley but she had never been this way. Wasn't this the back of the mountain and not open to skiers? Her heart froze. She moved into the lee of the wheelhouse, fumbled her piste-map from her pocket and pored over it. It was an artist's drawing taken from an aerial photograph. It showed the lifts as straight black lines and the various colour-coded runs wriggling down. *Snakes and ladders*, she thought. She orientated herself, identified the top of the T-bar and then traced ahead. She was right. Behind the T-bar was a narrow ridge which led across to a steep peak cut by a deep valley and rising to a glacier. The ridge was bordered by sheer-sided gulleys. Rock outcrops overhung the treeless valley which climbed sharply towards the summit, then it opened onto a snowfield which skirted the mountain's knife-edge. The sportswoman in Anita thought, *Fantastic skiing*, the teacher thought, *avalanche*. She felt sure this area was restricted and remembered seeing orange crash nets behind the T-bar. She stuffed the map away and went to look. Yes, there were the supporting poles and the netting but it had been rolled back to give access. And unmistakably, ski tracks went that way. Six. Icy fear congealed inside her as she headed forward.

By the time she reached the Snocats she was desperate. She began to call. Her voice was whipped away on the wind, but she kept calling.

"Becky! Dean! Hello! Can you hear me? Anyone?"

It was hard to stop her voice rising to a shriek as panic pushed against the shutters of self-control. There came an awful grumble and a sense of vibration. So, her instinct had been right. She could see from the abandoned workings that there were avalanche barriers under construction. She stood still and listened. The noise echoed and faded to silence. No more shouting. What had possessed the kids to keep going this way? Weary of the weight, she left her skis by the Snocats and trudged upwards, following the disturbed snow, desperate to find them yet dreading what she might find. A voice repeated in her head, *What will I say to their parents? What will I say to their parents?* It would not be hushed. She wept behind her goggles and a frightened little girl's voice moaned, *No, oh no, oh no.*

Close to the summit she was a tiny figure on the immense snowfield, a fly on a tablecloth. Huge, black, hollow air buffeted her frailty. She felt she might be plucked off the steep slope and hurled into space at any moment. It would be a relief. She sobbed aloud and looked up. Oh, thank God! A light! A yellow pinprick that blinked on and off. Thank God, thank God! Thank God for the list of safety items to be carried at all times, including a torch. Thank God at least one of them had taken notice. She screamed out, ignoring the risk, "Hold on! I'm coming! Dean! Simon! Lisa! It's Miss Shepherd! I'm coming!"

ICE

The light went out. She threw herself up the slope towards the patch of black from where the light had come, a great, ice-crusted rock guarding the glacier.

"Where are you? Where are you?" she called hysterically. "Shine a light, for God's sake!"

Behind the stone, a yellow eye opened once more.

❄ CHAPTER TWO ❄

At last there was grimy snow in patches by the roadside. For hours the coach had sped from the airport on greasy autobahns, tracing the flat valley floors. The passengers stared through streaked windows at dripping trees. The holiday representatives who had met them at the airport said there was snow in Unteriberg but it was hard to believe. This looked little different from grey, wet England. But now they were climbing, winding around bend after bend, the engine straining. Instead of the geometric blocks of factories and industrial plants that were scattered along the flat land there were now wooden farmhouses with stacks of neatly piled firewood. The little towns had ski-racks outside the shops and some cars sported chains on their wheels. The black rock-faces at the roadside glittered with icicle-encrusted cascades, and there were giddy glimpses of half-frozen lakes hundreds of feet below. Pines clung to vertical slopes as the road wound and climbed. It was late afternoon and the light was disappearing but the sky was clear of the heavy, lowland murk. It was not just chill now but briskly cold. Conversations sprang up after the post-flight gloom.

"I shall certainly go for my three-star this week." Geoffrey Hampton, a solicitor with one season's (that is, with one week's) skiing behind him and already an expert, was patronizing the two ladies seated ahead of him. Dot and Kath, on their first ski holiday, had introduced themselves and asked him whether he could ski.

"I need to polish my parallels for the blacks, practice some compressions on the moguls and tidy up my pole-plant but that's all. Straightforward stuff, really. You'll pick it up."

This was gibberish to the women, as the solicitor well knew.

"Ooh, it does sound complicated," said Dot. "You seem to know all about it." Dot may not have known much about skiing but she knew how to flatter an ego. She and her friend had plotted this trip during their tea-breaks at the sweet factory. They had seen a holiday programme on the telly which emphasized sunshine, young ski instructors, cream cakes and après-ski. It had also pointed out that you could start at any age. Both were single, over forty and fond of food.

"I suppose you have to be very fit," prompted Dot.

"Oh, I keep myself in trim," said Geoffrey, led by the nose. "Work out, play a bit of squash. You need to be pretty flexible when you're wedeling."

Dot winked at Kath. "What did you say? Widdling?"

Geoffrey blushed. "No, no, wedeling. Down the fall-line taking very short turns."

"I don't expect me and Kath will be doing any of those dangerous-sounding things. We've never done it before, have we, Kath?"

"Not unless you count dry-ski," giggled her friend. She was wearing all her ski clothes to save room in her case. The travelling had moulded her into a crumpled, pink-and-lime-green Michelin man. "Remember, Dot? Now, what did we learn?" She began to count off on her fingers. "How to knock over a ski-instructor, how to set off down the slope without your skis, how to swipe somebody with your skis by turning round when you're carrying them…"

"How to put your friend's eye out with a ski-pole," interrupted Dot.

"I never did! Anyway, you shouldn't have come crashing into the back of me. I wouldn't have minded but we were in the changing rooms at the time."

"Well, it was those boots. Felt like a deep-sea diver."

"Felt more like a falling tree."

They were like excited school-children. This was their first holiday together. Dot, who for years had looked after her chronically ill mother, had been liberated by her death. Kath had had a small win on the lottery. This was a bit of an adventure.

"So, Geoff," (Geoffrey winced.) are you going to teach us to be an expert like you?"

Geoffrey had lost the initiative.

The noise from the back of the bus increased. A crowd of lads were vying for the attention of a group of girls, deep guffaws angling for feminine giggles. Their energy and youthful health pulsed along the aisle accompanied by the scent of duty-free spirit. Duty-free. Tom Shepherd listened to them enviously. His freedom had come as a curse, unwanted and unexpected five years previously, when he was told that his wife, Anita, had disappeared on the mountains towards which he was now inexorably drawn. Clever, beautiful, vivacious Anita had been snatched from him and lost. He had not been able to see her to say goodbye so his hurt had remained locked and festering inside. Unable to confront the certainty of his loss, his thoughts flinched whenever they strayed close to the town of Unteriberg, snug below its guardian mountain. A nightmare visit for the inquiry into her disappearance was enough to pronounce the place guilty. He had fled home to sterile bachelorhood and overwork, not wanting to hear of skiing ever again. But time had done its curative work and when the call came he knew it must be answered. The town that Anita had loved, that she had wanted to show Tom, had reached out a hand to him. His wound was less sharp although the scar still ached. He hoped that by staying where she had stayed and skiing the mountains she had loved he might exorcise the pain.

Activity had failed him. His job as deputy manager of a leisure centre allowed him to volunteer for unsociable hours. He was never late, never sick, always keen to attend courses, run seminars, visit other institutions, do anything to avoid being alone in an empty apartment.

His boss knew his need but he also recognized someone who was good at his job. Business was expanding and it required people like Tom. He was good with clients, never morose, always positive and helpful. If he occasionally blacked out to a bottle of scotch at home, nobody but he knew. But then he had found the letter.

ICE

He had been working late, sorting computer files, when the name "Unteriberg" sprang off the screen. It was in a letter from head office to his manager suggesting that the company should offer ski holidays and they ought to look for suitable areas. Although the major resorts were already fully franchised to big companies, there were still some small villages and towns where foreign visitors rarely ventured. The skiing was often limited but some were looking to the future and were developing new ski areas. Unteriberg for instance. Somebody was needed from the company to check it out.

This had deliberately not been dropped on Tom's desk. Usually he was the one who went on inspection visits for new ventures but it looked like his boss was being tactful. He wondered if anyone had already been given the job. The name had slapped him, bringing his loss into sharp focus. He had tried to smother Anita's memory but she was always there. He felt he must recall her in all her youth and energy and with all his love if he were ever to let go. They had meant to holiday together in Unteriberg without schoolchildren but he could never arranged his time off. There seemed no urgency. Sometime would do. And sometime had arrived but with a sting he would have to bear. He would ski her favourite runs, drink "heisse chokki" in her favourite cafés and feel close to her last days. It might bring him peace.

He had spoken to his boss the following day. No, he hadn't given anyone the job, yet. Tom was not supposed to have known about it. He had wanted to spare him the memory. Tom was reassuring.

"Look, Bill, I appreciate your concern but I really would like to go. It's been a long time now. This will help me bury the past. I'll do a good job for you, you know that."

"Oh, yes, I know that, of course. But are you sure you're ready for this? I could easily send someone else, you know."

"Absolutely. I really want to do this. It'll be good therapy. And remember, I can ski. None of the others can. I'm in a better position to judge the possibilities of the place. Why Unteriberg, though?"

16

"Well, the problem with these small places is that often there isn't enough piste to stretch the advanced skiers but Unteriberg is about to open a new ski area. I understand they've been working on it for years but there've been some problems. Anyway, it's almost finished now and they will be able to offer advanced runs and glacier skiing which, as you know, extends the season considerably. If we can get in early and tie up some deals with the locals we could be on to a winner. But I don't want to drag you through the past."

"Thanks. I appreciate it. But you'd be doing me a favour to let me go."

So it had been agreed and here he was. He felt less tranquil about it now. Not so much healing the wound as scratching the scar.

Of course, the papers had had a field day. "Alpine Tragedy. Teachers Negligent." "Death in the Snow!" "Irresponsible Teachers on Freebies!" What was claimed was just not true. Tom knew from Anita that the staff could not be with every youngster every moment of the day and night. They did everything possible to ensure the children's safety but mountains were inherently dangerous. The children had been well kitted-out (he had helped Anita draft the letter to parents about ski-gear), they were constantly counted and checked, there was a gigantic first-aid bag, each pupil's medical history was known, emergency numbers were set up, all were fully insured, every evening there were organized activities and they never skied unsupervised. Anita always returned exhausted. She used to say that she never had an anxiety-free moment until the last child had been returned to its parents in the school car-park. But the press wanted a scapegoat and Anita was not able to defend herself.

Tom had flown out after the shattering phone-call, to attend the inquiry. It had been a nightmare journey travelling with the parents of the dead children. The staff had aged, too. None would ever take students on outings again, one would never teach again. It had been their job to face the parents. At the inquiry they had testified to Anita's total professionalism but it had not helped.

"The weather had turned severe, yes, Mr Williams?" the magistrate had asked. "Would it be normal to allow skiing to continue?"

"That decision was always left with the ski-school," Paul Williams had replied, firmly. "Once our students were with their instructors we relied on them to ensure the safety of the children. We checked that they were with their instructors at the beginning of each session. They had paid extra so that they had a supervised lesson in the afternoon as well as the morning. Most ski-schools only offer morning lessons to school groups but Mrs Shepherd always insisted that her ski groups would have no unsupervised skiing. The children were always met at the end of each session and checked."

The magistrate wanted to know whether it would have been more prudent to have a member of staff skiing with each group. Paul Williams was exasperated.

"It's not that simple. There are only four members of staff and yet six ski groups. The teachers themselves are of different skiing abilities so they can't just tag on to any group. We did ski with the groups when we could and spent most of our time going from group to group making sure that all was well. But we couldn't be everywhere at once. And some instructors didn't like having staff in their classes. It detracted from their authority. We had to trust the ski-school to be responsible."

It was Marco's testimony that had caused the damage. He looked very much the professional in his ski-school blazer with its subtle, prestigious crest. His steely-blue eyes looked candidly from his bronzed face as he spoke to the inquiry board. He explained that he had been a qualified instructor for six years, had never had any sort of accident with a group and was devastated by the loss of the children.

So what had happened?

"The weather was bad. Clear sun to blizzard in a half hour. I decided immediately that we must go down. My group were on the Steinplatz T-bar when the weather began to change. I was at the rear, as is our practice so that we can see if there is trouble. The children were a badly-behaved group and were acting foolishly on the lift. One of them fell and brought down the five others following. I told them to wait, I would come back up. I skied down with the rest of the group then took the T-bar up again. They did not wait. By that time the visibility was poor. I called the emergency services and joined the search. It was foolish of Frau Shepherd to go to search on her own. It made it more difficult for the rescuers."

The surviving students in Marco's group sang his praises. He was "ace", "dead good", "wicked", "cool", and they were vague and contradictory when asked what happened after he brought them down the mountain. The ski-school was exonerated. The bodies of the children had been discovered the following day after a helicopter search and their final route retraced. It looked as if they had become disorientated and had headed up the mountain only to fall to their deaths. A tragic accident. The only mystery was what happened to the teacher. The magistrate in his summing-up made some critical comments about the behaviour of English children abroad and the responsibilities of the teachers in charge. These last remarks were fastened onto by the press. Tom Shepherd felt angry all over again as he remembered.

In the seat across the aisle Mrs Bryon dug into her capacious hold-all and unearthed a flask and three packets of sandwiches wrapped in grease-proof paper. She passed a pack to her husband who was sitting by her next to the window and one to the seat in front where their only child, Caroline, was sitting. Caroline had been a late surprise. At fourteen, she looked more like a grandchild than a daughter. Her parents had arrived at comfortable and self-centred middle age when she made her appearance but they had seen no reason to change their lives. Keen walkers, nature lovers and joiners—Ramblers, RSPB, National Trust, YHA—they wore their badges with pride. Mr Bryon had a walking stick adorned with little shields. They had been visiting Unteriberg for years, healthily striding the langlauf trails, breathing deeply and repeating the same things about the clear air and the wonderful scenery. Now Caroline trailed behind them. Her abiding image of these trips was of her father's big bottom wobbling along in front and the ghastly "special" sweaters her mother knitted every year, one each, same colours, same pattern, different sizes. Team Bryon. The Three Bears. Not for her the glamour of downhill. Her parents disapproved. Damaging the mountains, they said. Plod, plod.

"Ham and pickle, George. Caroline, cheese and tomato. And mine's the egg mayonnaise. Crisps, anyone? Shall you pour the tea, George?"

Mr Bryon took the flask, unscrewed the top and passed it to his daughter. She shook her head. She hated the old flask, its nasty green plastic cup, the twist of grease-proof that wedged the cork stopper, the metallic smell of the tea. It accompanied them on all their jaunts and it made her sick. She stared out of the window, trying not to hear her father's voice. What she would give to be able to join the rioters on the back seat!

"We're getting close now, Hilda. Can you see those Alpine choughs? Caroline! Alpine choughs, look."

She nodded, dumbly.

"Did you remember the rope, George?" asked Mrs Bryon.

"In the big suitcase."

"Well done, dear."

Mr Bryon did not trust continental fire regulations and always took a thirty-foot coil of rope with him—just in case.

"When we get to the hotel I'll make sure that we have the two nice quiet rooms at the back that I requested. We don't want the trouble we had last year with balconies over the street. All those young men hanging around and shouting up. I can't think who they thought they were shouting at."

Caroline re-wrapped her half-eaten sandwich.

"Then we'll have a little lay-down before changing for dinner. I'll speak to the reps too so that we can put our names down for the evening sing-songs. But an early night tonight, everyone. Caroline? Don't you want that sandwich?"

Caroline silently passed it back.

"Perhaps she'll eat it later," said her mother.

The bus lurched around another hairpin. A tiny, framed picture of the Madonna swung on its chain above the driver's seat. A cheer went up from the back. A young man sporting a blue and purple jester's hat sprang to his feet and posed dramatically in the aisle, half crouched, arms kung-fu style, palms down.

"And the world snow-board champion has just entered the half-pipe and is looking to complete a tricky air and re-entry," he gabbled into an imaginary microphone. His friends laughed and cheered as the bus once again wound through a hundred and eighty degrees and he went crashing onto the laps of two girls. "And, wipeout! Radical!"

The driver's voice came over the microphone. "Setzen sie, bitte! Setzen sie!"

With much noise and confusion the young people sorted themselves out, the word "fascist" emerging from their area more than once. Mr Bryon breathed heavily, tight-lipped.

"I hope they're not at our hotel," he muttered to his wife.

Tom Shepherd, across the aisle, looked closely at the teenage girl in front of them.

"Excuse me," he said to Mrs Bryon. "I don't think your daughter is well."

Caroline was ashen-faced with beads of perspiration across her brow. Mrs Bryon gave Tom a resentful look and leaned forwards between the seats.

"Caroline? Are you all right, dear? Are you ill?"

It was not the time for enquiries. Tom hastily screwed his newspaper into a bag, swung across the aisle towards the girl and thrust it in her lap just as, with a small cry, she was sick. When it was over he put a paper handkerchief into her hand and took the sour bundle to the front of the bus and told the driver to stop. He threw the bag into the trees then suggested the girl might like some air. He left it to her mother and a few minutes later they were travelling again, mother and daughter sitting on a front seat where the movement was less. The girl rewarded him with a quick, grateful look as he returned to his seat. He smiled a "no problem" smile at her. He had travelled on plenty of coaches with young people, taking teams to fixtures. He had learned to spot the signs quickly.

The two reps who had ticked them aboard had been hugger-muggered over clipboards and paper ever since and now stood to address their flock. They wore blue and yellow company sweaters with name badges. The young man's said "Alec", and the girl's, "Shelley". Alec, tall, earnest and bespectacled, spoke enthusiastically into the microphone.

"Well, folks, we're nearly at Unteriberg and I would like to take this opportunity to welcome you all on behalf of 'Skiworld Tours'. I won't say too much just now," (muffled cheers from the back seat) "because tonight we have a welcome evening at the Hotel Ledermann to which you are all invited and where there will be complimentary drinks." (Louder cheers from the back). "My name is Alec and my glamorous assistant here," (Huge cheers from the back) "is Shelley. Our job is to make sure everyone is happy, to sort out any (hopefully few) problems, and to help you organize your skiing and snow-boarding. We will also be offering lots of apres-ski activities for you to sign up for. Now, tonight, when we arrive you will be dropped off at your various hotels or chalets where you can find your rooms, unpack and have dinner. Then at nine o'clock, Shelley and I will be in the Ledermann. We stop there first, so those who aren't staying there can see where it is. It's easy to find, right on the main street. So, we look forward to seeing you all there. If you have pre-booked ski-passes, ski-school or hire equipment then that will all be dealt with there. I'm sure you're all dying to get on the slopes. Any questions?"

Voice from the back. "What's the snow like?"

Alec grinned and ran his hand through his short, curly hair. "The best I've seen. All the runs are open. There's snow right down into town. We had fresh snow three days ago and since then it's been cold and clear." His bronzed face was animated. "It's fantastic. You can't see now but the snow is piled six foot deep at the roadside. They had to plough to keep it open. So no problems there. You'll all have a brilliant time, I'm sure. Did you want to add anything, Shell?"

Shelley flicked back her blonde hair. She was wearing black, skin-tight ski-pants which terminated in a pair of huge, furry boots. She looked as if she was standing inside two Afghan hounds. She wiggled her way down the aisle clutching a bundle of plastic bags.

"No, I think you've covered everything. I'll just give out the info packs. There's a street-map of Unteriberg, a piste-map of the ski area, some information about the town and tickets for your complimentary drinks. There's also a list of apres-ski activities for you to think about which you can then book tonight. OK?"

A voice from the back. "Where're you staying, then, Shelley?"

She flashed a brilliant smile. "Secrets."

Tom sifted through the leaflets. He reminded himself that he was here to do a job for the company and to put his wife's memory to rest, but he could not help an excited, involuntary anticipation in response to Alec's boyish enthusiasm about the skiing. He recalled early trips with Anita when there had been just the two of them, he full of thrills and spills, she more controlled. A better skier. He used to love watching her snaking gracefully through the moguls, flowing with the contours, her favourite buttercup-yellow ski-suit brilliant against the snow. Whenever she stopped he would speed dramatically towards her, stop with a spray of snow and fling his arms around her. Her face would be flushed, eyes sparkling, and he would feel the life thrilling through her body. Tom felt a pricking behind his eyes and blinked.

The road levelled and straightened and there were lights and buildings. The bus slowed to a crawl along a narrow, cobbled street. Tom could recall nothing of Unteriberg from his one, awful stay except his anger that life continued normally. With that turmoil gone, he saw now what Anita had loved—an ancient Swiss town hunkered down below the ragged teeth of mountain peaks, a community that had served its monastery-church since medieval times, which farmed, which had a market and which, only recently, played host to an increasing number of skiers. Houses and shops rubbed shoulders along its length, white walls decorated with gothic writing, grey walls faced with wooden shingles like fish-scales. There were ornately-carved balconies, elaborate wrought-iron signs and snow-laden, overhanging roofs dripping with icicles. Warm light from shop-fronts and windows spilled out onto snowy pavements which were pitted with footprints from the strollers and window-shoppers warmly clad in furs and boots. Tom had a brief glimpse of souvenir shops, cafés, sports shops and (he could have sworn) one shop displaying surgical appliances and then they were stopping outside an old four-storey hotel and Alec was saying, "OK, folks, this is the Ledermann. For those staying here (it's a great hotel, by the way) if you'd like to get out and collect your bags from the driver, Herr Brucke will be ready in the foyer to welcome you. Remember, we all meet here at nine for the welcome evening."

Tom rose and filed out of the bus. The Ledermann was an expensive hotel and he noted that the couple with the daughter were staying here, as were two giggly women and a single man in a suit. Tom saw a glance of relief pass between Mr and Mrs Bryon as the back seat remained in noisy occupation. He guessed the snow-boarders would be self-catering. Tom was a little disappointed. He had enjoyed their racket, all that energy and fun. They might have livened up what was beginning to look like a stodgy set of fellow guests. He reminded himself that he was one of the stodgy ones too. He rescued his skis, boots and suitcase from where the driver had dumped them on the pavement and turned towards the beckoning light at the hotel entrance. The icy air made him gasp after the stuffy interior of the bus. As he looked up at the glittering night sky he saw, suspended over the doorway, a beautifully-crafted wrought-iron sign. "Hotel Ledermann" depicted an alpine man in shorts, braces, boots and feathered hat. Herr Brucke smiled in the foyer, shaking hands with his new arrivals.

"Wilkommen! Wilkommen!"

✳ CHAPTER THREE ✳

I t would always be deedly-deedly music. The TV in Tom's room was churning it out when he tuned in the next morning for local ski conditions. Jolly accordion tunes with oompah rhythms. Now in the cable-car, squashed against the early risers, sleep-drugged and breakfast heavy, deedly-deedly trickled from tinny speakers in the roof. People swayed dosily, spoke quietly or were silent. It would be different on the way down. A day's activity would be relived in chatter and laughter. Now all anyone wanted was to absorb the gathering warmth of the climbing sun as it filtered through the scratched plastic windows. It was going to be crystal clear. When the streets of Unteriberg had been in shadow that morning and Tom was blearing at his TV, remote-controlled cameras on the roof of the mountain café showed salmony light staining the upper slopes. Accompanied by deedly-deedly. The trouble was, Tom was beginning to like it.

He had not worn skis for five years but as he stepped into the bindings, the solid click as they bit down onto the back of his boots was very familiar. An instant transformation of sensation made the skis an extension of his natural movements. He raised and lowered each leg, savouring the weight and the effortless slide over the hard-packed snow. He squinted up at the deepening blue sky, the sun prickling his skin like an electric charge. From all around came the clip of bindings and the creak of good snow, tiny sounds in the immense hollow clarity of alpine air, delicately scented with pine and sun-cream. The snow dazzled. Tom knew his first run must be something gentle to get the feel again. Take no risks. He pushed off towards a blue piste-mark and let the falling ground suck him down. A stiff, awkward first turn, a wobble, and then came relaxation. His knees flexed automatically, the contours became a map to read and he flowed into the mountain, breathing easily, alert, the wind cold on his face, his shoulders embracing the fall-line. As his spirits soared towards the distant mountain ridges he whooped aloud. He swung around slower skiers as his toes became more sensitive to weight shift and his whole body transformed into the biting edges of his skis. The wide piste wound gently through pines and shallow gullies, offering an invitation to snake up and down their banks and lean against their resistance. Rising ground tempted him. Don't lean back. Loss of contact, steering gone, knees bent, slap down, more speed, the hiss of the turns audible now, a drop, lean forward, abandon yourself to the hill, knees judder over ruts, flatten out, hurtle towards the lift, knees bend, plant the pole, unweight, plant, weight, turn, skid, spray, stop, breathe deeply, hear your heart pounding. Take it easy? No risks? No chance!

The long chair-lift hauled him steadily through the pines and then beyond, above the tree-line. After each ridge the cable looped ahead again, the chairs rising and dipping like washing on a line. The hot sun and gentle movement made Tom feel sleepy. He wedged himself comfortably into the corner of the seat, the weight of his skis resting on the bar underneath, and he turned his face to the warmth like a sunflower. The endless English months of grey, cold and wet began to thaw. He thought of Anita and let the sun heal the wound.

He was taken to the highest skiing point on the mountain. Various runs snaked away, marked for difficulty. The blacks, which ran beneath the chair-lift and the cable-car, he would save for another day but he felt ready for red. It was quiet here. Few people had ventured this high yet. As he glided forward off his seat he felt tiny against the vast whiteness. A blaze of sunlight flooded down through the thin air, a cool breeze whipped over the last ridge and the snow felt dry and crisp. Tom squinted into the steely distance. Mountain peaks reached to the horizon, enfolding blue, treed valleys and icy lakes. Above there was wispy high-level cloud and a vapour trail, needle-sharp. He rolled down the top of his ski-suit and drew off his sweater.

The drying perspiration on his roll-neck chilled and refreshed him like an icy shower. He folded his sweater into his rucksack and re-zipped his suit, feeling lighter and freer. Later, this mountain would have to be viewed as a business proposition but for now it was his playground. The red markers posted a gentle route towards the shadowy side of the mountain then it wound back to the sunny face before it began to drop. The gentle approach allowed a few practice turns before it got serious in a heart-stopping drop, a tight bend and a long screaming run over jumps, through trees , down mogul fields and flat-out schusses. Tom visualized Anita ahead of him. She loved this kind of terrain. He chased the image as he used to do in reality, aiming to catch her but she was always just out of reach. He skied faster but the yellow-clad figure with its long hair streaming from the favourite white headband would not be caught. Then, as he exploded over the brow of a ridge, he saw her clearly. She was trudging up the steep slope in the wake of six youngsters who themselves were scrambling upwards, apparently unaware of her. The stab of pain in Tom's chest took his breath away. He opened his mouth to call her name and at the same time caught an edge. In seconds, his flowing, graceful motion was a thumping fall, a blur of snow, skis and sticks.

Face down, feet higher than his head, both skis off, sunglasses missing, snow up his sleeves and down his neck, he lay still, reorientating, breathing hard but in no pain. He carefully brought his legs below him. No damage, just undignified. He shook the snow from inside his sleeves where it burned with cold. With skis recovered, boots beaten free of compacted ice and sunglasses retrieved and wiped, he stood up to see if anyone had noticed him making an idiot of himself. A group of schoolchildren were laughing at him as they were being organized by their young teacher. She wore a yellow ski-suit and a white head-band. Time for a heisse-chokki break.

The sun-terrace was a kaleidoscope of colour. Pine tables and benches were vibrant with ski-wear. A forest of skis sprang out of the snow and flags in primary colours fluttered against a shimmering background of white and blue. The scent of coffee, chocolate, glühwein and Jagertee competed with cooking and cigarettes. Heavy boots, unclipped for comfort, clumped across the pine boards, their wearers moving with the hip-swinging gait of racing walkers. Breath steamed, conversations blended and music tinkled. The inside of the café was dark after the glare as Tom lined up for his drink. The tiled floor gleamed, slick with snow-melt. A skating rink. How would you explain a skiing injury done in a café? Lie. He took his mug outside, like everyone else not wanting to lose a moment of the sun. Sheltered against the café wall, a row a deck-chairs cradled sunbathers, shiny-faced with aromatic oils. Tom excused his way to a space on a bench facing the slopes and put his mug down. He slipped on his sunglasses and studied the huge snowfield facing him dotted with tiny black figures. Ants on a tablecloth. Nice place. Possibilities.

Seated opposite, a middle-aged man was also looking at the slopes appraisingly. He appeared to be on his own and was dressed for skiing but in greys and blacks rather than the preponderant garish colours, as if he were more at home in a office. Tom suspected that beneath the warm jacket there lurked a shirt and tie. He caught Tom's glance and smiled.

"Es ist schön, nicht wahr?"

"I'm sorry, I don't understand. English." The absurd excuse, as if "English" said it all. Which it did.

The man smiled again and raised his eyebrows fractionally.

"That is quite all right," he said with only a trace of accent. "I speak some English. I said, 'It is beautiful'. You are here on holiday, yes?"

Tom warmed to his friendliness although wondered whether he just wanted to practise his linguistic skills. He wore spectacles with dark shades that flipped up like a letter box.

"A bit of holiday, a bit of work," Tom replied. "And you?"

"The same," he said. "From what part of England are you?"

Tom told him. "You must have been to England," he guessed, but was surprised to learn that the man had never visited. "You speak my language very well. I suppose I'm typically English not speaking another language. Did you learn it in school?"

"Yes, but I have also spent many years in Australia."

"Ah, that's why you're so fluent. You're lucky the accent didn't rub off as well."

Tom had meant this as a throwaway remark but the man took issue.

"You know," he said, slowly stirring his spoon in his coffee, "that is so English. You always judge each other, how do you say—'put each other into boxes', yes? It is always class with you. In Australia, everybody talked the same."

Tom felt wrong-footed, unprepared for a discussion on English attitudes to status on a bright morning on the ski slopes. But there was some justice in the man's remarks.

"Well, that's me put in my place," he said wryly.

"I do apologize," the man said hastily. "I have been impolite. I do not always think before I speak. Please, shake hands. My name is Kristian. Kristian Weller.

"Tom Shepherd. And there's no need to apologize. You're right, really. We are quick to criticize. But do your countrymen have no faults? You are Swiss, I suppose."

"Oh, yes, from Zürich. And of course we have faults. Many. We are often accused of being obsessed with money."

"And are you? Is that what you are? A gnome?"

Herr Weller laughed. "Yes, yes, I know this expression. No, I am not a 'gnome'. I am an engineer. I was working on a bridge construction in Australia which is now complete. Now I am here to help with the work on Spirstock?"

"Spirstock?"

"Yes, you know, the mountain over the ridge." He pointed upwards to where the chair-lift disappeared. "The tow-lifts are still to be installed and the avalanche protection system completed. They have been wanting to develop the area for many years. They wish to have high-level, glacier skiing. It will create wealth, you understand." He smiled. "We Swiss, eh?"

Tom's heart began to beat. "I thought that area was too dangerous," he said quietly.

"Yes, in the past, but we have advanced technically, you see. It has been er—prone—prone, is that right?—to avalanche but we control that now. Barriers are stronger and we also predict very accurately when the risk of avalanche is high. It is possible to create controlled falls with the use of explosives. Many new areas have been developed in this way."

"I thought I read somewhere of an accident there, in the past," Tom said, cautiously, his face studiedly neutral.

Herr Weller looked blank. "No, I know nothing of that. Of course, I have been out of the country for many years."

"Perhaps that's why it has not been developed."

"No, I think not. I understand the technical difficulties are very severe and there have been problems with the workforce. The contractors have used outside workers. There is still local opposition."

"Why?"

"Oh, some people feel there are enough visitors to their town. There is an ecological question, too. Are we damaging the mountain, you understand? You seem very interested, Mr Shepherd. May I ask what your work is?"

"I manage a sports centre in England and, yes, I'm interested. I told you I'm here for work as well as pleasure. We are thinking of organizing holidays to Unteriberg, aimed at intermediate and advanced skiers. The area you are creating might be crucial to us but safety is a concern. I am very pleased to have met you, Herr Weller. I have to compile a report to take back with me so I hope you won't mind if I ask you questions."

"Not at all, not at all. Please, call me Kristian. It is quite a coincidence we should meet like this. Perhaps I can show you the site sometime? My company will be pleased to know that English skiers are already interested in Spirstock. Where do you stay?"

"The Ledermann in Unteriberg."

"I will telephone you there when I have made the arrangements. I must return to Zürich today but we will meet again in a few day's time, yes?"

"Thank you, Kristian. I shall look forward to that. Are you skiing now?"

"No, I have to see to the work now. It is easier in the good weather. Of course, most building will take place next summer. But it will go ahead this time, I am sure. It is only some of the older people who are objecting. Hotels and cafés want more business and the skiing is limited at the moment. Once we are on the glacier the season could extend into the summer months."

Tom rose, shook hands once again and pulled on his gloves. "I shall hear from you soon, then. Good to have met you." He dredged up his schoolboy German. "Auf Wiedersehen."

Kristian smiled. "Sehr gut! Auf Wiedersehen."

By midday, Tom knew enough to stop. Overall he was fit but his underused ski muscles were begging for a rest. When do most accidents happen? When you're tired. That had been drilled into him over many years. He dawdled over erbensuppe at the café and then slipped down the gentle blue run towards the nursery slopes which were prettily framed by pine trees and caught the afternoon sun. Groups were dotted like clumps of brightly-coloured flowers all over the area. Tom remembered how exhausting it was at the learning stage with all the side-stepping, snow-plough stopping, kick-turning, falling down and getting up. But he also recalled the fun of it as shrieks of laughter drifted across to where he stood watching. The slope had its own T-bar, a very gently graded one and slow. It was this that was causing most of the hilarity as instructors taught their groups how to hook on, ride and let go. It was policy to quickly give pupils the basic skills on lifts so that they would be able to take them higher up the mountain where there would be more skiing and less walking. Tom watched, entertained and glad of a rest. He heard a squeal and a giggle as a plump lady sat down on the T-bar and was dumped ungraciously on her bottom.

"Oh, bloody hell, Kath! I'll never get the hang of this contraption!"

Tom recognized the woman from his hotel, the one called Dot. She sprawled in a tangle of skis as the bar bounced up the slope without her, winding itself in as it went. The operator killed the motor. The queue waited patiently.

"No! No! No! That is no good! You do not listen! You do not sit on the bar! You stand up, you put the bar behind your ass, you hold the handle, it pulls you. It is easy! What is the matter with you? Are you stupid? I say again and again, do not sit, but you do not listen. Gott in Himmel!"

The voice sent a chill through Tom. He remembered its arrogant confidence and hard tone. He looked intently at the red-suited man who was shouting at Dot. Marco Kreiz. Five years older but hardly changed. A few more lines on his face but still black-haired and bronzed with the jutting moustache advertising his masculinity. Tom had not spoken to him at the inquiry but had instinctively distrusted him. Now all the nightmare images came back. Dot struggled to her feet, Marco watching contemptuously as he lounged against the wheelhouse and lit a cigarette.

"You have no strength! No fitness! Why do you try to ski like you are?"

Dot's natural instinct to find fun in the situation was struggling in the face of her hurt at the abuse. She smiled uncertainly and stood up shakily. Tom felt for her. His own learning days had been free of anyone like Marco. All he remembered was fun, friendship and final success. He was wondering whether to intervene when another voice that he recognized struck his ears, a thin, well-spoken English voice, nervous but determined to have its say.

"I say, that's not right! No, really, you will not speak to us like that. We have not paid a great deal of money to be shouted at. You will not upset these ladies like this. We are here to learn to ski and to have a holiday. If you cannot speak civilly, then I will make a complaint to the head of the ski-school."

It was Geoffrey, the solicitor, solicitously helping Dot with her skis. She looked at him with gratitude, Marco with amazement. Tom could not understand what Geoffrey was doing on the nursery slope. He had overheard his bravura talk on the coach and had assumed he would be shredding the upper slopes. However, watching him wobble uncertainly as he accompanied Dot to the back of the queue, Tom realized that the athletic figure he had drawn of himself was far short of reality. Nevertheless, Tom was impressed by his challenge to Marco who seemed uncertain, took a long pull from a hip-flask before casually waving the next skier onto the lift. Dot and

Geoffrey were joined by Kath who had herself fallen and been relegated to the back of the queue. She had jarred her shoulder, too, although had not complained. Dot spoke.

"He's a shouter, that Marco, isn't he? I suppose it must be boring for him with all us beginners. Ta for sticking up for me, Geoff."

Geoffrey tried to look stern and manly. He had surprised himself. An only child, and now, in his early forties, still living at home with elderly parents, he was not the assertive type. He tried to build the confidence he lacked by having expensive ski-wear and technologically advanced equipment but his limitations had quickly been discovered by the instructor of the intermediate group he had joined that morning. He had forgotten all that he had learned the year before. He was demoted to Marco's group and had been mortified to find Dot and Kath there but they were delighted to have him. Dot appeared to believe he had made a special request to ski with them. That was the impression she gave. Because of his one week's experience, he was the star of the group. He had never been the star of anything before. His self-esteem soared.

Dot made him feel protective which naturally made her attractive. Quick to smile, her eyes glittering with fun, she was unlike any woman of his acquaintance, girlish and cheeky. She made him feel young. He ran his hand through his greying hair.

"Well, we can't let these chaps get away with it, can we? How are you? Any bruises? Do let me help you with those skis. Just bend your leg. I'll knock the snow away from your boots. You just put your hand on my shoulder to balance. That's it. Now, when we reach the head of the queue again, we'll get on the T-bar together. It can be easier with two, OK?"

Kath stood silently behind them. Her shoulder hurt and she was frightened of the lift. All morning, her natural confidence had been chipped away by Marco. She was the slowest learner in the group and he had no patience. When she fell, which was often, he left her and took the group on to the next stage. By the time she got her skis back on she did not know what the group was doing and trailed behind, falling more often. She was very tired and close to tears. The rest of the group seemed much younger and were urging Marco to push them on as quickly as possible. With Dot now under Geoffrey's wing, she felt isolated. This was not how she had imagined it when she was laughing with Dot across the jelly-babies on the conveyer belt.

By the time she reached the front of the queue, she was shivering. She knew she would fall. The rest of her group had gone. Geoffrey had held the bar for Dot, standing by her side and carefully positioning it, reminding her not to sit down. With a shriek and a wobble they had set off up the slope, he encouraging her all the time. Marco scowled at Kath and indicated with a flick of his head that she was to take the bar. She stood frozen with fear. He slouched towards her and pushed her into position, jarring her shoulder again. Distracted by the pain, she did not see the lift operator take the bar and hook it beneath her. Not ready for the pull, she was hauled off her feet. Instinctively hanging on, she was being dragged on her back when the winch was stopped. She lay, weeping.

"Out of the way! Move! Schnell!" Marco's voice was harsh and contemptuous. He stormed up to her, grabbed her arm and dragged her roughly off the piste. Then he nodded at the operator to start the lift and the line of skiers began their ascent, each staring at the prostrate, weeping Englishwoman as they passed. Marco stood over her.

"You are worse than your friend! Always I wait for you! Only you! You never learn, never listen. Up!" He wrenched at her arm and she cried in pain.

Tom Shepherd had seen enough. He shouldered his way through the gawping people and pushed Marco out of the way.

"Leave her alone!" he said. "Can't you see she's frightened and hurt?!"

"So. Who are you?"

"That's none of your business. What is your business is to look after the people in your group."

Marco snorted derisively. "I teach the skiing. I know what I do. You go away." He took a step towards Kath who shrank back. Tom stepped in front of her.

"I told you, leave her alone. I've been watching you. You might be able to ski but you're not fit to be an instructor."

Marco's face darkened. His hands curled into fists. Tom stared at him, inviting him to make a move. He was quite prepared for a fight, even though the last time he had battled with anyone had been in the school playground. He felt compassion for Kath's distress and he hated bullies. Marco saw the resolve in Tom's face. His face changed from anger to disdain.

"OK. You so clever. You take her." He skied to the front of the queue, deliberately barging against Tom as he passed him and grabbed the next bar as it arrived. With insolent ease he swung it behind him and slid up the hill. Tom crouched beside Kath who was sitting up and sobbing bitterly. He put his arm around her shoulders and spoke quietly to her. He heard the words, "Scheiss-Englisch" spat out as Marco passed them.

"It's Kath, isn't it? Staying at the Ledermann? Me too. I'm Tom Shepherd. We were on the coach together coming up. You're with a friend, aren't you?" It did not matter what Tom said, he simply wanted to give her time to stop weeping. "Where does it hurt? The shoulder? Yes, very easy to jar that. Done it myself. Can you stand up? Yes? Right, here we go, then."

He supported Kath to her feet. Her tears had streaked her make-up and the thick layers of clothing were bunched and rumpled. She had been too hot all afternoon but had not had the courage to remove her thick jumper or take off her woolly pom-pom hat. She had read all about hypothermia. Now she was scarlet-faced and perspiring.

"Thanks," she sniffed. "I'm sorry, what did you say your name was?"

Tom introduced himself again.

"You've been very kind. Can you help me get my skis back on? I can never seem to get my feet straight. I suppose I'd better try the lift again and catch up with my group."

Tom was moved by her courage. She ought to be having more fun than this. He gently shook his head.

"Not just now, I think. Let's walk down to the 'Eis-bar' over there and I'll buy you a stiff drink. I think you need it."

"But I don't want to give up," she said, plaintively. "I want to learn to ski."

"I can see that," said Tom, "but just now you need a rest more than anything. It is only the first day. I'm taking a break myself. I've already had a faceful of snow this morning."

Kath smiled uncertainly.

"That's better," said Tom. "Come on, what do you fancy? Coffee and schnapps? It doesn't make you ski better but you'll certainly feel better. If you want, afterwards I can give you a few tips. Show that bastard, Marco, eh?"

This time, Kath smiled openly, her natural optimism rising.

"OK. And make it coffee and rum."

Throughout the afternoon, Tom patiently built up Kath's confidence. She was timid but a willing learner. Once relaxed, Tom saw that she could become a good skier. He knew, from years of working in the sports business, that you could not always predict how a person might perform a particular skill just by looking at their physique. He took Kath through small stages, making it fun, watching critically, praising generously. He had seen Marco-schools of instruction before, the "Watch-me-aren't-I-brilliant-now-you-do-it" type. Demonstrating but not teaching. People needed images, routines, games that required a particular skill, tricks to break bad habits, repetition. And lots of praise. Focus on success. He knew Kath was progressing after she let out an involuntary whoop at a series of successful snowplough turns. She was transformed. Her eyes shone and she glowed in the afternoon sun. Tom had managed to persuade her that she would not die of frostbite if she removed her chunky jumper and let him carry it in his rucksack. She was more comfortable and moved more freely.

"I don't know what I found so difficult this morning," she kept saying.

When most of the groups were at the top of the nursery slopes and it was quiet, Tom persuaded her to try the T-bar again.

"We'll go up together. You'll see, it's not that difficult."

He stood side by side with her, watching the bars come round, explaining how they would need to ski on to the piste to catch their ride.

"We'll take our time. We're not holding anyone up so if we're not ready, we just wait until we are. I'll catch the bar, you stand next to me. Remember, don't sit down or you'll have us both off. And I'll never forgive you," he smiled.

Tom mimed to the operator to slow the speed. Kath was quiet and tight-lipped but she was full of grit and determination. Tom pulled the handle between them, positioned the bar carefully, checked that Kath's skis were parallel and said to her, "OK, here we go. Try to relax."

Just as Dot had done, Kath gave a shriek when the reel on the bar was fully extended and she felt herself tugged firmly forward. Tom's presence acted as a balance and she found that the lower slopes were disappearing behind her. The breeze from their movement cooled her hot cheeks and she began to enjoy herself although she kept her eyes glued to her ski-tips as they tried to go in different directions.

"God, this is better than walking," she said.

Tom was not comfortable. Considerably taller than Kath, for her to have the bar in the correct position, he had to place it almost behind his knees. Nevertheless, seeing Kath enthusiastic and happy gave him a good feeling. He always wanted others to find pleasure in the things that gave him pleasure.

"When we reach the top," he said, "you'll need to ski off to the left. Don't worry about the bar. I'll deal with it. Don't go until I say and make sure you're on the flat part."

He took the strain of the cable as they levelled off on the disembarking area, turned the cross-bar so that it passed easily between them and, with his arm round her shoulders, gently propelled Kath to the side. He released the bar and saw it smack the snow bank ahead as it reeled in. He had seen beginners smack similar snow banks as they failed to release their terrified grips. Kath would not be one of them. Another layer of confidence. When he approached her she was sitting on her side in the snow.

"Are you all right? Did you fall?"

"No," she said. "I needed a bit of a sit-down, that's all."

The nursery slope was laid out beneath them, its gentle gradient and wide smooth surface perfect for learning. Their extra height had brought further mountains into view and Kath stared awestruck.

"This is so beautiful," she breathed. "Thanks for having such patience. You could have been off skiing if you'd wanted."

"I've enjoyed it," Tom said, honestly. "I wasn't kidding either when I said I needed a rest. Now we can really ski. No more walking back up hills again. You see the bottom of the T-bar down there? That's where we're heading. Off you go, doing those linked snowplough turns. I'll follow. I won't try to overtake—honest."

"But which way shall I go?" asked Kath.

"Whichever way you want. You're a skier now. I put myself entirely into your capable feet."

Kath set off slowly, concentrating. The increased slope made her turns easier and, by not having to stop, she began to feel the rhythm of skiing. Gradually her speed increased, Tom following. He slowly became aware that Kath was humming a tune, one he recognized. It was the theme music for "Ski Sunday".

She stopped ahead of him so he drew level. She was breathing deeply and had a glazed expression. He and Anita used to call it "white fever". Once you've had it, you're hooked.

"So, how's Heidi Zurbriggen, then?" he asked.

"Pretty damn good," she gasped. "Look! Isn't that my group down there?"

Skiers were standing in a line further down the slope, a red-clad figure in front, lecturing. Dot's lime-green-and-pink outfit was clearly visible.

"Tom, will you follow me down, like before? I know it's childish but I've got to do this."

Before he could reply she was off, he knew where. They built up speed and Kath headed for her group. Without stopping she skied between Marco and his pupils, called, "Hi, Dot! See you in the bar!" and swept on down, Tom following closely on her heels. She reached the bottom, laughing.

"Another run?" asked Tom.

"You betcha. You couldn't teach me that snow-spraying stop, could you?"

Tom took a candle and lit it from one of the hundreds that glowed solemnly around the elaborate shrine in the contemplative gloom. A serious house, this. He had strolled into the monastery church late that afternoon as a tourist. Now he was not sure what he was. A non-religious man, certainly, but nevertheless he was moved by the presence of a thousand years of worship and belief. The enormous interior overwhelmed, dwarfing petty concerns. The atmosphere was oppressive in spite of pink and gilt decorations and alabaster angels poised for flight. The chill air filtered reluctantly through a fog of incense and everywhere were reminders of mortality. Side chapels housed tombs enclosed by spiked bars, reliquaries squatted in candle-lit niches, the skull was everywhere. The air murmured with prayers. Tom placed his candle among the rest, then knelt impulsively with other bent figures as they muttered or quietly wept. He felt fraudulent but his instinct carried him. The icon to which all prayed was a tiny wooden figure, rudely carved and dark with handling and age. The black madonna. A miracle worker, able to cure the sick and the lame. The evidence was hanging on the walls in the entrance porch—walking sticks, support frames and crutches, many worm-eaten and ancient. Tom put his scepticism on hold. This was the only time he had lit a candle for someone. Anita had told him about this church and its monastery which loomed at the head of the little town, a real town unlike the soulless, purpose-built ski-resorts with their concrete apartments, fast food, hotels and night clubs. Unteriberg was founded when mountains were impenetrable barriers, not playgrounds. Everything focused on this church, the clock tower chiming the hours, each road terminating in the cobbled courtyard with its many-spouted drinking fountain, the gilt cross on the domed roof drawing the eyes heavenward. Anita had told him that when she first came here they had skied the slopes behind the monastery and at the end of the day had skied into the town through the monastery quadrangle, even slaloming around the occasional brown-clad, sandal-shod monk. Tom had laughed in disbelief but Anita swore it was true. Anita. Quick to laugh, quick to tears. He still lived in the flat they had shared. He thought of its sterile surfaces, the neatness and order he had imposed, missing her lively clutter, the shoes kicked off and left, magazines lying where she had last been reading, the kitchen a bomb-site, impulsive flowers, sudden, inspired, mad meals, wildly expensive perfume. He kept her scent bottles by the bed. There had been no-one since. Because she had not been found, he could not part with her. The tranquility which had begun to settle on him was suddenly displaced by a knot of grief so painful that he drew in his breath sharply. He looked up to see if anyone had noticed and there, across the aisle, her back to him, this time unmistakable with the white headband enclosing her fine, pale hair, was Anita. He almost cried out, stumbled to his feet and ran across to clutch her shoulder. She spun round, shocked, grey eyes reflecting her fright. Anita's eyes were brown.

"I'm sorry, I'm terribly sorry," Tom gabbled. "I thought you were someone else." He thought she may not understand what he was saying but her alarm subsided.

"Oh, you made me jump!" She looked at Tom's face which was still rent by his emotion. "Are you all right?"

Tom backed away in confusion, scared that this should happen twice. She watched him, half-smiling. She was nothing like Anita, pale and serious-looking, her hair more golden, and where Anita had a small, neat mouth, this girl was almost vulgarly full-lipped. Her grey eyes shone behind thin-rimmed spectacles and with her black coat and long scarf she appeared schoolgirlish. She carried a folder and had a pencil in her hand. She had been sketching when Tom approached her. Before she shut the folder, Tom had glimpsed carefully drawn carvings, architectural mouldings and statues. She turned back to a figure carved into the stone wall, opened her folder and recommenced drawing.

In the church doorway, Tom paused. This visit had not had the calming effect he had hoped for. He should have accepted

Kath's invitation for a drink in the hotel instead of coming here. He placed a donation in the collecting box and signed the visitor's book, a leather-bound volume with entries going back over many years. He flicked through its pages, refusing to acknowledge what he was hoping to see. Nothing. It was not the kind of thing she would have done. There were older entries in a series of volumes racked on a shelf. The earliest visitors were mostly Swiss although there were some English names there too. Probably on the Grand Tour, Tom thought. He picked up an English information leaflet and read: "This church is build of 1200s on the place of one ancient, holy house where live the pauper holy man who craft the Santa Maria. Wonders there have been after his passing and folk are wandering many miles to cure. A spring sources the famous fountain. It is needed to drink each spigot for no harms."

Feeling foolish, Tom stepped into the courtyard and made his circuit, sipping the icy water.

❄ CHAPTER FOUR ❄

Tom was in his kitchen preparing dinner. He could hear guests in the next room talking and laughing. He did not know who they were but he knew he had to impress them. Anita should have been home but had not arrived. The kitchen door was locked and he had barricaded it with chairs but they kept hammering and asking was it ready. The floor was slick with oil and he had opened all the windows to clear the blue miasma which made his eyes sting. A cold wind blew in but it only stirred the smoke. On the hob, pans bubbled and hissed. In the dining room they were calling for ice-cream and he reached reluctantly towards the walk-in freezer. He knew there was no ice-cream there but he pulled open the heavy door. No light came on. It had been faulty for years. The walls were covered with mould and it smelled of corruption. His gorge rose but he had to look deep inside. He stepped forwards and the door quietly thudded shut behind him.

He started awake, shiny with sweat. The monastery bell clanked four. He lay on his back, breathing deeply and staring into the darkness, the unfamiliar furniture of his room slowly emerging as his pupils dilated. All was quiet but there was an extra hushed quality that made him want to pop his ears. He pushed aside the duvet, climbed out of the big, wooden bed and crossed to the window. He drew aside the heavy curtains. Snow. It cushioned his balcony railing and whirled heavily down, grey goose-feathers in the street lights. Tom shivered and dragged the duvet from the bed to wrap around himself. The street was empty, the last tyre tracks already disappearing, parked cars shrouded, pavements sheeted. He brought a chair to the window and, cocooned in his quilt, watched the balcony fill up with snow, each soft layer slow and soothing. The monastery bell counted the muffled hours.

Hot coffee nudged him gently awake. Herr Brucke, laying tables, had been surprised to see him so early in the dining-room. A man of few words, he grunted, "Morgen," and slid quietly into the kitchen as Tom took a window table. It seemed a good day to start work so he had brought his documents down to browse through. He was spreading them out when the hotelier returned with the coffee-pot.

"Entschuldigung, bitte," he murmured as Tom created a space on the table. He left the pot on the table but not before he had glanced sharply at one of the documents. It was a draft version of a leaflet which Tom's company was planning to use to promote their ski holidays. One of his jobs was to look at the area to suggest information that might be included. He had sketched in a bold heading, "Ski Spirstock!" and it was this that caused Herr Brucke to purse his lips. As he walked slowly away, dark brows creased in thought, an old man's voice, high-pitched and querulous, called from the kitchen, "Josef!" Herr Brucke hurried through the doors. Tom heard his deep voice speaking urgently, followed by silence.

He found the development plans at the old Rathaus. Its rows of windows, each bordered by painted vine-leaf festoons, stared at the hotel from across the high street. In flaky gothic lettering it proclaimed its earlier importance. Today it housed the tourist information office. Tom crossed the crunchy road surface into a brightly-lit, open-plan office where gleaming posters of Unteriberg "Im Winter und Sommer" decorated the walls. He glanced at the racks of postcards then moved towards a central display cabinet which contained drawings, maps and a model. A lady in a dark-blue suit, the cantonment shield pinned to her lapel, stood up from behind her desk and asked, in English, whether she could help. The cut and colour of his clothing unmistakably declared his nationality.

"Yes, please, if you have a moment. This expansion of the ski area," enquired Tom. "Is it definitely to go ahead?"

She joined him at the display, clipping across the tiled floor in her businesslike shoes. In her silk scarf, worn like a cravat, she reminded Tom of an air-hostess.

"Oh, yes, certainly. In winter next there will be skiing on Spirstock. You are here to ski, yes?" She took in Tom's athletic build and smiled. "The meisterskier, hm? You wish for more black runs? Next year. I will show you."

The cabinet contained a scale model of Unteriberg nestling beneath its rim of jagged peaks, gentle ski runs snaking through clumps of tiny trees. The monastery with its gold-capped towers, clock and fountain was minutely reproduced. Tom thought architects must be like big kids with toys when it came to modelling. Except that real kids would play destructive games. Monster attack. Avalanche. A miniature Spirstock frowned over the town. The helpful tourist lady was pointing out two winding black trails carefully painted down the vertiginous face of the mountain.

"There you have them. Ski runs for the brave. You will see also that it will be possible to ski Spirstock for the inter-mediate—you see the red runs here are not difficult."

Ski runs for the brave? A brochure heading? Would that put off more than it would attract? Think about it. Good red runs, too. It looked a real possibility. A tiny chair-lift marched from the present highest ski point almost to the summit and there were four drag lifts indicated.

"What are all these buildings here?"

"Well, that one at the base is a café, there is an ice-bar also here and here, and at the top, a club."

"A club!"

"Well, a café/bar/hotel/club. It is to attract the young folk. They ski all day and then dance all night. It will have sun balconies, saunas and steam rooms, a swimming-pool and so on. It is new because we build so high on the mountain. A place for adventure."

"They'll never finish all this by next season, will they?"

"Oh, it is building three years now. Yes, it will finish. The avalanche is no longer a problem with new technique. In the summer the construction is complete. We have a good company now, from Zürich. No more stops."

"I hope so. I want to bring groups of skiers out from England next year and we have to begin working on the publicity material now."

"Ah. I felt your interest was more than ordinary. Yes, we have guarantee that all is complete for the winter. No problem."

"But there have been problems?"

"Yes, but all finished now. The workers from Zürich are expert."

"I would have thought that local builders would know the terrain best."

There was a pause. The lady fiddled with her brooch and tightened her lips. She appeared to come to a decision.

"No company from here would make the work. I am from another valley so I do not understand why. Many old people do not want the construction at all. They say the area is dangerous. They do not understand new technique. The younger folk—the shopkeepers, café owners and so on—see it will make money for the town. They have tried to build many times but always there is trouble. When the new company comes they want to use local workers but no-one will work for them. So, they bring in workers and now it will be complete. I hope you will come next year with your groups. You will have a good time." She smiled and stepped back to her desk to attend to a large fur-coated gentleman who was breathing heavily like an irritable bear and clutching postcards in a huge paw.

There would be new snow. Tom's fellow travellers in the rickety cable-car looked as if they had come to the same conclusion. When he left the office, the snow was thinning and the sky brighter. What would conditions be like on top? New snow. Unsullied, unbroken, waiting to be sliced and ploughed. The piste-map showed a cable-car slung over the shoulder of the mountain. It did not mention that it was the oldest cable-car in the area. Compared to the scarlet, brand-new supercable that had whisked him up the mountain on his first day, this felt like a tram. Its ridged wooden floor was black with damp and it creaked and groaned pitifully as it crawled from pylon to pylon. There were only a handful of passengers but it was cramped. They looked like skiers who knew what they were doing. One man, bearded and bronzed, wore a ski-school jacket. He was standing next to Tom. His skis were new, the brilliant paintwork unscratched, edges still razor sharp, the compact, aerodynamic bindings no doubt hideously expensive. He noticed Tom's admiring look and smiled.

"Fortunately I do not have to pay for them. The company gives them to the ski-school. Today I have free time. Powder snow, mmn? Excellent." He indicated with his head towards the mountain top, grinning.

"If we ever get there," Tom said as the cabin once again rattled and shook over the trolley wheels.

"Do not fear," the young man said, confidently balanced as the car swayed and swung. "We Swiss are very careful. All cable-cars maintained regularly." His eyes twinkled. "Every ten years. This is due next year." His teeth were very white against his brown face.

Tom laughed with him. There was a camaraderie in the sporting world which he felt privileged to share even though he was worried about his powder-snow skills. It had been a long time.

It was hushed at the top. Few had chanced it yet. Most were still in the cafés in town, sipping coffee and checking the steely sky, waiting for it to clear. It was icy cold and there was no wind. The usual babble of voices was absent. Tom could hear the hiss of his skis as he glided to the start of the piste. Red poles marked the way like teachers' ticks. His cable-car companions were already gone, slinky patterns unwinding behind as they bobbed from side to side like kelly men. As soon as he hit the new snow, his skis became invisible. He was knee-deep in icy dust that flowed away from him like water. He concentrated on feeling the hard ground through his feet and legs. As his confidence grew, so his speed increased and turns became explosive, bursts of spray shouldered aside. A snow swimmer. Tiny ice particles stung like sparks. He hoped his bindings were tight. Years before, skiing with Anita in powder, her bindings had released in a fall and the snow had flowed over the top of them. It had taken half an hour of patting down snow like crop circles before they found them. He smiled and another layer of healing formed. He let the marker poles draw him back to the main ski network.

The flat grey sky eventually slid away like a steel door and sunshine flooded the mountain. Once more the slopes were the glistening backdrop to a kaleidoscope of movement. Tom looked down from the top of the T-bar as he lubricated his face with suncream and lipsalve. He had avoided this lift so far, but if he was to exorcise his nightmares it had to be faced. He turned to look up into the teeth of Spirstock, at the snarling ridge that had ripped away his happiness. It was breathtakingly beautiful. An iceberg in a cobalt sea. He stared at the huge snowfield which was almost too bright even through his sunglasses. It seemed to beckon.

Compared to the crowds shearing the lower slopes to shreds, there was icy calm and emptiness. Poised for development.

English voices drifted up to him. They came from the direction of Spirstock. Tom was surprised. There should be no skiing there, yet. He looked along the track to the mountain and saw a group of snowboarders sitting in the new snow like a colony of seals. Beyond he could see the constructions he was to inspect with Kristian. It was a chance to have a snoop on his own. Kristian had not called and was unlikely to be visiting today because of the earlier weather. Tom slid through a gap in the barrier netting and slipped down towards the young people. They were having fun. Free of the crowds and playing on a cushion of soft snow they were watching each other doing tricks, cheering successes, jeering wipe-outs, laughing. A makeshift ramp was their focus and Tom was struck by their skill and daring. Jumps, one-eighties, three-sixties, rail-grabs, forward rolls. This area could be a dedicated snowboarders' park. Build a permanent ramp, create a half-pipe, put in a lift. He skied down to them. Groups of young people were part of his job at the leisure centre and he always found them friendly and easy to talk to. He knew many older people found them threatening, probably because they tended to be loud and liked to be part of a group—Tom could remember being the same—but he liked them. Tom knew this particular crowd. They were the ones on the coach from the airport. He popped his rear bindings with his ski-pole, stepped out and flopped into the snow with the spectators.

"Looks like hard work," he said to the young man next to him. His baggy shapeless clothes were in marked contrast to the skiers' brightly-coloured outfits. It was when you looked closely you saw that the material was tough, flexible, padded and insulated. Just what you needed for a sport that demanded the skills and toughness of a gymnast. Tom rather envied their freedom—no poles, soft boots. Was it too late for him to start? Mmmn.

"Yeah, knackering, man. This is the raddest place but walking uphill kills you. It needs a lift."

"Are you all together?"

"Yeah—Portsmouth Uni Snowboard Club. I organized this trip. Where're you from? Oh, ta." He accepted an offered glucose tablet.

"Just outside Southampton. Did you know this area is being developed?"

"Apparently so." He looked up at the new pylons and the piles of building material.

"I work for a leisure company. We're interested in this place for group holidays."

"Well it needs a snowboard park with lifts and all."

Tom nodded. "I bumped into the engineer in charge of all this the other day. I'm meeting him again. I'll have a word."

The young man called across to another amorphous bundle, this one distinguished by a purple Wee Willie Winkie hat. "Shaz! There's a guy here with contacts in the area."

Shaz shambled up. "Hi," she said, breathlessly. "Haven't I seen you before?"

"On the coach coming up. Tom Shepherd. I'm at the Ledermann."

"Right, yeah. I remember. We're in a chalet. Cheap and cheesy. I'm Sharon, by the way. He won't have introduced himself 'cause he's dead ignorant so I'll tell you, he's Olly. And if he told you he organized this trip he's lying. I did all the real work."

"Yeah, yeah, yeah. Nag, nag, nag," said Olly. "I tell you, it's the last time. You get it all set up and then guys just let you down last minute. 'Can't go.' 'I've had a row with my girlfriend.' 'I'm broke.' 'I've got a job.' But this place could be wicked."

"Have you thought about booking through somebody else— let them do all the donkey work?"

"Ah, but," broke in Sharon, "that means Olly loses his free place, don' it moi ole toight-fisted lover."

"She's from Truro," explained Olly.

Tom laughed. "Well, my company is interested in organizing ski holidays and I think we must include snowboarding. If I can persuade Herr Weller to make this into a snowboarding area, would you be interested in booking through us? We're only down the road from you. I could certainly do you a good deal."

Olly looked at Sharon and raised his eyebrows. "Maybe," he said.

"I tell you what," Tom said, fishing in his pocket. "Take one of the company cards and we can chat about it at another time. I'm getting a numb bum."

"Yeah, OK. Hey. You want to watch this kid, though."

Above the ramp, a boy who looked about sixteen, was beginning his run. He was taking a longer approach than the others, flowing loose and relaxed, knees bent, arms hanging. He burst off the lip vertically then appeared to hang motionless, completely inverted until suddenly tucking his board underneath him in a backward somersault and landing smooth and controlled on the down slope. A round of whoops and cheers rang out.

"He's never at university," said Tom. "He's too young."

"No, he just hangs out with us. He's local. He reckons the snowboarding scene here sucks. It's all langlauf and downhill. He's a good kid. Called Rudi." Olly pushed himself to his feet, removed a large gauntlet and held out his hand. "Looks like it's my turn. Show the young turks how it's done." He shook Tom's hand. "We'll see you around. Nice to talk to you."

"You too," said Tom. "Take care."

"You must be joking," said Olly, grinning. "Come on, Shaz, you loverly Cornish cream-tea. I'll follow you."

Tom watched them sweep down the slope, shrinking in size as they went.

Now that he was so close to the new building, Tom had to take a look. He could get the details later from Kristian. He traversed the creaking, soft snow and crossed the narrow neck of rock which linked the lower slopes to Spirstock. Sturdy metal barriers now guarded the edges and under the powder, the snow was hard-packed from the tracks of the sno-cats. As the ground began to climb again and open out there was a large levelled area where the new café, already half-built, rose from a jumble of timber, building blocks, steel girders, cement mixers, diggers and piles of plastic bags, their sharp edges softened by snowfall. Icicles hung from every horizontal surface, glittering and dripping as the sun licked at them. Tom pictured himself sitting on the sun-terrace of the completed building, sipping a beer and drinking in the air and the view before taking the new lift to the glacier above. It would be stunning and his company could be in on the ground floor. He smiled. Perhaps "ground floor" was not quite the expression. He felt positive and optimistic. He squinted up towards the peak, his eyes tracing the thread of the chair-lift already in place. The engine house, at the rear of the café, was locked and barred. Tom felt it was the right moment to walk a little way up the slope. He needed to face the mountain on which the children had perished and where Anita had disappeared. He unclipped his skis, stuck them in the snow and plodded uphill beneath the chair-lift. He was warm with the exercise but the air was colder at these higher altitudes. The wide snowfield narrowed into a steep-sided valley. He imagined skiing routes as he progressed, something he did even back in England whenever he was in hill country. The possibilities here were enormous. He pictured vertical drops, heart-stopping jumps and high-speed turns. As he emerged from the valley, a vast, shimmering snowfield opened up. Enough, he thought. Far ahead was a glint of blue-green glass, the glacier ice. His heart was pounding and he squatted in the snow and turned his thoughts to Anita. As his breathing slowed, calmness enveloped him and he found himself saying goodbye to her in a way that he had not been able to before. He felt close to her. He shut his eyes to see her more clearly, the lashes filtering tears that crystallized on his cheeks.

He was cold and stiff. A wisp of high cloud had slipped a gauzy veil between himself and the sun and the temperature had plummeted. He could also not shake off a feeling that had been growing on him that something was wrong. His neck prickled. He stood up and stretched his thighs, bending each leg in turn, catching his ski-boot and pulling. As he balanced on one leg, a movement at the lip of the valley caught his eye. Two creatures, tiny silhouettes at this distance, were stepping delicately across the skyline. Chamois. Tom had never seen them before. He held his breath and slowly straightened his leg. The two animals froze, heads turned in his direction, nostrils investigating the air. The three made a tableau until the animals, with the wind behind them, felt secure enough to begin snuffing again at the new snow. To gain a closer look, Tom inched his way up the valley edge, side-stepping in slow-motion, his eyes fixed on the creatures. He was halfway towards them when there came a noise of thunder behind him. It reminded him of visits to his grandmother as a child when the coalmen shot bags of glittering black fuel through the opening in the pavement, rumbling deep into the cellar. Her tiny terraced house would shake. It used to scare him. It terrified him now. The chamois catapulted away and Tom's head whipped round to see, on the opposite valley side, a huge slab of snow detach itself and, with a roar, hurtle into the valley where it exploded like a shell, spitting out boiling clouds of ice and snow and then thundering on in a wild charge down the valley. *Of death*, thought Tom, shaking, *if I hadn't gone on safari*. The frozen breath of the avalanche brushed his cheeks and told him to leave. Immediately. The ground where he stood began to look treacherous. Something did not want him here. There would be no second warning. He stumbled clumsily downwards keeping above the torn jumble of ice, rock and snow that spewed down the valley floor. He expected to see broken pylons but the protective barriers had done their job, dividing the river of destruction so that it flowed around them. By the time he reached the site of the café, the energy of the fall was spent. And so was he. Sweat channelled down his back as he leant, gasping, against the engine-house wall. As his heart-rate steadied, so his thoughts cleared. He should have noted the signs. Steep valley sides, new snow, warm sun after frost—a deadly recipe. But now he had something further for his report. More barriers needed and mortars placed to release unstable snow. He located his skis and began the trudge back to the lower slopes which suddenly seemed attractive, warm and welcoming.

❋ CHAPTER FIVE ❋

Caroline Bryon scowled at her cards. She loathed "Knockout Whist" and "Beggar-my-Neighbour" and "Sevens" and all the other puerile games that her parents insisted on playing. She had just learned the word "puerile" and it featured largely in the ever-increasing list of things she hated. Father Bore and Mother Bore (she was rather proud of that) were in the Ledermann lounge, torpid after platefuls of veal and chips. Caroline was bored and edgy with hunger (she had left her veal on principle and most of her chips on dieting requirements.) She was wedged by her mother's spreading bulk into the corner of an upholstered bench, its ornately-carved wooden back digging into her. At least she was out of the knitted jumper and bobble-hat horror that had poisoned her day yesterday while her father, harrumphing with pleasure, had led them along the old familiar trails. Because of the bad visibility that morning they had spent the day scouring shops in the town looking for bran-sticks for her father to sprinkle on his morning muesli. Now Caroline wore her tight jeans and new, skinny-rib top that her mother disliked so much and which accentuated her stalky figure. It made it difficult for her to be identified as the daughter of those two lumpy old people. She hoped. She looked up at the cuckoo-clock above her father to see how much longer she had to endure before being released for bed. She was willing it to fall on his head when she caught the eye of a young woman sitting alone at the next table. It seemed to Caroline that there was a hint of sympathy in her smile.

At a table, conveniently close to the bar, the ski-reps, Alec and Shelley, held court. Alec liked to call it his evening surgery. He and Shelley had done the rounds of the company's clients in Unteriberg and had sorted out ill-fitting boots, lost lift-passes, broken showers and had fielded the usual litany of complaints. They had arranged tobogganing, swimming, ski-biking, yodelling competitions, excursions and ski-tests, had provided weather forecasts and dealt with all the other matters that the day had created. In fact, Alec had done the work. Shelley had simply looked gorgeous in her scarlet boob-tube, black leggings and pointed leather boots, had smiled dazzlingly at all the young men and occasionally flicked back her lovely blonde hair. But no-one was complaining. Alec enjoyed helping people, was conscientious and was fluent in German. He provided the friendly, efficient service. Shelley enjoyed being looked at and provided the glamour. There were always the ski-instructors for the women. It was ski-instructors who were the subject of their discussion at the Ledermann. Geoffrey, the solicitor had approached them.

"It simply is not acceptable," he was saying. "He may suit some of your clientele but I find his methods quite offensive. I had to have stiff words with him yesterday. The way he behaved towards these ladies was intolerable." He gestured to Dot and Kath who were seated nearby.

Alec listened politely and wrote notes on his clip-board. He had heard every variety of complaint about instructors in his time as a rep so this was nothing new but he was disturbed by the frequency with which Marco's name occurred. Geoffrey's earnest face was flushed with indignation, wine, and the unfamiliar role of gallant protector but he felt capable and debonair in his blazer, slacks and silk cravat. He had escorted Dot and Kath around the town all day and been decisive about what to see and where to eat. Dot saw how much pleasure it gave him and easily became the helpless female. She only took control when she and Kath did some shopping-therapy at the apres-ski fashion store. They now wore the result—silk blouses (Dot, white, Kath, pink), multi-coloured, loose-fitting trousers and zip-sided, black leather bootees. They had spent too much and were a great deal happier for it, pleased to wear similar clothes as a visual symbol of their friendship. With duty-free perfume liberally employed they both felt cool, comfortable and glamorous. They sipped coffee and amaretto and let Geoffrey champion their cause.

Alec was placatory. "Don't worry, it's no problem. I'll get you a change of group for tomorrow. Lots of people change groups after the first day or two. I think Franz has room. You'll like him, I know. He runs the ski-school and is very careful and painstaking. I'll sort it out tonight and call here first thing tomorrow to let you know where to meet him. OK? The forecast's good for tomorrow. Lots of sunshine."

"But what about this Marco fellow?" Geoffrey insisted. "Something should be done, you know. He was rude to Dorothy and he treated Katherine abominably." He went back to join the ladies.

"It doesn't matter, Geoff, honestly. Leave it. We're in a new group, so let's just enjoy the holiday." Her confidence restored by Tom, Kath did not want to dwell on the past.

Geoffrey huffed a bit but was startled into silence when he felt Dot take his hand below the table and give it a squeeze. She favoured him with a grateful look, turned to face Kath, raised her eyebrows and gave her a wink. Time to rein him in a little. Kath hid her smile in her coffee cup.

"Right," said Alec. "Good. Now, Shelley has the list of the evening entertainments. Is there anything you want me to put your names down for? Horse-drawn sleigh-ride?"

Tom appeared in the doorway and took in the scene. He had skied until late that afternoon, gripped by white fever. The light had been failing and the lifts closing when he skidded to a halt by the cable-car. A group of instructors, having delivered their pupils to the top station, had gathered at the start of the one black run, a steep, difficult run that would take them beneath the cable-car, through the trees and down to the foot of the mountain. Tom had simply tagged on to them. It had been a wild, exhilarating run, a non-stop, high-speed career through gullies and moguls, compressions, jumps and steep, tree-lined tracks on virgin snow. Grinning, he had swept up to the scarlet-clad group in the car-park, his legs burning and face rasped. Because the buses had gone he was given a lift into town so he bought a round of drinks at a Kellerbar in town as thanks and reached the Ledermann as dinner was being served. He ate wearing his skigear and only then went to shower and change. On his return, as he stood in the doorway of the lounge, planning a quiet drink and an early night, faces turned towards him. There was the elderly couple who had the daughter who was sick on the coach. The girl was sitting with a young woman at a neighbouring table, a table covered with books, files and sheets of paper. The two were chatting animatedly. The girl was transformed from the sulky adolescent she had been on the bus. She was animated, her eyes alive with interest. Her parents kept glancing distrustfully across at her as they clutched playing-cards in their plump fingers. She ignored them. It took some time for Tom to realize that the young woman was the one whom he had grabbed in the church. He felt impelled speak to her but was stopped when a female voice called across the room, "Tom! Come over here and join us!"

Kath, delighted to see him, insisted on buying him a drink. He gave her a warm smile, pleased to see her restored to the bubbly state that was her natural self. He joined the group around Alec and Shelley.

"This is one's personal ski trainer," Kath said, plummily. "Epsolutely essential, one feels. One never trevels withite one."

"You'll be getting the bill later," Tom told her. "Hello, everybody. Tom Shepherd."

"Did you go up today?" enquired Alec. "You look as if you did."

Tom's face was glowing.

"Yes. I thought I might see you there with the new snow."

Alec looked wistful. "I would've done but I had admin to do. Shelley went with some of the instructors, didn't you, Shel? She said it was great."

"Brilliant," she said, looking towards the door. There was a hubbub of noise in the foyer, loud talk, laughter, the clumping of feet.

"Do you want me to give you a call next time you're free?" Tom asked Alec. "You can show me all the runs that I've missed."

"Great, I'd like that," he said. Alec had found the instructors cliquey (unless you looked like Shelley) and he was tired of skiing on his own. "So, how was the new snow?"

"Erm, loose," said Tom. "It was fantastic on the lower slopes but I went for a look at the new development on Spirstock and it attacked me."

"Avalanche?" asked Alec.

"Yep. Bit scary. It missed me but only by luck." A vision of the fountain by the monastery flashed through his mind. "There's still more work to be done, I think."

"God, you shouldn't have been there. It's supposed to be restricted. It's always had a bad reputation," said Alec seriously.

A figure stood silently behind Tom. Herr Brucke, carrying a tray of drinks, had approached noiselessly and had been listening to their conversation, his heavy features like stone. He slammed the tray down on to the table and returned to the kitchen. Dot giggled nervously.

"He is moody, isn't he?" she said. "I don't think I've ever seen him smile. What's his problem, Alec?"

"Dunno. He's just a serious Swiss, I guess. This hotel has been in his family for generations. You'll see the old man occasionally. He still tries to run things in the background."

"So, Geoffrey," said Tom. "How's the skiing? You seem to have become an extra instructor like me. I saw you on the first day."

Geoffrey, always prepared to be defensive, was taken aback by the implied compliment. It was one thing to impress two non-skiers like Dot and Kath but to be so naturally included into the magic circle of experts by this quiet-spoken, easy-mannered man gave another boost to his self-esteem. Paradoxically, it brought a layer of natural modesty to the surface."

"Oh, I did very little, you know. Just a few hints here and there. Dorothy is a very apt pupil." He sounded like an end-of-term report.

"Give over, Geoff," Dot said. She addressed the rest of the group. "He's lovely. Ever so patient. Never gets cross." She smiled fondly at him. It was true she was flattering him outrageously but she did enjoy his old-fashioned courtesy, something no man had shown her before. She also sensed his vulnerability.

He blushed brightly. "Well, I have negotiated a group change for us all and I'm sure we will all make good progress from now on. It is hot in here, isn't it?" he said, and daringly removed his blazer.

Shelley, bored with the present company, brightened as Olly and Shaz tumbled into the lounge propelled by the rest of the snowboard crowd. Tom noticed that young Rudi was with them. They transformed the quiet buzz of conversation into a party atmosphere in an instant, crowding around the bar, shouting orders to each other, arguing, laughing and wafting clean, cold air through the room. Their charity-shop grunge clothing made it seem as if a company of strolling players had hit town. Two young men lifted Shelley, screaming happily, out of her seat and up to the bar and began plying her with punch. Olly approached their table.

"Hi, Alec. Hello, Tom. So this is where you hang out. Hi folks." His open face took in Geoff, Dot and Kath. "What're you drinking?"

Tom stood up. "No, no, this is my shout. Is Sharon with you? What'll she want? Right, you take my place. I'll see if I can catch Herr Brucke's eye."

Olly did not argue. "Great, thanks. I'll give you a go on my snowboard sometime."

"I might just take you up on that," replied Tom, seriously.

Ruth Francis rescued the papers that had slithered off her littered table. As a post-grad student researching the European monastic system she had been working in her room but had brought her materials into the lounge where she felt less solitary. She looked like a school-girl with her slender figure, spectacles and the cascade of unruly hair constantly being tucked behind her ears. She had spent the day in the Unteriberg monastery library, steeped in the decaying smell of the past. This evening, with her eyes tired from reading and translating medieval German all day, she had felt the loneliness that sometimes came upon her when she paused from work. When Caroline Bryon had returned to her the sheet of paper that had wafted across the floor, Ruth had reached the stage when she needed a break She had noticed the girl's boredom and saw in her someone who also could do with a break. Ruth liked young people and she had discovered that she enjoyed the teaching work she was required to do as a graduate. They were now poring over Ruth's sketches, their heads close together.

"What's this?" asked Caroline. She was looking at a figure that Ruth had sketched a number of times, a crude representation of a man, the sort a child might do. A gingerbread man, except that he wore no smile.

"I don't know, yet," replied Ruth. "Have you been inside the church? I found this carved in the stone of the north wall. It's quite hidden away and the guidebook doesn't mention it. It's too well cut for graffiti and anyway, it's not the sort of picture a casual graffiti artist would create."

Caroline, who had done her share of graffiti in the school toilets (her parents would be horrified) agreed. "What are these marks?"

"Something else I don't know." The figure was decorated from top to toe with broken lines. "When I saw it, it reminded me of something I'd seen. You know the film, *Moby Dick?*"

Caroline shook her head.

"Well, there's a character in it called Queequeg and he's covered in tattoos. I think that's where I've seen something like it. But I've no idea why anyone should carve it on the wall of a church. It looks old, don't you think?"

Caroline had also seen something like it although she was too embarrassed to say. The previous summer, the family holiday had been at Lyme Regis where they had indulged in the usual deadly mixture of deckchairs and newspapers, afternoon teas and little jaunts in the Rover. One little jaunt had taken them to Cerne Abbas and there, looming over the village, was a giant, a carved chalk-hill figure with an enormous erection. Caroline still blushed at the memory, her father's averted eyes, her mother's fascinated disgust. Now, in front of her again, in miniature and thankfully shorn of its manhood, was the same primitive. Ruth was reaching to pick up the sketch when someone bumped hard into the table. With a little scream she watched helplessly as books, papers, pens, maps and coffee cups cascaded to the floor. A man with close-cropped dark hair, brown kindly eyes and a comic expression of shock and contrition was staring at the mess he had created. She had seen him before.

"I'm so sorry," Tom said, squatting down and gathering up the materials. "I seem to be fated to give you shocks." He had been trying to find a way through the students, now engaged in a noisy drinking game, when he had been jogged. "I don't think anything's damaged." He replaced the books and papers on the table and collected the empty cups. "Let me replace your drinks. Coffees? OK." He took the crockery to Herr Brucke at the bar, left his order and returned. "They'll be along in a minute. Can I join you for a while. I'd rather not be inveigled into their games. I prefer to ski with a clear head." He smiled at Caroline. "You look a lot better than when I saw you last. How's things?"

Caroline smiled back, shyly. "All right," she said.

"That's good. I'm sorry, I don't know your name. I'm Tom."

"Caroline!" called a voice from the next table. Mr Bryon was manoeuvring himself out of his chair. "Mother and I are going to bed."

Mrs Bryon struggled off the bench. "Come along, dear. Another busy day tomorrow."

Caroline reddened but stayed seated. "You go. I'll be along later. I'm not tired."

"Oh." Mrs Bryon stopped in her tracks. This was not like Caroline. "George! She says she is staying here."

Mr Bryon was equally nonplussed. He humphed a bit, hurt that she so clearly preferred other company to that of her parents but he could see that he and Hilda might be a little dull for the youngster. It was the unexpectedness of the declaration of independence that had shaken him. But she was enjoying herself and looked the better for it. He loved her dearly and would not spoil her evening.

"Very well, dear. Just don't be too late. Good night all." His smile embraced the whole group, then he took his wife's arm and escorted her out of the room.

Caroline was surprised at the ease of her victory. She felt a welling of affection for her father. His awareness of her needs made her feel very grown-up.

She sighed melodramatically and raised her eyes. "Yes, it's 'Caroline' as you heard. Parents!" she said, but she smiled.

Ruth quietly stacked her work together. She did not want to show it to this clumsy stranger. She should have remained in her room as she had originally planned and not been tempted out for company. It was one thing to entertain a bored teenager but her work was too important and personal to expose to the prying eyes of another adult.

Tom was beginning to regret having broken into the relationship. He was aware that the studious-looking young lady was inconspicuously preparing to leave as he was asking Caroline about her skiing. She removed her spectacles, slipped them inside a case and dropped them into a large raffia bag bulging with books and papers. Tom stood up.

"I'm sorry," he said to her. "Please don't leave on my account. I should get back to the others over there." He waved vaguely across the room.

Ruth looked directly at him for the first time. She thought he was probably older than she was but his slim, athletic build and, at present, his awkward earnestness made him seem quite young. He was wearing black jeans and a simple, navy shirt and his freshly-showered look made him appear vulnerable. Her feelings of threat faded.

"No," she said, tucking her hair behind her ears and smiling, "it's all right. I'm just making sure that my books are safe when you start throwing the new coffee around."

Her grey eyes, undefended, swam with quiet humour. Tom, unprepared, felt something like pain inside him. He stared stupidly for a few seconds, then laughed and sat down. "I'm not normally clumsy," he said. "Hi, Tom Shepherd." He reached across the table and shook hands formally. The touch of her slim fingers was a shock.

"Ruth Francis."

"You're not here for the skiing, I take it," Tom said, gesturing towards her books.

"No, I'm studying."

"Ah," said Tom. "The monastery."

"That's it."

"And how's it going?"

"Not bad."

"Is it a project you're working on?"

"Sort of. You on holiday?"

"Sort of."

They smiled warily at each other. Olly and Sharon loomed up to the table, raised glasses and called, "Cheers! Don't forget the snowboarding!" then dived back into the crowd. Caroline looked longingly after them.

"Why don't you ask if you can join them tomorrow?" Tom suggested.

Caroline looked down at her feet. "No," she murmured. "I've got to go with mum and dad tomorrow. Anyway, they wouldn't want me. They're all older than me."

Tom stood up and, using his arms as a snowplough, parted the crush until he found Olly again. After a few brief words he returned with him in tow.

Olly was one of those big lads who put on their adult bulk early. It gave him a confidence and presence that made his contemporaries defer to him instinctively. He enjoyed company and habitually formed groups around himself. He approached Caroline, radiating energy.

"Yeah, come with us tomorrow. I'll get young Rudi to teach you. We've got a spare board. Have you got ski-boots? Ah, cross-country, right. What size feet are you? Yeah? I think we can find some boots—lots of us have got soft and hard boots. We'll meet you at the top of the cable, half-past nine, OK? Well, if you can't, it's no bother. We'll leave the stuff in a locker. We'll be there, whatever. Hope you can make it. We're just off to the bar round the corner. It's a bit more lively than here. You coming, Tom? Anyone?" His gaze took in the rest of the table. "Anyway, it's the Storchen, if you decide. Cheers."

"What do you reckon?" Tom asked Caroline.

"I dunno. I dunno what mum and dad will say."

"It looks good fun. And I've seen Rudi. He's amazing. He's about your age. Look, that's him. Why not have a word? He's Swiss but he speaks good English."

Tom pointed out a small lad with cropped, orange hair. If you had thought for a minute that it might be his natural colour, the thought would be dispelled by the green stripe that ran from forehead to neck. His long-sleeved, mud-coloured T-shirt hung shapelessly over grey, baggy trousers and , at the moment, his studded nose was deep inside a glass of coke. Irresistible.

"Shall I?" asked Caroline of Ruth.

"Yes, why not?" she said. "Just don't introduce him to your parents."

Caroline giggled and stood up. "OK," she said. "Here goes."

Tom and Ruth smiled again at each other after Caroline had gone. "Tough age," said Tom. Ruth nodded. "Are you working tomorrow or do you go skiing sometimes?"

"I'm going to Zürich. I'm meeting someone there."

"Oh, I see," said Tom.

"Look, this coffee is taking ages. I think I'm going to leave it. Thanks anyway. Enjoy your holiday." Ruth stood up just as Herr Brucke approached across the room, tray in hand. She looked rueful and sat down again. However, Herr Brucke did not reach the table. He stopped, staring at them in horror. They stared back, then looked quizzically at each other. Tom shrugged and whispered, "He's a very funny bloke. Everyone says so."

With a hissed, "Mein Gott," Herr Brucke turned on his heel and rushed back into the kitchen.

"He wasn't looking at us," said Ruth. On the table, ringed with coffee stains, was her sketch of the tattooed man.

❄ CHAPTER SIX ❄

Marco was bored and drunk. By getting rid of the fat Englishwomen and their stuck-up friend he had thought to free himself for some advanced skiing but the remnants of the group, willing and daring though they were, were still only on their fourth day. The mixture of teen-agers and young couples had progressed but they were beginners and they were tired. It was hot at the top of the chair-lift and as the group collected they flopped into the soft snow to await their instructor. Marco glided casually towards them, poles tucked under one arm. His, "OK, we go," was met with a chorus of groans.

"Can't we just stay here and sunbathe for a bit, Marco?" asked Melissa, switching on her winsome puppy look. "Please. We're ever so tired." She was sixteen and her wealthy parents were off free-skiing somewhere. With her designer ski-wear and inno-cently knowing looks she had been given a great deal of individual attention by Marco. With the schnapps he had swigged on the chair-lift glowing inside him and Melissa's hungry look feeding his ego, Marco decided to show his group what real skiing was. He gave an exaggerated sigh and pointed to where, not far below, there was a ramp of snow underneath the chair-lift.

"We go there, yes? We make the jumps. I show you first. You watch." Without pausing he planted both his poles, jumped up and spun round one hundred and eighty degrees to face down the slope, and was off in a racing start, accelerating rapidly. Other skiers, realizing his intention, stopped to watch. He hit the lip at speed and launched into a low flight. At the peak of his trajectory he casually rotated three hundred and sixty degrees then dropped to a featherlight landing, spraying a curtain of snow as he dug out an emergency stop. There was a ragged round of applause from the onlookers. His group looked down in awe.

"I hope he's not expecting us to do that," murmured Liz to Jim. "This is supposed to be our honeymoon, not a survival course."

Her husband laughed. "No, he's just showing off, that's all. God, that was incredible. Oh, shit. Look."

Marco was beckoning them down. The group looked at each other in disbelief. There followed a swift discussion as to who was to go first. Jim, all agreed, was the best skier and so should be the first to defend the reputation of British pluck. There was no doubt about it. It was exciting in Marco's group. And terrifying.

"Oh, thanks guys," he said. "All right, here goes." He turned to Liz. "It's OK, love. Just go slowly, that's all."

"Slowly?" she replied. "I'll be walking down and side-stepping up."

Jim set off towards the ramp, controlling his speed in a wide snowplough. As he approached the jump he had to bring his skis parallel. This alteration brought about a sudden acceleration. He watched helplessly as his skis rose up in front of his face, his head went back and he took off. It was not a lengthy flight. He landed on his back, his sunglasses bounced off and snow flowed down his neck. A voice near at hand was shouting, "Why you lean back? You lean forward always!" Thanks, Marco, thought Jim. You might have mentioned that earlier. There was another, more distant sound. It was the rest of the group laughing. He brought his skis below him across the fall-line (aptly named, he now recognized), and scrambled to his feet, favouring the group with a two-fingered gesture. Marco was waiting for the next victim.

Liz did not quite walk down as she had threatened but, having seen Jim fall, approached the jump so slowly that she did not have enough momentum to reach the lip. She was halfway up the ramp when she slid to a halt, there was a momentary pause, and then, as her face froze in horror, she began to slide backwards. She collapsed into an untidy heap at the base of the jump and began the slow process of untangling herself from her equipment. She was concentrating on this when she heard, "Get oot o ma way! A cannae stop!" Moira, unwisely, had set off as Liz had reached the ramp, assuming, wrongly, that the way would be clear by the time she reached it. Liz had removed one of her skis when Moira hit the other one. No-one could complain about her failing to lean forward. She went over the ramp head first, diving to a halt at Jim's feet.

"A cannae see! A cannae see!" she wailed, looking up at him. Laughing, he bent down and removed her goggles which were packed tight with snow.

"The other way of stopping, I see," he said. "You all right? Liz?" he called to his wife. With her skis over her shoulder she was plodding towards him. Moira, whose skis had become crossed behind her when she had belly-flopped, could not figure out which ski was on which leg and was stuck like a crab on its back. Jim and Liz had to remove her skis before she could stand up. All three moved to one side and sat down to watch the entertainment.

"Great spectator sport," said Jim as, one by one, the class attempted the jump in their individually disastrous ways, in spite of an increasing number of people bellowing, "Don't lean back!" as they approached. Finally there was Cameron. Not the most skilful of skiers but the most daring. He loved Marco's on-the-edge approach and was fearless. Unlike the others, he approached flat-out, skis parallel. In the final few metres he heard, "Don't lean back!" and acted on the advice. He took off smoothly, wobbled uncertainly in the air, came down with a slap on the hard snow, did the splits, recovered and snow-ploughed to a halt, still on his feet. He was greeted with whoops and cheers from the group. Marco slapped him hard on the back.

"Das ist gut," he said. It was the first praise any of them had been given. Marco's teeth gleamed beneath his black moustache. "Now I show you," he said. He ran back up the slope, skis herringboned for grip, then turned to face downwards, waiting, watching the chairlift.

"Now what's he going to do?" asked Melissa.

"God only knows," said Cameron. "Forward roll? Double twist and pike with tuck?"

What he did, none could have predicted. The chairlift was busy and weighed down with passengers. Marco waited until an unoccupied chair came into view then set off on his run again, pushing hard with a skater's step to give himself power. When he hit the lip, instead of crouching forward for a long, shallow flight, he stood upright and leapt high into the air, straight into the path of the approaching chair. He spun one hundred and eighty degrees and was scooped up neatly into the passing seat, sending it swinging wildly. He leaned back, took out a cigarette and lit up. Cheers and applause burst from the onlookers, especially the other passengers on the chair who had thought they were about to witness a disaster. His group watched his back recede to the top, saw him alight and snake down to rejoin them, cigarette still between his lips.

"That was totally unbelievable, Marco!" breathed Melissa, her eyes shining.

Marco nodded, barely acknowledging her. "We take the chair now. Rest at the top. You follow." He set off quickly, his pupils scrambling to their feet and hurriedly pursuing him in a trail of snowplough turns. Marco muttered, "Scheisskopf," as he recalled the lift operator at the top. His pupils had not seen him being shouted at and called "stupid" and "crazy". He spat with contempt for the small-mindedness of the locals. In the seven years since he had arrived in Unteriberg he had never been accepted in spite of investing his money in the area. Even that had only been possible on Spirstock. All the lower slopes were run by local families and they froze him out. He had made a killing when he sold his nightclub in Innsbruck and even after buying the disco in Unteriberg he still had money sitting uselessly in the bank. Then came the possibility of developing the higher slopes. Oddly, the local people had not wanted anything to do with it so he had been free to set up his own development company for a purpose-built hotel and discobar for skiers, climbers and walkers. There had been problems all the way. Local companies would not take on the job, there had been accidents and work had been suspended, the risk of avalanche was high, and bad weather had often shut down progress for weeks. But since the chair-lift had been installed, materials were now being transported to the very edge of the glacier where his vision of the most spectacular ski-lodge-and-nightclub in the Alps was taking shape. By next season he would begin to recoup his investment and after that he would make serious money. He smiled at the thought. The local peasants would regret trying to close him out. No serious skier would want to mess about on the lower slopes when there was glacier skiing to be had. There would also be the lucrative summer trade too. As he glided off the chair past the dark face of the operator he enjoyed the thought that those hostile looks would have to change to respect.

"I wonder why he brought us here," mused Jim. He and the group were lounging on the deck of the unfinished base café on Spirstock.

"I don't care," breathed Liz. "Just be grateful we've got a break." Lying back, cushioned against her jacket and sweater, she was luxuriating in the brilliant sun, eyes closed, face shining with freshly-applied cream.

"Where's he got to, anyway?" Jim stood up and looked around.

"Jim, love, just relax will you," said Liz. "Sit down and look at the view or something."

"You tell him, Liz," murmured Moira, sleepily. She too was sprawled out in the sun, every limb aching. She had taken off her boots and her stockinged feet steamed gently. "A dinnae want tae move frae here for an hour at least."

Marco was pleased. The avalanche barriers had done their work and diverted the latest torrent of churning snow around the pylons. It was evidently recent, but ingenuity, technical development and greater knowledge was now able to control this unstable mountain. On both sides of the valley there were mortar emplacements which could trigger snow slides whenever the risk of avalanche was high. They were capable of being electronically fired from remote positions and would harmlessly expel the mountain's armoury. For the first time, Spirstock's brooding menace would be tamed. Marco imagined the empty chairlift weighed down with passengers ascending to his café to spend their francs, queues of people waiting at the bottom with their lift-passes from which he would get a hefty cut, and the slope sprinkled with figures. Hundreds and thousands on an iced cake. And hundreds of thousands in the bank. He took a long pull at his flask, tilting back his head. Up there, where the black specks of choughs spiralled silently against the shimmering sky, was where the Hotel Kreize already had its foundations. The foundations of Marco's fortune. Giddy with his vision and bursting with self-confident energy he looked down at his class of beginners basking on the verandah of the base café. A brilliant skier and recognized as such by the ski-school, he was more at home on skis than walking and was totally fearless. He was mostly given advanced classes but Franz, the head of the ski-school, insisted that he take his share of beginners too. It was only fair. He did not like Marco but he needed his services as more people were coming to Unteriberg each year. Marco did not enjoy being told what to do. It was time for another demonstration.

Liz sat up with a shriek as snow scattered down on her face and bare arms. Icicles crashed from the eaves as Marco launched himself off the café roof, flew overhead, cleared the verandah and touched down on the slope below, light as a bird. He turned and dug his edges, grinding off speed to bring himself quickly to a halt, stepped out of his skis and stood one upright, an automatic reflex from his competitive days when sponsors needed the cameras on their logos. His group watched him in astonishment. Cameron had seen the whole thing, only realizing at the last minute exactly what Marco was going to do. The rest, alerted by Liz's scream, had seen a flying figure against a blue sky. It was awesome. When Marco rejoined them he could not have wished for a more flattering response. Melissa stared, adoring, Cameron admiring, and the rest unbelieving.

"I'm crazy, huh?" he said, and slid down next to Melissa, propping himself up against the wall of the café. "We take more break now." He swigged another mouthful of spirits then closed his eyes against the warm sun, soon breathing regularly and deeply. Moira watched him.

"Crazy?" she said, quietly. "Fuckin certifiable!"

There was general agreement.

Half-an-hour later Cameron was itching to get going again. Sitting around in the sun was a waste of good snow time. As the only beginner in a group from St. Andrew's he had been separated from his friends by the ski-school and was desperate to rejoin them, free-skiing. Good at sports and a quick learner, he was fit and not in the least tired. He glanced at Marco who had slumped to one side and was snoring, stood up and found his skis.

"What you doing, Cam? Jim was watching him through slitted eyes.

"Thought I'd practise ma turns a wee while. You comin?"

Jim looked at Liz lying next to him, her arm tucked through his, eyes closed and a gentle smile on her peaceful features as she bathed in the warmth. "No, I don't think so. I'll not disturb Liz's beauty sleep. She needs it."

He was given a sharp dig in the ribs. "Just watch it, you," murmured Liz.

Jim chuckled. "Have fun, Cameron," he said.

Cameron clipped up his boots, shouldered his skis and plodded up the line of the chair-lift. He just needed enough height to be able to put together a few snowplough turns and perhaps have a go at those sexy parallels that looked so easy. The snow here had been disturbed by something but there were smooth areas to thread a way through. He stopped by one of the pylons and looked down as Marco had done. Below were Marco's tracks, serpentining until they neared the point where the snow-laden roof of the café merged into the hillside. There they straightened and cut at right angles across the roof, disappearing abruptly at the edge.

Cameron's stomach churned with excitement. He could never resist a challenge and he was sure it could not be difficult. His leap that morning had given him an adrenalin buzz which he was keen to repeat. As long as he kept his speed under control and remembered to lean forwards he knew he could fly like Marco. He placed his skis across the slope and stepped into the bindings. They made a satisfying click. He had had trouble on the first day with loose bindings, his skis releasing irritatingly frequently so he had borrowed a screwdriver and wound them up tight. Now they felt snug against his boots. He twisted his torso to face the fall-line and leaned forward to plant both poles below his skis. Then, leaning hard against the top of his poles to stop himself moving, he slowly shuffled round until his skis faced downhill in a wide snowplough. He took a deep breath and stood up straight, releasing his poles as he did so and smoothly slid away down the slope. He traced Marco's tracks, snowploughing where Marco had made parallel turns and lining up for a straight schuss as he approached the roof. The difference was the speed. A parallel turn, much quicker than a snowplough, retains more of the skier's momentum. As soon as Cameron left the roof, gravity tugged hard. He leaned forward but was hauled down into the yawning space. His ski tips dropped and hit the wooden deck, throwing him forward and slamming his face into the boards.

The sound of the crash violently yanked those dozing on the verandah from their dreams. There were cries of shock, and questions shouted as they scrambled to their feet. Sprawled face down, Cameron screamed with pain, blood pouring from his smashed nose and mouth. But the pain was elsewhere, his face quite numb. His right leg, the one with the ski still attached and the sheared bone poking bloodily through his salopettes, was fuelling his dreadful shrieks. The dark blue material, already soaked black with blood, dropped scarlet gouts through the gaps in the wooden planking and stained the snow beneath.

Jim was the first to reach him. He dropped to one knee.

"Christ, man! Whit are you daein? Jesus, what a mess! Cameron? Cam? Can you hear me, man?" The rest gathered round, frozen in horror by Cameron's noises. Moira could not look at his leg. She reached out a hand to touch his shoulder when a voice said, sharply, "Don't move him!"

It was Melissa, Queen Guide, Duke of Edinburgh Gold, Outward Bounder, First Aider and St. John's Ambulance. She moved authoritatively to Cameron's side, unaffected by his screams. She ignored the split mouth and missing teeth and concentrated on the leg. She looked towards Marco who was still slumped against the café wall, peering blearily at his class, wondering what had happened.

"We must stop this bleeding or he'll die," she said, simply. "Jim, get a tourniquet from Marco. You know what I mean? And some painkillers. He'll have something in his pack. Moira, take off your jacket and cushion his head. Gently!" She removed her own jacket as she spoke and draped it lightly across Cameron's shoulders. "We'll need more covering. He'll go into deep shock and we have to keep him warm. Jim, have you got that tourniquet? Here, give me the pack. Make Marco get help quickly." She delved into the pack, found a length of rubber tubing with a wooden handle at one end and slipped it around Cameron's thigh above the fracture. She wound the wooden handle until the rubber tightened and squeezed tight into the gory salopettes. Her hands were scarlet but rock steady as she watched the flow of blood slow to a drip. "Has Marco called for help yet, Jim? Good. Right, pass me your coats," she said to the group. They willingly handed them over to cover the broken figure. His ruined face, now turned carefully to one side and cushioned in Moira's expensive jacket, was deathly white between the blood. His screams had stopped but he had begun to shake violently and grunt. Melissa spoke quietly to him.

"You'll be all right, Cameron. Help's on its way. Just hang on for a little while. That was some fall you had. It'll make a great story when you get home. It's OK, it's OK. Swallow this, if you can. It'll ease the pain." She did not know whether he could hear her but she wanted to keep his attention and stop him drifting into unconsciousness. She turned to Liz. "You see that tourniquet? Can you check your watch and let me know in five minutes. I'll need to release it and retighten it or it could do damage. Thanks."

Liz obeyed automatically. Now that the initial shock was wearing off she had time to be impressed by Melissa's competence. Who would have thought it? She saw that Marco was speaking urgently on his intercom. It was the first time she had seen him look worried.

The bloodwagon arrived swiftly, skied in by the head of the ski-school and his most experienced instructor. As soon as they saw the damage they knew that a high-speed ride down the mountain strapped to a sledge was out of the question for Cameron. Franz radioed for a helicopter as his colleague gave Cameron a morphine shot. Now that decisions and action were out of their hands the class stood around helplessly, looking down anxiously at their companion. Franz and Marco were in serious discussion.

"Someone'll need to let his friends know what's happened," said Jim.

Moira spoke up. "A'll dae that. I ken whaur he's stayin."

"What're we waiting for?" muttered Liz who was shivering in spite of the sunshine.

"The chopper, I guess. Looks like Cam was doing a Marco," said Jim. "You know what he's like—anything you can do…"

Melissa was still squatting by Cameron's side. She looked up. "I'll go with him to the hospital," she said quietly. "He'll need someone with him when he comes round. Moira, find out his parents' phone number when you see his friends. I'll ring them when I know what the hospital says. He'll be here for some time. They'll want to fly out, I'm sure."

Moira nodded, also wondering at Melissa's transformation. Melissa was unconscious of the surprised looks she was receiving. She turned back to Cameron and gently placed her hand on his forehead, instinctively thinking calmness and healing. Although unaware of it, for her this was a defining moment, something that would shape the course of her future life. She inspected her tourniquet again. The rescue team had looked closely at it when they had arrived and left it alone, nodding their approval at Marco. She looked at him now. He had regained his composure and was talking to Franz, every inch the man in charge of the situation. Melissa's disillusion was complete. She listened for the beat of the helicopter.

•

ICE

Tom and Kristian saw it first. That morning they had trudged up the line of the new chair-lift and were now enjoying the reward of a spectacular view, the whole canton spread out below like a model. The sun winked off the gilded dome of Unteriberg's church, a gold filling among the grey and white fangs. Iced lakes glassed the valleys. The building debris at the site of the top station was transformed into bizarre sculptures by the snow. The sky was clear but it was chill here and fingers of icy wind felt down their necks. They had scrambled across the foundations, Kristian enthusiastically describing how it would look next summer. The landscape defined the building, its main point of reference being the massive rock which marked the start of the high glacier. An elevated sun terrace was to be constructed against it and then the hotel would be built as a series of steps down the precipitous slope concluding with a lower terrace with steam baths and jacuzzis. Tom and Kristian had inspected the immense supporting girders already driven into the granite. The workmen, unable apparently to resist leaving their mark, had scratched a drawing on the black rock. It was oddly familiar to Tom.

Kristian was pleased by Tom's enthusiasm.

"This place will take one hundred and fifty people. It aims to be the best ski-lodge in the Alps. You must make the first bookings with your company next season. You will never have it so good again."

"'Cheap', I hope you mean."

Kristian smiled. They were enjoying each other's company. "I understand it is owned by a young Innsbrucker. I will find out for you."

A crimson dragonfly rose up from distant Unteriberg and headed their way. They heard the throbbing of rotor blades pulsing off the hillsides. It flew low and fast, skiers on the lower slopes stopping to watch its progress.

"Someone's in trouble," said Tom.

"Look!" pointed Kristian. Below, at the new base café site, orange smoke spiralled into the air. They made out tiny figures and an orange cross spread out on the snow.

"What could have happened there?" puzzled Tom. "It isn't open for skiing yet."

"We'll find out, yes?" Kristian plucked his skis out of the snow and stepped into them. As the helicopter rose from below, he and Tom skied down from above to converge on the scene of the accident. The helicopter settled on the orange marker in a swirling blizzard, its blades continuing to slice the air. Two figures jumped out and ran, bent double, to the ring of waiting people, a still shape at their centre. As they neared, Tom and Kristian saw them gently wrap it in a sheet.

"Looks like a fatality," Tom muttered.

"No, I think not. Watch." replied Kristian. One of the medics had attached a small gas bottle to the sheet, the sheet inflated and made a protective cocoon around the injured person. Now immobilized, he was carefully lifted onto a stretcher and carried swiftly into the helicopter, accompanied by a small figure wearing pale blue. The machine roared off and quickly disappeared down the valley.

"Perhaps we might help," said Kristian, removing his skis and striding towards the snow-covered deck of the base café where three figures wearing the scarlet jackets of the ski-school were talking seriously. The red stain at its centre made it look like a kamikaze pilot's headscarf.

Tom turned towards the four young ski-class members who were standing apart, solemnly murmuring amongst themselves. He asked a few questions of his own as he waited for Kristian to return.

"A bad fall, it seems," Kristian reported. "The class instructor is angry. One of his pupils has got drunk and acted crazy. He tried to ski off a roof. Said he'd seen it on James Bond."

There was a chorus of incredulity from the listening class.

"That's not what I'm getting," said Tom.

"Well, he was quite clear about it. They came here for a rest, away from the crowds. They were told not to leave the deck. It seems that this boy said he was just going for a walk and then he falls from the roof. Oh, and it's a coincidence but the instructor..."

Tom knew. "Let me guess. Marco Kreiz."

"That is so," said Kristian, surprised. "You know him? He is the person I talked about who owns the top station."

"We've met," said Tom, grimly.

Moira broke in. "That's no whit happened at aa!" she said, outraged. "Cameron didnae hae a dram. And Marco widnae ken cause he was sleepin at the time. He's tellin lies aboot it."

"I wouldn't be surprised," said Tom to Kristian. "He's a nasty piece of work, this Marco. Speak to the head of the ski-school. He's the one with the beard."

Franz was walking towards them as Tom was speaking. He was not happy with Marco's story but his English was not quick enough for him to understand what the class was saying. Marco followed at a distance. Franz spoke to Kristian.

"Will you tell the class," he said, "that, whilst it's a bad injury, he's in good hands. Unteriberg hospital is used to dealing with ski accidents." Then he added in a lower voice, "But why do some learners ignore their instructors? They seem to think they can do it on their own. Do you know these people, Herr—?"

"Weller. No, I don't, but according to them it did not happen like that." He was aware of Marco hovering in the background as he spoke quietly. "I happened to be here with Herr Shepherd inspecting the new installations, saw there was trouble and came to see if I could help. The class has been telling Herr Shepherd their story. It does not match with the instructor's." He turned Franz away from Marco. "Tom, tell me what they say. I will translate for Herr Riedler."

"They say Marco had been showing off, doing crazy stunts including jumping off this roof." As he pointed, Marco caught his first clear view of who was speaking. He gave Tom a murderous look. "They think he only brought them here because he wanted to look at the work. He'd been drinking steadily all morning and was asleep when the boy—Cameron?—" Moira nodded. "—tried to copy him."

Kristian translated rapidly and Franz pursed his lips. This was serious. Kreiz would have to be suspended until an investigation was completed. He turned to Marco and spoke briefly to him. Marco's response was sudden and violent. Before anyone could move he launched himself at Tom, knocking him over backwards and grasping him by the throat. Although taken by surprise, Tom's response was instinctive. As he hit the ground he brought his knee sharply upwards into Marco's groin. Marco's intake of breath and the relaxing of his grip told him he had found the mark. He pushed him off sideways and stood, leaving Marco bent double in the snow. Then something seemed to take over. He ached to see more blood on the snow, blood draining into the mountainside. He looked at the vulnerable bowed head waiting as if to be beheaded and drew back his heavily-booted foot. He swung hard but was barged to one side. His boot skimmed the side of Marco's head, neatly removing his sunglasses.

"Hey, man! There's no call for that. Take it easy. You don't wanna kill 'im." Jim had him by the shoulders.

"Yes I do," thought Tom, licking his lips. Then Kristian was in front of him, blocking out the sight of Marco. Tom's blood-lust faded. He felt drained and shocked. That was not me, he thought. That was not me.

"I'm sorry," he gasped. They were staring at him. He had not been aware of the look of deadly intent which had crossed his face as he swung his foot. "Something came over me. Can we get away from this place?"

Franz Riedler had been speaking quietly to Marco who was now on his feet, looking subdued. He came over to Kristian. "Herr Weller, would you help me, please. Herr Kreiz has been temporarily suspended. We will go to the ski-school and return the rescue sledge. Herr Kreiz will accompany us. Would you escort the rest of the group to the cable-car? Take it slowly, they are all a little shocked. They should not ski for the rest of the day. Tell them I will arrange another teacher for them for tomorrow."

"What does the instructor say?" asked Kristian.

"He says that your friend has a personal grudge against him."

❋ CHAPTER SEVEN ❋

"Now this is becoming embarrassing. I honestly do not do this on purpose." Jostled from behind as he queued for coffee in the crowded café at the top of the cable-car, he had shunted the person in front. Hot chocolate sloshed onto a tiled floor already wet with melted snow. Somehow Tom had known, even before she turned round to frown vexedly at him, that it was Ruth. Her annoyance melted into surprise.

"I'm supposed to believe that?" she asked, grey eyes amused. "You're just trying to get ahead of me in the queue. Do you practise spilling people's drinks or is it a gift?" The good-natured smile robbed her words of sting.

"Years of hard work," replied Tom, ignoring dark grumblings behind him. The room boomed with conversation and the clump of ski-boots. Through the smoke and steam he spotted a group of people preparing to leave. He pointed. "Look, grab that table and I'll bring you a fresh drink. Chocolate?"

Ruth nodded, abandoned her tray and staked her claim, an inside table on this achingly-cold day not something to be lost. That morning she had found flashes of the old skills she had when at fifteen years old she had been the envy of her friends on the school trip, a natural on skis, hurtling fearlessly down the slopes at St Moritz and Wengen. Her long-unused muscles complained now and she gladly flopped onto the wooden bench, stretched her legs and unclipped her boots. She thought back fondly to her boarding school, the old building with towered and turreted dormitories, dusty, woody-smelling class-rooms, tennis courts, netball courts and hockey-pitches spread among its park-like grounds. Clever, sporty and popular, she had progressed predictably from form-captain, hockey captain and prefect to Head Girl. She had wondered how her widowed mother, teaching languages in a state school, had afforded the fees. Now she was beginning to think that she knew.

Tom slid into the seat opposite and presented her with a mug capped with a mountain of whipped cream and sprinkled with chocolate flakes. He struggled out of his jacket, loosened the roll-neck on his shirt and ran his hands through his dark hair, smiling at her and radiating vitality. He was very different from her university colleagues with their pale faces and cardigans. She returned his smile guardedly.

"I suppose you're here to compare today's hot chocolate with the medieval version," he said, sipping his coffee.

"So not only do you spill my drink but you make me feel guilty too," replied Ruth. She scooped a mouthful of cream with a long-handled spoon and closed her eyes. "Mmmn. They probably had milk sweetened with honey. Not quite the same."

Tom realized why she looked different. She was not wearing her spectacles. The schoolgirl with the faraway look was gone. Now her eyes were deep, alert and appraising. "I'm just as bad," he said. "I should be working but the skiing is irresistible. I tell myself that I work better for taking a break. It could even be true."

She smiled. "I'm sure it is. I've reached the point where I must look further than the pages of a book. What are you escaping from?"

Tom reluctantly pulled his attention away from her cloud of fair hair. "Oh, words, words, words. I have to write a skiing report but I'd rather do it than write about it."

Ruth was surprised by the Hamlet. He did not seem the type. She could not know about the odds and ends he had picked up from Anita who had taught English as well as PE. "Who for?" she asked. Her old headmistress would have shuddered at the construction.

Tom explained briefly about his work.

"Well, you have more excuse than me," Ruth offered, once again ignoring her expensive education. "You can at least claim it as research."

"You could be my PA," said Tom with a grin.

She was wary. Why was he on his own? He wondered at her switches of mood from ease to anxiety. Why was she on her own? They sat in silence for a while.

"How's it—?" they both began, and stopped.

"After y—"

They paused, smiling. Tom made an invitational gesture to her with his right hand and raised his eyebrows interrogatively. Ruth took the opening.

"It's going well. Have you been inside the church?"

"You don't remember?"

"Oh, yes, of course. Sorry. What did you think?"

"Garish. Gloomy. Cold. A bit overwhelming. Not friendly. Except I enjoyed lighting a candle."

"Me too."

Neither asked for whom.

"It's a very old foundation. I peel off a layer like an onion and there's always something underneath, each time a little paler. I expect it will become invisible in the end. I'm working on the thesis that alpine monasteries were built on sites of pagan worship to demonstrate the power of Christianity. Unteriberg's monastery was originally a hermit's cave. The wooden madonna is reputed to be his. It is clearly older than the building. What I want to know is why the hermit chose this cave. Isolation? A clean water supply? Or did the place already have some kind of power? Pagan worshippers commonly invested places with potency—rocks, trees, springs. The past sometimes disappears behind the energy of the present. And occasionally it is deliberately obscured." Ruth's features, animated by enthusiasm for her subject, darkened suddenly. She stared into her mug and murmured something inaudibly.

Tom watched her expecting some kind of explanation but she was silent and preoccupied. He had the leisure to study her downcast lashes and full lips. Then she looked up, on guard again.

"Sounds fascinating," he said. "It must be like a treasure hunt."

"Well, the finds are usually few and far between. It's mostly just digging. But, yes, it is fascinating."

"You're right about history disappearing," he said. "Have you ever lived in a place where the locals have a name for somewhere or something which does not appear on any map? It seems to get passed down. Perhaps that's where you'll find your invisible history. Talking of which, have you picked up about Spirstock?"

"You mean, it's unlucky?"

"Yes. You know the development I told you about? Locals won't work there. They told me that at the tourist office. Now, where does something like that come from?"

"Perhaps I'll find out," said Ruth. She collected her gloves and sunglasses from among the debris on the table. "Time I went back to work, anyway." As she stood, Tom realized that what he had thought were her snow-boots were in fact ski-boots. He had assumed she had been here for the view.

"You ski?" he said, failing to keep the surprise out of his voice.

"Oh, yes," said Ruth. "It is possible to study history and know how to ski, too."

"I'm sorry, I didn't mean…" He pointed an imaginary gun to his temple and squeezed the trigger. He looked through the wooden-framed window at the bright, sunlit snow. "Look, it's clear out there now. It'd be a pity to miss it. Ski some more and let me join you. Please?"

Shadows quietly flooded the valleys. Peaks smouldered pink, shrinking like cooling embers. As Tom and Ruth were skiing out the last of the light on the lower slopes, up on Spirstock the new chair-lift wound smoothly on oiled wheels, cables thrumming taut. Hans Teuber watched helplessly as his favourite Pentax slipped from his cold grasp and tumbled into soft snow seven metres below.

"Scheisse!"

His companion gave him a rueful look. "So, Hans. There goes a day's shooting and a few thousand francs worth of kit."

The camera housed a reel of photographs of the Spirstock site—buildings, plant, machinery, views, potential ski-runs, the chair-lift—all to be part of an interim report for the money-men. Hans had been shooting some final frames from the spectacular vantage-point of the descending chair when the cold had bitten into his bared fingers and fumbled the camera from his grasp. He felt foolish. He had been expensively hired for the day and had travelled from his studio in Bern to do the job. His wife, whose brother ran a hotel in Unteriberg, had pulled strings to get him the contract. He had to be professional. The camera would have been cushioned by the snow. He scanned below, quickly memorizing features to pinpoint where it had fallen.

"You go down, Werner," he said, otherwise you'll be late for the engineer's meeting. I'll go up again. It's not far from the top. I'll find it."

"You want me to come with you?"

"No, it's not necessary. I won't be long."

"I'll wait at the bottom. I can call the hotel to say we'll be late. Anyway, I have the keys to lock the engine-house. Here, take my ski-poles. They'll help in the soft snow."

"Thanks. Sorry for the delay."

"No problem." Werner smiled. "They won't begin the meeting without the chief electrical engineer. Let them wait. It's getting dark. I'll switch on the pylon lights."

The ground rose to meet them, Hans flipped up the safety-bar and Werner gently slid off his seat and trotted to a halt. The chair carouselled behind him and began its ascent once more, with Hans hunched into one side of the seat, quickly disappearing into the gathering dark. Werner watched the wheel in the engine-house spin quietly, enjoying the sight of good design working well, then he turned to the panel of dials, switches and coloured cables that were his business. He read it like a book, flicked a switch and turned to look at the necklace of light threading its way up the mountain face.

After an hour he was worried. Empty seats hummed endlessly round. There had been no communication from the top station and no response to his call. He waited a further fifteen minutes, watching for that one occupied chair with Hans triumphantly waving his camera. Nothing. Just increasing cold and thickening darkness, the lights now slicing sharp spaces out of the gloom. He made his decision and stepped into the path of the next chair. It spooned him up and rose. A bitter wind clawed his face as he drew down the plastic hood and swung the leg guards, with their insulated, waterproof flaps, across his knees. It would take twenty minutes to reach the top. He peered up into the blackness towards each stark pylon outlined in its pool of greenish light.

Something was moving below. Werner levered up the hood to see, braving the ice particles which flayed his skin like steel filings as the final tower pulled towards him. From the shadowy snow a running figure emerged into the light.

"Hans! Hans!" he called.

Hans did not look up but plunged and flailed down the steep slope, occasionally giving a hasty glance over his shoulder. He was fighting against the pull of the deep snow as if in a nightmare, staggering towards the sanctuary of the light. As he neared the pylon he found more grip from the trodden ground and stabbed his poles violently to hurl himself forward.

"Hans!"

This time he did look up. Werner saw a terrified white face with the black O of a mouth. He was trying to call out when he stumbled and pitched forward down the slope. Paul saw him desperately plant a ski-pole, body-weight and inertia driving him against it. As the metal bowed, Hans began to catapult like a vaulter. Then, with an audible crack, the stick snapped. He dropped as if he had been shot. The sheared spike drove into his throat just above the Adam's apple and emerged through a fountain of blood from the nape of his neck. Horrified, Werner twisted round in his seat to stare at the sprawled figure below, skewered into the mountain. He was carried smoothly overhead into the dark.

"Maybe we should make our way to the cable-car. It's getting late." The clock-face by the T-bar showed the time of the last ascent. Ruth checked her watch.

"A last run?" Tom could have skied for hours. His blue eyes glittered with energy. The afternoon with Ruth had brought home to him how weary he was of being on his own. They had thrashed every run. She skied like he did, impetuous and risky, matching him easily for pace. The lines she took were ones he would have taken, turning in places he would have turned. Her early caution was replaced by an abandon which surprised Tom. She embraced the mountain, threw herself into jumps and turns, loose-limbed and fearless. Her last runs, however, had been more careful, as if she was somehow reining herself in.

"No, I don't think so. My ski-legs are complaining."

"Fair enough. Race you to the cable-car, speed-freak."

She laughed. "You can talk!" she countered and was off down the fall-line before he could move. He grinned and set off in pursuit, his longer skis and extra weight making for a slower start but giving him the edge for overall speed. She used the ground instinctively, making tiny adjustments to her line to maintain pace, crouching low on the schusses. He carved his turns more crudely, bouncing from edge to edge. She arrived at the knoll above the cable-car station just ahead of his ski-tips, juddering to a halt and raising her arms in triumph. He slid alongside, spraying her with snow and shaking a mock fist. As he came to a sudden halt he overbalanced and they both fell, laughing.

"Cheat!"

"Bad loser!"

He had instinctively clutched at her as they tumbled and he still embraced her as they lay in the snow. He smelt her perfume, could feel her body panting against him and saw the desire which flooded through him matched briefly in her eyes. It was swiftly replaced by mistrust. He scrambled awkwardly to his feet and held out a hand to help her up. She ignored it, stood up unaided and began brushing the snow off her clothes.

"Sorry about that," he said. He tried to keep it light. "Your fault entirely, of course, stopping on the brow of a hill."

She smiled briefly and removed her skis. He felt her freezing him out.

"A drink in the bar when we get back?"

"Thanks, but I must work." She was engrossed in clipping her skis together.

"Will you ski tomorrow?"

"No, I don't think so. I have to go to Zürich sometime and I don't know how long it will take."

What had he done?

"I'm sorry if I dragged you away from your work," he said. "Thanks for your company, anyway. I really enjoyed it."

She stopped fiddling with her skis and looked at him directly, her flushed features relaxing.

"I'm sorry, Tom. No, you didn't drag me away from my work. I dragged myself. And I had a great time, thanks. But I really do have things to do." She watched him mask his disappointment.

"OK," he nodded. "But I would like to know how you get on with your research. It is possible to work in a leisure centre and be interested in history, too."

"Ouch!" she said with a smile. "Touché. Come on, let's get in the queue before this lot arrives."

The chair-lift was disgorging a group of men who were talking earnestly and animatedly to each other as they trudged in their snow-boots towards the cable-car. Their overcoats, scarves and hard-hats made them distinctive. Ruth and Tom slipped into the cable-car station ahead of them. As they waited for the gondola, a voice called out, "Tom! Herr Shepherd!"

Tom turned to see Kristian Weller bustling towards him, his hand outstretched. They shook hands vigorously, Weller full of enthusiasm.

"Hello, hello. I am so glad to bump into you. I have just come down from Spirstock with my colleagues here." He waved a hand towards a cluster of men who were stamping their cold feet and lighting short, pungent cigars amid a roar of conversation. "It all looks very good." He lowered his voice and leaned towards Tom conspiritorially. "We have been able to keep the news of that young boy out of the papers. There are some very influential people here. So, no nonsense spreading about bad luck, eh?" He laughed again. "We have a meeting tonight in the Ledermann to collate our reports for the consortium in Zürich and then it will be full steam ahead. I would like to meet you after our gathering and we can talk about bringing skiers in for next season, yes?"

"Excellent!" Tom responded. "What time? About nine? In the bar, right." He turned to Ruth. "Looks like we're both working tonight," he said with a smile. He turned back to Kristian and lowered his voice. "I must say, I was worried that the accident would put a brake on progress. Are you sure it's all sorted?"

"Oh, yes, absolutely. And the route up to Spirstock has had the barriers replaced. There are large notices warning skiers to keep away. There will be no more accidents there, I can promise you."

❋ CHAPTER EIGHT ❋

I ncense stung the air enclosed within vaulted shadows. The atmosphere fell heavy and chill across Tom's shoulders, turgid with candle-smoke and the white breath of prayers. He raised his high collar, zipped it and peered over the rim. Smiffy from the Bash Street Kids. So much for Anita's attempts to lure him into literature. But as the sombre threads of plainsong wound among the footsteps and whispers, he was ambushed by the thought of the melodies being up at the holy end. Shadowy figures moved behind a wrought-iron screen and deep male voices echoed off the cold stone. Tom peered through the grille, pondering on the conviction that drove people to offer their lives to a belief. He saw a bowed head, a tanned and wrinkled profile. The monk was tall, his brown tonsure showing through cropped, grizzled hair. He growled the sacred words, brows corrugated in concentration, coarse, labourer's hands hugging the rough folds of his gown. Tom's eyes were drawn down from the hooked nose to the sandalled feet with yellow, horny nails protruding mummy-like from the open leatherwork. When he raised his eyes he saw he was being studied in return by a pair of deep-set eyes, black in their shadowy sockets. Then in one movement, the monk and his brethren drew their brown cowls over their heads, turned and processed slowly through a dark side door, their chants thinning away.

Tom shivered warmth into his chilled limbs. His newly-used muscles had tightened and he was taking the day off. He thought of his report, papers neatly arranged on the table in his room where he had placed them yesterday evening prior to his meeting with Kristian. He should be there now, writing a confident appraisal of the new ski area but since yesterday's events, no one was confident any more. Spirstock was closed as the search continued for Werner Kohl. The body of Hans Tauber had been brought off the mountain and the contractor's meeting that evening became a disaster committee. When Tom had reached the bar he could see something was wrong. There was an oppressive hush across the tables and Kristian's face told of calamity.

"We have trouble."

Tom was horrified to be told of the grotesque accident but the news of the missing engineer chilled him even deeper.

"And what now?" he had asked.

"They search again tomorrow in the light. All work is halted. I do not know. We must wait. It seems we must wait also for drinks tonight," Kristian had added heavily. "Brucke is not here. There is a new girl who is very slow. A drink, Tom?"

"Thanks. Coffee." He paused and added, "And a schnapps."

"I will join you. There is nothing more we can do at the moment."

Tom looked around the room and spotted Kath at a table on her own finishing a mouthful of gateau. She caught his eye and smiled guiltily. He winked.

"Do you mind if I ask the lady over there to our table?" he said to Kristian. "It looks as if she's been abandoned. I skied with her the other day."

"Yes, of course, please invite her."

And so they had spent the rest of the evening being entertained by Kath's comic accounts of her beginner's group. Her fresh-eyed wonder at the mountains and her admiration for Franz who had taken her group and made the learning fun was a timely reminder of what skiing was about. She had lifted their gloom with her enthusiasm.

Tom had not intended to visit the church the next day. Instead he had planned a gentle stroll around the shops to ease his stiff muscles but every direction he took seemed to lead him back to the church until he gave up trying to avoid it. He had gone inside but found no comfort there. Everything spoke of pain and sacrifice. He stood slowly and rubbed his hands down his thighs to release the knots that ravelled tightly whenever he rested. He must visit Alpensee that evening and soak away his stiffness in the iodine pool. He stumped down the aisle under the cold gaze of alabaster angels frozen in mid-flight and paused to stare through the bars of caged tombs like a visitor at a zoo. Fat, bone-coloured candles embossed with heraldic devices stood guard, guttering with sickly light. Tom suddenly felt nauseous and shaky. He stumbled into a side-chapel and slumped onto a bench, breathing heavily. Icy dampness spread across his brow and salty saliva flooded his mouth. With head between knees he fought to control the sickness and claustrophobia. Assuming that he was deep in prayer, no-one disturbed him. Eventually his queasiness passed but he could not shake off the feeling of being buried alive. He stood shakily, rested his wet forehead against the cold stone-work and closed his eyes. When he opened them he was staring at the faint outline of a man scratched in the stone. He pulled back sharply. Away from the wall the figure was almost invisible. It was primitive, the way a child might draw, with twiggy fingers on the end of its arms and decorative markings on its head and body. Tom had seen it before. Twice. Once in Ruth's notebook and yesterday on the rock by the top station at Spirstock. He had a feeling of being crushed by a great weight. He turned and lurched towards the exit and the light. Something was nagging at him. He burst out into the bright square, glittering icicles winking with sunlight around the fountain, the cobbles glassy. Like a drowning man reaching the surface, Tom drew in lungfuls of sweet air, his heart hammering. It was the fingers. The figure on the mountain had five fingers on one hand but only four on the other. He had hardly registered it at the time. Just a crude, casual piece of graffiti. So why did the figure in the church share the same detail, the same hand? He shivered in the shadow of the building. He felt himself being dragged under again and wrenched himself away from the shade into the light, turning his face to the warm sun.

The sun had long since abandoned the mountains to the freezing night by the time Tom lay warmly enclosed in the hot water of the outdoor iodine pool at the Alpensee water complex.

He looked up into the black sky. Snow filtered through the golden steam and feathered his face as powerful underwater jets pummelled his back and legs. He recalled as a child waking cosily in bed, his unheated room icy, the windows frosted but feeling all the warmer for his pinched nose. He had the same dilemma too. How do you face leaving it? He came to the same decision.

"Just five more minutes."

At night Alpensee bubbled with violet, turquoise and gold liquids like an alchemist's laboratory, sending luminous steam rising into the icy air. Bathers wrapped in a warm mist came upon each other suddenly like ships in fog. Snow lay thick all around. Water channels routed swimmers back to the main indoor pools from the jacuzzis and swirl pools but not from the iodine pool. That required a brief, semi-naked tiptoe through the snow for the short, sharp shock that was supposed to be good for you. Tom had worked out many years ago that you only felt better after unpleasant experiences because they had stopped. Nevertheless, from the shouts and shrieks around him there were clearly some who were indulging in the full traditional therapy of a roll in the snow between plunges. Screams and splashes were followed by gentle groans of pleasure filtering through the mist. Suddenly he was face to face with Olly followed closely by Sharon.

"Tom?" Olly's face loomed closer. "Oh, hi. God, you need foghorns round here." He sank below the surface and rose again, his hair smoking. "Yeuch! That tastes foul. Feels brill, though, dun't it, m'lover?" he said to Sharon, giving her a cuddle. She placed her hand on the top of his head and pushed him under.

"Don't mention Penzance or he's bound to go 'poirates, ah-haaa,'" she said to Tom as Olly burst to the surface doing his "Creature from the Black Lagoon" impression.

"Have you done the snow-roll, yet?" Olly asked, spluttering and spitting. Tom shook his head. "Aw, you're missing a treat."

"Sounds like torture to me," he said as screams and shouts continued to echo through the darkness.

"No, that's just the gang having a snowball fight."

Tom peered in the direction of the noise. A breeze briefly parted the vapour enough for him to glimpse a snow battle raging between young men and women clad in bathing costumes. He also saw other bathers, mainly middle-aged, who were taking their healthy exercise seriously and with dignity, watching from the pool in disbelief. The mist mercifully closed again leaving disembodied laughter and the occasional misdirected snowball floating their way.

"English! Tuh!" said Olly mischievously. He placed his hands on the poolside and levered himself out in one smooth action, his muscled arms glistening, his body a column of steam. Then he lowered a hand for Sharon and hauled her out, slender, gleaming and slippery as a fish. "OK, Shaz? Let's go join the winning side. See you around, Tom," he said as they were swallowed by the night.

Tom laughed quietly. It would not be long before an efficient, uniformed attendant would tell them, "Das ist verboten." At least it might save them from frost-bite. He steeled himself for a hypothermic dash across to the water-channel that would guide him back indoors. He gasped as he hauled himself out of the warm, enclosing water into a clinging skin of frost. He visualized polar-bear cubs born on icebergs. Silly sods. Perhaps wearing more than just swimming shorts helped. He hobbled over the biting snow like a barefoot holidaymaker on a pebbled beach and vaulted hastily down into the warm water channel. The enveloping heat was pleasure on an orgasmic scale. Perhaps these Swiss did know a thing or two he thought as he pushed through the plastic flaps back into the main building.

The indoor pool shimmered like cut sapphire, its surface sparkling under a cascade of water endlessly plummeting from the roof. Rich green plants everywhere suggested the tropics. Tom shallow-dived from the side tingling with well-being and ploughed three quick lengths, the cooler water injecting him with energy. On his fourth turn he realized two figures sitting on the side were watching him. One, a boy, bent over like a stringless puppet, had a spiky mop of orange and green hair and wore enormous, baggy shorts which hung loosely from his skinny hips to below his knees. His girl companion, sitting demurely on her hands, wore a black, one-piece costume that clung to her immature figure. She caught Tom's eye and waved. He swam across and hooked his forearms on the side.

"Hi, Tom," she said, and smiled. She was a different girl to the shy, sulky person she had been. Her wet hair, lying black and shining on her thin shoulders, had straightened into a natural, carefree look which suited her. She sat with easy grace, her body relaxed, her animated face flushed with mountain sunshine and young health.

"You know Rudi, don't you?" she said.

"We've seen each other but we haven't spoken," Tom said, giving Rudi a friendly nod. "Hello. Tom Shepherd. Nice to meet you."

Rudi leaned forward and formally proffered his hand.

"Hello, Herr Shepherd."

Caroline burst out, "I've been snowboarding! It's excellent! Rudi's been teaching me. He says I've picked it up quickly. We're going again tomorrow."

Tom looked at her having so much fun. Enjoy it all, he thought.

"I've just seen Olly and Sharon," he said. "Are you with them?"

"Rudi is but I came with Ruth."

Tom snatched a breath. "Ruth's here? Where?"

"I don't know. Somewhere around. We were in the pool when Rudi arrived. She went off to do her own thing. We're meeting up again later."

A bell rang. Rudi sprang nimbly to his feet and reached down his hand. Caroline took it, shyly glancing at Tom as she did so, and was helped up. She then primly held her nose and jumped feet first into the pool. As she surfaced, Rudi grinned at her and threw himself in headfirst in a lollopy, comic dive making frog's legs as he did so. Tom heard Caroline's light laughter for the first time.

"What's going on?" he asked as they trod water next to him.

"Wave machine," said Rudi. "Bondi. Pipeline. You like?"

"Oh, I like," replied Tom as the first pulse of water rolled towards them. The pool filled rapidly with swimmers and he found himself separated as he became part of a noisy jostle of flotsam bobbing like corks as the sheet of water flapped underneath them. He gave it a few minutes but, preferring the real thing, allowed himself to be washed towards the sloped shallows where he stepped out, aiming to find somewhere away from the echoing shouts.

Inside the sauna there was a meditative quiet. Perspiration welled from his temple and trickled down the expanding network of runnels on his head and body. The semicircle of tiered, wooden benches looked like a darkened lecture theatre, the audience perched in various attitudes, some bent forward resting forearms on knees looking at the floor while others stared blankly ahead. On the highest level, some lay flat on their backs, eyes closed. An occasional, muted comment briefly punctuated the hot, dim air then disappeared like water dropped on cotton-wool, being replaced by the susurration of deep breathing. Tom sat with palms flat on the boards, arms straight, head bowed, and watched the drops fall from the pelt of dark hair on his chest. The inside of his nostrils stung as he slowly drew in the dry, searing air and felt heat thread through every fibre in his naked body. The heavy wooden door occasionally opened and thudded shut as figures came in and out, men and women of all ages and shapes in continental unselfconsciousness about their bodies. Someone poured water on the hot stones over the stove and the hiss signalled a sharp rise in humidity. Tom watched the sand trickle through the timer. Five more minutes.

Ruth. He saw her silhouetted briefly in the doorway as she slipped inside and stood wrapped in a white towel, looking for a place, her eyes adjusting to the dimness. Then she saw him. Tom waited for her to leave or to choose a place as far from him as possible. Instead, looking pleased, she stepped daintily towards him and seated herself by his side.

"Hello," she whispered. "I'm glad you're here. I love saunas but I'm always a bit nervous when I'm on my own."

"Hi," he whispered back, his heart pounding. "I knew you were around somewhere. I've just seen Caroline."

"Is she all right?"

"More than that," he said with a smile. "Love's young dream."

"Oh, good. I thought I'd leave them some space. Rudi seems a nice sort of lad." She smiled back at him. "How long have you been in here?"

"Not long. I thought I'd do another five minutes."

"That's about as much as I can stand in one go." She leant her head back, closed her eyes and breathed out long and slowly, her hair falling in damp tangles down her back. Then she untucked her towel and let it fall to her hips, her white skin shining.

Tom looked down but he could still see a slender girl seated with her back arched, small breasts with pale pink nipples stretched taut, thin, girlish hips and thighs enclosing a luxuriant shock of dark, curled hair. He felt a stirring between his legs. Her unconcern at his nakedness and her own un-abashed sensuality had taken him by surprise. Showed how much he knew about women, he thought, urgently conjuring up a memory of a nil-nil draw he had once witnessed in the rain at Bristol Rovers. He stared resolutely at his feet.

"How's work?" he murmured.

"Fine," she breathed. "Zürich tomorrow. You?"

"Problems."

"Mmn?"

"Tell you later."

"OK."

Ruth breathed deeply and slowly, visualizing each muscle group in turn, consciously relaxing from head to toe, a technique she had been taught at school by the drama mistress. She was completely at ease with her body, her advanced-thinking headmistress instilling in the girls a belief in the equal importance of loving and understanding your physical self as well as your intellect. Oxford had been a narrowing experience rather than an expanding one. Most of the young male undergraduates still believed in seduction and dominance. They misinterpreted Ruth's ease about her own sexual needs as girl-school promiscuity. She was angered and disappointed by their immaturity and came to prefer the company of the tutors and professors. At least they were interested in her academic development and they simply assumed sexual equality. She gained a reputation among the undergraduates for being highbrow and cold with an unfashionable enthusiasm for her studies. Her First came as no surprise. Ruth enjoyed the pleasure it gave to her ailing mother but she kept her loneliness and isolation to herself. Then Aleksis had arrived at Oxford. A brilliant historian, he was Ruth's academic tutor for her post-graduate thesis. Their affair had lasted six months. He was young with dark good looks. His habit of pushing the heavy black locks of unruly hair away from his eyes seemed to Ruth to reflect revolutionary thinking and his attempt to control his wilder ideas. She found him exciting and he found a willing disciple. From late night discussions to sharing her bed had seemed a natural progression. The fact that he was married and had two children did not seem to be relevant to their relation-ship which appeared to her to be an entirely separate thing and as much intellectual as sexual. That was until the awful evening when she answered the door of her flat and found a small woman in a headscarf standing there, weeping. Suddenly Ruth was a scarlet woman, a destroyer of marriages and blighter of children's lives. It was not a game any more. Aleksis had suggested she made the European research trip and had arranged the funding. He was not such a revolutionary, it seemed. Ruth was glad to take it.

She glanced at Tom whose eyes were closed. He was different. Aleksis had a skinny frame and soft, rather girlish skin. Tom was compact, his shoulders and arms tight with muscle. Bent forward as he was she could see the concave ridging of his stomach. And yet he was gentler in manner than the imperious Alek. She had noticed his courtesy with appreciation. A shiver of desire moved within her. She wanted to reach out and stroke his shoulders and down the dark hair of his spine. But not another married man.

When Tom opened his eyes she was gone. The upper bulb of the timer was empty. He stood up quickly then sat down again as a wave of heat and giddiness swept over him. More slowly he wrapped his towel around his hips , stepped down to the door in a half-crouch and pushed his way out, grimacing against the brightness. From the dark, arid peace of the sauna he entered a bright, wet tumult of pools, reflections, steam, shouts and echoes. He recognized Ruth's long hair as she stood under a shower, her back to him. He watched the water darken her fair tresses and run from the tips down between her buttocks, transforming her from underworld temptress to mermaid. Time for his shower. Cold.

As he was dressing he made a decision He could not face his room at the Ledermann. It would be too much like the solitary evenings he spent at home. He wanted noise and company, especially Ruth's company. She had somehow slipped through his self-imposed barriers. Her voice was in his head, he breathed her fragrance, she whispered to him. He felt gripped by adolescent obsession. Her elusiveness made it urgent that he find her now, otherwise something important would be lost forever. He swung his bag on his shoulder and made for the main entrance, his hair still damp. He thought he must be ahead of her. She was not in the foyer so he fed the drinks machine for coffee and sat down to wait, feeling nervous.

When she emerged she was with Caroline and Rudi. She saw Tom first as he sat reading a leaflet, his right ankle crossed onto his left knee. He was wearing pale grey ski-jeans with dark snow-sneakers and was shrugged into a high-collared black fleece. He glanced up and stood as she approached, his blue eyes piercing into hers. He looked so fresh and full of life she wanted to slip her arms inside his jacket and hug herself against his hard body. She had guessed he would be waiting and she basked in the warmth of his smile. She was glad it was Caroline who spoke to him first.

"We're going to the disco! All the snowboarders are going! Will you tell mum and dad where I am and that I'm with Ruth?"

It was a blow. Marco Kreiz ran the only disco in town. He could not face that. His smile faltered and he stood silent. All the things he was going to say evaporated and he was left staring. Caroline and Ruth stared back. He felt foolish. Something new-born and fragile shrivelled and died inside him. He rescued his smile and turned to the young girl who was looking disappointed.

"Yes, of course. I'll tell them that you're off with a red-hot snowboarding young Swiss punk," he teased, winking at Rudi who was waiting in the background, gloriously grungy in his granny jumper complete with designer holes.

Caroline opened her eyes wide. "No!" she breathed, horror-struck, then saw the look in his eyes. "Don't you dare!"

He did not think he could be jokey much longer and was glad to see Rudi take Caroline's hand and rush her through the glass doors out onto the crisp pavements. Ruth followed them without meeting his eye. Tom stood quite still for five minutes, head bowed like a mourner at a graveside. Then he headed out for the long, cold walk back to the hotel.

She was waiting for him. "Join us after you've spoken to Caroline's parents." Her warm breath was a wraith in the dark. "Please." She took his hand and looked into his troubled eyes.

"Where?"

"'Marco's'"

"Yes."

Ruth walked away into the dark. What am I doing? she thought. She could still feel the pressure of his wedding ring against her hand.

The two heavies guarding the portal to the night-club stood immobile like Egyptian statues. Tom ducked under the black arch below the pink neon sign and descended the dark steps into a throbbing underworld. At the end of a stone-flagged corridor, dimly lit by a single red bulb, double doors appeared to bulge like leaky lock-gates with the strain of holding back the weight of noise. A cadaverous girl clad in a black shawl, fish-net stockings and thigh-length boots took a huge amount of his money in return for a stamp on his wrist and a voucher for one free drink. She pointed a black fingernail towards the doors and Tom pushed through into pandemonium. Heavy pulses of sound from a grey wall of speakers hit him like fists.

His eyes jinked as laser lights flickered over a jumping cauldron oozing smoke, sweat, perfume and alcohol. He peered into the gloom, his senses making frantic adjustments but could only register chaos and confusion. He battled towards the only other source of light to swap his voucher for a beer, then leant his back against the bar to try and find Ruth. He quickly spotted the snowboarders at the centre of the action. Caroline and Rudi were with them, he showing off for her, she loving it. The alcoves around the edge of the room all contained couples and as the lasers turned to strobes he saw Ruth's flickering image as if in an old movie. A man was leaning towards her, his arm lying along the back of the seat behind her shoulders. Ruth was smiling and talking. Tom excused his way round the walls until he was close. The man was broad across the shoulders and his short-sleeved, expensive-looking shirt revealed swelling biceps and muscular forearms. A wafer-thin gold watch nestled among the dark hairs of his wrist. He was speaking.

"Come, I buy you a drink. How about it? Is no good, you a lonely lady. I like happy people. I see a pretty girl in my club, I make her happy. What you wish? It is no problem. I don't pay. My club." And he laughed.

Ruth had begun, "Well, I, er—" when she saw Tom and gave him a look which clearly said, "Help". The man saw her expression and swivelled around. His face instantly transformed into fury and he stood up. He stepped up close to Tom and breathed tobacco and alcohol into his face.

"Bastard!" he hissed. "You make me lose my job." He pushed Tom hard in the chest who staggered back. "You make trouble always." He pushed again, this time an open-fingered prod against his shoulder. Tom kept his arms by his sides and backed away. Marco's lips curled in contempt. "You go! No drinks here." Push. "I know you. I know why you make trouble. English stupid people. That is why they die on mountains."

Tom stopped. A hot wave of hatred distorted his features. He was aware of Ruth's horrified face as he lunged at Marco. He yearned to tear that neck, to beat those sneering features but, as in a nightmare, he could not move. Two heavy figures had quietly emerged from the darkness and gripped him tightly by the arms. He thrashed like a fish on a hook. Marco punched him hard across the mouth, splitting his lip. Then he gestured with his head towards the door. An arm went around Tom's throat, cutting off his air, his arms were twisted up his back and he was roughly pushed through the doors and driven stumbling up the steps. At the top, a boot caught him in the back and he sprawled onto the icy pavement. As he rolled onto his back he saw his attackers talking briefly to the doormen. All four looked as if they had been constructed on the same production-line—bull-necks, shaven heads, unshaven faces, flat noses, small eyes, ringed ears, tattooed hands and bulky bodies. There was no sign of Marco. Tom was dragged by his collar down an alley that ran by the club, kicked in the stomach and left, face-down in the snow, gasping for breath. His lip stung and dripped blood. In spite of the pain he was impressed by the bouncers who had been so quietly efficient. They showed no anger, had not spoken a word to him. He felt he had been professionally processed rather than beaten up. Still, you would expect the best for the amount of money he had paid to get thrown out. His chuckle turned to a groan as his bruised muscles contracted. He rubbed snow across his mouth to clean off the sticky mess that he could taste and slowly got to his feet, leaning against the wall for support. He had never thought of himself as a hooligan before.

As he trudged back to the hotel he realized he had lost Ruth. Black depression quickly replaced the adrenaline rush and his despair was an admission of his hope. The stone slab which had sealed him in for five years had been sliding open to let in a narrow shaft of light. Now he heard the hollow scrape as it thumped back into place. He was not a young tearaway. It had just been an ugly brawl. God only knew what Marco was telling her. He could still see the shock on her face. He would phone his boss tomorrow and take the first flight home. Dead ends.

In the lobby cloakroom of the Ledermann he checked the damage to his face. A vampire stared back from the mirror. Dried blood was caked around his mouth and chin where he had smeared it with snow. He filled a bowl with warm water and lowered his face gently into it, soothed by its softness. The water turned yellowy-brown like the iodine pool. So long ago. He dabbed his face with a towel and looked again. There was a small cut on his lower lip, nothing more. "Didn't she spread, eh?" Where was that from? Another of Anita's attempts to "couth him up" as he used to say to tease her. Some play or other. Sorry, girl. Not doing too well at the moment. Need to soften the edges with a few drinks.

Alec was regretting having called in at the Ledermann. He had wanted to see Tom to arrange some skiing but had been cornered by the Bryons.

"But surely not as late as this," Mrs Bryon said as he tried to explain that nightclubs opened late which was why they were called nightclubs. "We don't know what's wrong with her, do we, George? First she won't ski with us, then she's gadding off to some swimming baths and now sending messages about some discotheque or other. It isn't like her at all. Is it, George?"

Mr Bryon was not so sure. He shared his wife's anxiety but was aware of a transformation in his daughter. He had seen her eyes sparkling, her skin glowing in a way new to him. She looked, well, attractive. He began to wonder about the boys beneath the balcony last year.

"Well, at least she tells you where she is," said Alec brightly. "Most just run off with their ski instructors," he added, laughing.

As reassurance this was not very effective. He saw them exchange looks of horror and back-pedalled rapidly.

"Only kidding, you know. She'll be fine, I'm sure. Look, do you want me to pop over to Marco's and check?"

"No. George'll do that, won't you, George?"

Again, George was not sure. He had an inkling of what it might be like for his teenage daughter to have her dad come to fetch her from a disco because it was past her bedtime.

"I don't think that's such a good idea, Hilda," he said. "She is with that Miss Francis. I'm sure she'll look after her."

"But it's nearly midnight."

The bar was empty except for their corner. Herr Brucke quietly wiped table-tops, his sleeves rolled up, his waistcoat protected by a white apron. He kept glancing in their direction.

"I think he wants to close the bar," Alec murmured.

The hotelier cleaned a final table and came towards them. To their surprise, he pulled up a chair and sat down.

"You want us to go?" asked Alec.

"No, no, please, no. I join you, yes? You wish for more drinks?"

Alec would have preferred to leave but it was unusual for Herr Brucke to be sociable and he did not wish to appear churlish. Also, the man looked worried.

"Er, well, yes, thanks. I could probably squeeze in another beer. Two more Ova-Maltines?" He looked at the Bryons who looked at each other, then nodded. "What about you, Herr Brucke? Can I buy you a drink?"

"Please, it is Josef," he said. "Yes, thankyou, I will have a schnapps. I bring them." And he rose and busied himself behind the counter. Alec raised his eyebrows towards the Bryons and lowered his voice.

"This is unusual. I've repped here for three years and never seen him join the customers. And he has always been 'Herr Brucke' or 'Der Hotelmeister.'" Alec shook his head. "Very odd." He looked up towards the door and his face brightened. "Oh, good, it's Tom." He beckoned. "Come on over! What do you want, it's my shout? God, you look worse for wear," he said as Tom approached and he saw the bruised and swollen lip. "You been head-butting trees on the slopes?"

Tom smiled painfully. "Yeah, something like that," he said, glad not to have to explain further. "Thanks, Alec, I'll—"

"Have you seen our Caroline?" Mrs Bryon interrupted, poking Tom's aching shoulder for attention. "She's not back yet. We're worried sick." An unspoken "and it's your fault" hung in the air.

Tom was not in the mood for accusations but he saw that beneath the abruptness there was real worry. He knew teenagers well. He thought, "You ain't seen nothin' yet."

"She's fine," he reassured them, "and having a good time. Ruth will bring her back soon, I'm sure. Schnapps, please, Alec. Really, there's no need to be anxious. I saw her at Alpensee, too. Loving every minute." He did not specify what.

The Bryons appeared relieved. Alec called the extra order to the bar and leaned towards Tom.

"We have the honour of the Hotelmeister's company tonight," he told Tom with a significant look on his face. "And we're to call him 'Josef'."

Tom was not impressed. It did not seem such a big deal. As this would almost certainly be the last time he would sit here, he did not care whether Brucke joined them or not, as long as he delivered a large schnapps. Soon. When it came he downed half and let the soft explosion begin paralysing his thoughts. The world took a step back. Herr Brucke, seated opposite, gloomily sipped his drink and stared silently at the table-top. The Bryons began synchronized stirring, their spoons clinking rhythmically. It felt like a wake, Alec thought. It brought to his mind the news that was filtering through.

"Did you hear about Spirstock? Apparently one of the engineers has been killed in an accident."

"He was the husband of my sister," said Herr Brucke, abruptly. "Photographer, not engineer."

Great, thought Alec. Another fine conversational opening. He looked at the heavy jowls of the hotelier, blue with whiskers, his sad, baggy eyes droopy with years of late nights. He reminded Alec of a bloodhound.

"Oh, God, I am sorry," he said with genuine remorse. "I had no idea."

"Yesterday I identify him. I talk to Helga on the telephone. She is in Bern, you understand." He sighed heavily. "She cries. I tell him not to work on this mountain. He laughs at me. He thinks I am simple peasant." He scowled at the table-top then stared accusingly at Alec. "You people, you know nothing. Leave Spirstock alone."

Alec looked to Tom for help but he was lost in his own thoughts. The bottle of schnapps was on the table and Tom poured himself a second large shot. He raised his eyebrows towards Brucke who nodded and he refilled his glass too. When would Ruth return? The drink was making him more depressed yet he could not move. He had no desire to hear more of Brucke's doom-laden tones but he wanted to see the safe return of the teenager whom he had come to like. Alec, too, deserved some company. He blanked out the thought that he was only waiting to see Ruth.

"I thought the risk of avalanche had been eliminated," said Alec.

Herr Brucke snorted. "You think that is all the danger there is, yes? My family live here always. We know things. Hans did not die in avalanche. And where is the other man, hm? They come from outside the valley, they smell the francs," (he rubbed his thumb and forefinger together) "and they do not listen to we who live here." His eyes grew more urgent. There was an edge of fear in his voice. "It must stop. You tell your companies."

"But tell them what?"

Herr Brucke looked out through the window to the illuminated hotel sign. "It must not be disturbed," he said quietly.

Alec opened his mouth to speak as Caroline burst into the room. Tom looked up hopefully. No Ruth. He resumed his stare into his glass.

"Hi!" she said, breathlessly, running up to their table and giving her father a kiss. "What a wicked club! Can I go again, tomorrow, dad?"

Her mother pursed her lips. "Caroline, do you know it is past midnight? We have an early start tomorrow to catch the train to Zürich for the art galleries. I think it is high time you were on your way to bed, young lady. And you are not going anywhere where there is wickedness."

Caroline's brightness, which had momentarily lifted the mood of the table, was snuffed out. Her smile froze, she blushed scarlet and her eyes welled with tears. She spun on her heel and ran out of the room without another word. The awkward silence was broken by Mr Bryon.

"I think perhaps that was a little harsh, mother. We might have asked her about her evening, don't you think?"

Mrs Bryon was shocked by her daughter's reaction. Her words, born out of worry, had sounded worse than she had intended. She felt she was in the wrong so naturally she entrenched her position more deeply.

"Nonsense. She can tell us all about it in the morning. Surely you are not happy with her frequenting dives of wickedness?"

"I think you'll find 'wicked' is simply a term of approval, Mrs Bryon," put in Tom, mildly.

"Well, there you are then, picking up these ridiculous expressions. I thought you said she would be fine, Mr Shepherd. I don't call storming off like a proper little madam, 'fine', do you? It seems to me she has been coming under some bad influences. And now, if you will excuse us, we are late enough as it is." She levered herself off her chair and stalked with dignity out of the room. Her husband followed her, giving the company a smile of apology as he left.

"Time for me to be off , too," said Alec, slipping on his rep's jacket. "I'm free the day after tomorrow, Tom, if you fancy some off-piste."

Herr Brucke stood up heavily. He gave them both a piercing look. "Remember what I say," he said, nodding portentously. Then, turning towards Tom, his face broke into a surprisingly sympathetic smile. "I leave the bottle with you. It will ease the pain."

Tom sat alone, staring at his glass. "Of what?" he thought. He did not want any more drink. He wanted Ruth. He did not care any more what she might think. He could not let her slip just because things got in the way. If this night passed without him seeing her again he knew he would regret it for the rest of his life. He pushed the glass away and turned towards the doorway. She was looking at him, the lobby lights behind her transforming her hair into a golden halo. Her grey eyes were large and concerned. She walked towards him and he, like a sleepwalker, went to meet her, his mouth opening to speak. She shook her head with a smile, took his hands in hers and gently kissed him on his bruised mouth. Then, without a word, she led him out towards the stairs.

❈ CHAPTER NINE ❈

Beams of light projected through the shutters and gilded Ruth's back as she lay asleep, curled like a cat. Tom, propped on one elbow, watched the slight movement of her shoulders, half-expecting to hear a purr. He marvelled at her smooth skin and leaned forwards to breathe in her warmth. She lay on her side, sunlight igniting the fine down on her arm as it rested on the white pillow. He ran his tongue between her shoulders and saw her back arch. She straightened her long legs until they protruded from the bottom of the cloud of duvet and pointed her toes. Her arms reached up and her fingers curled over the heavy, pine headboard. She stretched long and luxuriously, her small breasts almost disappearing as they flattened, her stomach concave under her rib-cage, then she rolled towards him, breathing in slowly. The duvet cover smelt clean and starchy, its coarse surface scratchy. With a long sigh, her whole body relaxed and she half-opened her eyes and looked at him.

"Hello," she murmured with a smile. "What time is it?"

"Ten-thirty. We've missed breakfast."

"I didn't miss it."

They had made love twice, at first urgently then more slowly but had stayed awake through the night, saying little but simply wondering at each other's presence. Tom absorbed gratefully the sweetness and tenderness of a woman, Ruth felt the comfort of a man's hard, warm flesh cradling her with passion. They had fallen asleep at dawn.

"Shall I open the shutters?" he said.

"Mmm."

He stepped across to the French windows which opened onto a wooden balcony. With the glass doors open and the shutters pushed back, sweet cold air breathed into the room, carrying the scent of snow and the glitter of sunlight. Tom stretched his arms wide to embrace the day. Ruth studied the arc of his shoulders and the packed muscles of his buttocks as he was silhouetted in the doorframe. When he turned he saw that she had put on her spectacles. Her blend of innocent head-girl and sexual woman aroused his desire again. He returned to the bed, wondering at the softness of her milky skin now tinged with gold. She lay watching him, the duvet drawn back, one arm resting over the curve of her slender hips, the other cradling her cheek. As he approached she lay on her back and drew him down to her, placing his stiffness between her small breasts then tracing him down her body, across the neat pit of her navel towards her dark jungle. He left an iridescent trail like the path of a snail. He gently removed her glasses and kissed her eyelids, brushed his lips across her forehead and slid his mouth slowly down the cushion of her cheek to find her melting lips, so different to Anita who was firm and feisty and who had fought him with her passion. Ruth drowned him. As he sank into her soft mouth she guided him into her nether moistness, drawing him in fully in one movement. She drew her knees up and arched her back as they blended into one flesh. He slid his hands around the curve of her waist and cupped the small globes of her buttocks, pulling her around him. Her body curved away like the earth.

"'Licence my roving hands,'" he murmured, the taut bow of his back juddering with release.

"'My new found land,'" she whispered.

He sank against her breasts, his face nuzzling the sweet dampness of her white neck, his hand entwined her golden hair. She folded him in her arms and gently stroked his shoulders, wondering at his need and her response to it. They breathed like runners at the end of a race, joined heart to heart and melted into one.

"Tom?"

"Mmm?"

"Are you sorry?"

"What for?"

"This."

"No. Are you?"

"No."

"Why do you ask?"

"You're married."

Tom raised his head. Her grey eyes glistened. He put his lips to their corners and tasted her sweet salt.

"I'm not married," he said, quietly.

She searched his eyes. They were steady, calm and tender.

"I was married. She died."

He raised himself on his elbows, gently withdrew from her and lay by her side staring at the pine ceiling. She curled towards him and he cradled her in his arms.

"I'm sorry," she whispered.

"Don't be," he breathed. "It was five years ago."

Ruth reached across and intertwined her fingers with his.

"You still wear your wedding ring."

"Yes."

"Why?"

Tom breathed deeply, absorbing the perfume of her soft curls.

"You don't have to tell me," Ruth said.

"No, I want to."

He wrapped her closer and she snuggled against him, as right as a jigsaw piece. Street sounds wafted through the windows mingled with the chimes from the monastery.

"She disappeared. I know she's dead. I knew it even before I answered the phone-call which told me the news. But she was never found. The last time I saw her she was boarding a coach at four in the morning with thirty-five teenagers. That's how I see her, busy, in charge, full of life. She was twenty-five. It's been hard to let go when I've not been able to say goodbye. Whenever I've thought of taking off my ring, it felt as if I was killing her. Is that crazy?"

"No."

"She was lost along with six schoolchildren on a ski trip."

Ruth knew the answer to her next question before she asked it. "Where?"

"Here."

He felt her go very still. Even her breathing stopped. Then she unlaced her fingers from his and rolled onto her back. The ghost print of her warm body cooled rapidly.

"So that's why you're here. I thought you were working, writing a report about the skiing."

Tom was suddenly terrified. He was going to lose her. He sat up and took both her hands in his. He gently pulled her up so that they could look into each other's faces. He framed her cheeks with his hands.

"Oh, Ruth. Do you think I am using you as some kind of therapy? Yes, I came here to put the past to rest but you were never part of that. And I did tell you the truth. I am working for my employers on the skiing here. I didn't expect you. From the day I saw you in the church you have been in my head. I tried to ignore it, told myself I was lonely, I was misreading my feelings. But I'm not. Last night, when you came to the bar, I was on my way to find you. I thought I'd lost you at Marco's. It was breaking my heart."

Ruth watched his face. "Was she like me? Who did you think I was in the church?"

"No, not like you at all. From the back, perhaps, the long hair. But I was seeing her everywhere, then. On the plane, in the hotel, on the slopes. I think I was a bit crazy."

"What was she like?"

"Full of life. Quick to laugh, quick to cry. Organized. Sure of herself. Strong. A good teacher."

Ruth tucked her legs under her and knelt facing him, her hands in her lap. He did the same.

"So what happened?"

"Are you sure you want to hear this?"

"Yes."

"I've never really talked to anybody about it before. It's not very clear what happened. The inquest said accidental death but there were too many unanswered questions. Anita, that was her name, Anita came in for criticism but it was a cover-up. She was always so careful, so responsible. She'd taken kids skiing for several years. They'd had the occasional bumps and scrapes but you expect that. Everything else always ran like clockwork. It was the way she was. She couldn't be negligent."

Tom was now half-talking to himself, unearthing once again his instinctive feelings that there was something wrong with the inquiry. His voice was quite steady.

"I could never go with her, couldn't get time off work. She rang me from here the night before the accident, just to chat. All was well, the usual stresses and strains of taking kids abroad of course but nothing unusual. The following evening I got the news."

Ruth watched him, gravely. He found it easy to tell her. The anger and grief that had always strangled his tongue was calmed by her quiet, grey eyes. He told her how he had flown out, what had been said at the inquest and what the newspapers had written. How his fury could find no vent, his anguish no relief. The memorial service at home had not laid her ghost to rest.

So he had numbed himself with work, alcohol and solitude. But then he'd been offered the chance to come to Unteriberg again. And he'd found Ruth.

She put her hands on his shoulders and laid her soft cheek against his morning stubble. Then she drew the duvet around them.

"Did you know you quoted Donne to me when we were making love?" She smiled. "I didn't have you down as a poetry man."

"Did I?" He laughed quietly. "Anita used to try to get me to read more, without much success. Still, I seem to have picked up odds and ends. She read bits out to me when she was marking. She taught some literature as well as sports."

They lay down again, wrapped in each other's arms, the duvet cocooning them tightly.

"Swiss roll," said Tom.

Ruth giggled. "We should get up," she said, cuddling closer.

"Why?"

"I've an appointment in Zürich this afternoon. A train to catch."

"Ah-ha, zis is very mysterieuse. I weesh to know all your leetle secrets, Mademoiselle Ruth."

"Actually, it is a bit of a mystery," she said, smiling. "I'm trying to trace my family."

"Really? I thought you were researching medieval churches."

"Well, yes I am. But I have other reasons to be here."

"Like me?"

"Yes, I like you," she said.

"Don't try to be clever wiz me, mademoiselle." He bit her ear gently. "And I like you too."

"I needed to get away from Oxford."

"A man?"

"Mm-hm."

"Is he like me?"

"No, not like you at all."

"This feels like déjà vu."

"Pardon."

"I said, this feels like déjà vu."

"That's odd. I'm sure I've heard that somewhere before."

"Wha—oh, very funny."

"Sorry. I suppose it's only fair that I should offer my confession in exchange. You know what this reminds me of?"

"'Tess of the D'Urbervilles.'"

"I'm impressed."

"Saw it on the telly."

"Don't spoil it. I was beginning to believe I was not sharing my bed with a moron."

"Fossil."

"Our first quarrel."

They kissed slowly, breathing in each other's breath.

"He's my tutor. Married."

"Ah, I see," said Tom.

"It is true that I'm researching European religious foundations but I could probably get most of my information from libraries in England. But I had the affair with Alek and it ended badly." She shuddered at the memory. "He offered to fund a continental trip to get me out of the way and I was glad to take it. But something else happened at the same time which is why I chose to come to Unteriberg."

"What?"

"My mother died. She'd been ill for some time. I had to go through her things."

"And your father?"

"He died before I was born. Mum talked about him a little at the end. He was a research mathematician. Mum taught modern languages in a school near his university. She said they met in a pub. They'd only been married five years, mum was expecting me, and he contracted meningitis. She brought me up on her own and reclaimed her maiden name, Francis, for both of us. I think it was a symbol of her independence. When I left home I asked her how she'd paid for my private schools, the music lessons, the trips abroad, university and so on but she always dismissed it with a throwaway phrase, you know, 'scrimped and saved', 'begged and borrowed', that sort of thing. She'd told me years before how she'd been an adopted child and had been given the privileges she was now giving me. She knew nothing of her real parents. But during the final days in the hospice she said some odd things. I heard her say 'Frank' a number of times. I thought at first it was the name of an old boyfriend—my father was called Michael—but then she said, 'Leah, my name is Leah Frank.' When I said, 'It's Francis, mum, Laura Francis,' she said, 'Ask Uncle Otto.' I had never had any relatives as far as I knew. I'd certainly never heard of an Uncle Otto. After she died, as I was going through her belongings I found a photograph."

"What of?"

"'Of what?'"

"What?"

"'Of what?'"

"Don't start."

Ruth smiled, then became serious once more.

"I'll show you."

She reached down the side of the bed to where her holdall bulged with books and files and fished out a small notebook. Pressed between its leaves like a dried flower was a small, sepia-

and-white photograph, ragged at the edges and soft with handling. She passed it to Tom. It showed a young man, perhaps in his twenties, holding a baby in his arms. The image was blurred but the expression on his face was clear. It was fear. He was dressed for winter in a long overcoat and he wore leather boots. There was snow on the ground. Behind him, out of focus, was a cascade of icicles and beyond that, a large, shadowy building. The baby seemed to be wrapped in sacking and the young man was clutching it to himself. Tom thought of a wild creature at bay. He turned the picture over. On the back, in pale, grey ink was written, "Otto Schneider und Leah Frank, 1942". He sniffed the old card. It smelled sad.

"Your mother?"

"I think so. Look again at the photograph."

Tom turned it over again. The same hunted expression stared out at him.

"Look at the background."

He studied the blurry icicle spikes. They were regularly spaced, in tiers. It looked like a wedding cake. He had seen something like that recently.

"It's the fountain! Frozen! And the building is the monastery! Your mother was born here? Is that your grandfather?"

"I don't know. I really don't know. It wasn't too difficult to identify the place—the fountain is unique—but there was something else I found. A letter to my mother from a solicitor's office in London about an enclosed cheque and with it, another letter written in German. It was addressed to the same law firm advising them of the francs enclosed, to be forwarded to Leah Frank, anonymously, in the usual manner. The address was the Stadtmuseum, Zürich and it was signed 'Otto Schneider'. It was dated two weeks before she went into the hospice. I think the letter from Zürich was enclosed by mistake."

"You should contact the museum," said Tom.

"Done it."

"And?"

"I'm meeting a Professor Otto Schneider, authority on medieval churches and curator of the Stadtmuseum, Zürich, this afternoon."

✳ CHAPTER TEN ✳

The earthy smell of parchment and leather filled the room. Subdued lighting ignited the warm, autumnal colours of fat volumes packed into the oak cabinets lining the walls and projecting into bays and alleys. Sloe, chestnut, damson, myrtle. It felt like a cosy burrow—a hobbit hole, thought Ruth—where you could delve quietly into the past. Seated across the gleaming mahogany desk with its low, green-shaded lights, was an elderly gentleman wearing a crumpled, grey-striped suit. It looked as if it had been expensive and smart when new but it now sagged comfortably around his portly shape like a pair of old pyjamas. From the breast pocket protruded the curved stem of a pipe. There was ash on his lapels. He was poring over a roll of parchment, reading the medieval Latin quickly, his eyes alert and sharp as he adjusted the angle of his head to accommodate the ornate lettering through his half-moon spectacles. His face had surprised Ruth. She had somehow expected pale asceticism but here was a complexion that could have belonged to a hill farmer. His round cheeks were flushed with outdoor glow and his white hair sprang out around the brown, bald patch as if being tugged by blustery winds. It looked at odds with the stillness of the museum library. However, his long, sensitive fingers with their beautifully manicured nails, at that moment busy tracing the lines of faded letters, gave him away. Behind him was a cabinet of books arranged with their leaves facing outwards, each volume attached to the shelf by a thin chain which hung down in a long loop. It looked like a protective curtain of chain-mail and would have made a striking portrait to match her poster of Brunel on the wall of her flat in Oxford. But it was the "Die

Fotografie ist verboten" notices that really protected these delicate pressed leaves of history.

Schneider looked up and removed his glasses. His brown eyes were still journeying through the past. He slowly focussed on Ruth and smiled.

"So, Ms Francis, a fascinating thesis, I think. Since I received your letter from Oxford I have found a number of texts which you may find germane to your research." He indicated the piles of papers, parchments and books stacked on the desk. His voice was gentle, his words precise. "It is a much-debated question, how Christianity replaced ancient beliefs. It is generally accepted now that many Christian establishments were deliberately sited where there was evidence of an earlier cult. It marked the ability of the new religion to eclipse former beliefs. No doubt it helped too, in the conversion of the heathen in that they already associated these places with power. However, it is more difficult to establish how long the old ways of thinking lasted, side by side as it were, with the new, which is where your interest lies. We know that the Christian calendar overlays an earlier cycle—feasting, fertility rites, sacrifice and rebirth etc. The difficulty for you is that there is so little written evidence. The church had a stranglehold on literacy so documents of the period invariably support the orthodox view. This, for instance," (he indicated the roll of parchment he was carefully holding open) "is correspondence from Rome to the See of Zürich authorizing the establishment of a monastery on the site of the chapel of St. Bulof, Unteriberg. You say you are particularly interested in the Unteriberg monastery? Well, St. Bulof had died probably five hundred years before this letter was written. One of many early Christian saints who espoused a life of poverty and simplicity. It is likely he came to the mountains for isolation and closeness to God, lived in a cave, fasting and praying and preaching to anyone who had the hardihood to seek him out. There were others similar. But what you are looking for is what came before and here you're in very muddy waters indeed. The early pagans certainly venerated the mountains. The sites that have been identified and excavated suggest that they associated places with power—a certain tree, a special spring, a cave, a particular mountain. But so much of that tradition was oral and if it lingered would be distorted over time. Whether you can untangle anything of value I don't know." He gave Ruth a kindly smile. "That doesn't mean you shouldn't try."

Ruth thought of the conversation she had had with Tom about local place-names. Tom. She smiled warmly at Herr Schneider.

"Yes, you're right. It is difficult, I know." She looked at him closely, trying to trace the features of a young boy in his face or some echo of her mother. There was nothing. "I have been talking to people where I am staying in Unteriberg. They seem to have a strong tradition of an unlucky mountain but that is all.

Herr Schneider's gentle features clouded. "Spirstock?"

"Oh, you know of it?" said Ruth.

"I was born in Unteriberg."

"Really?" Ruth acted more surprised than she was.

"Yes, Unteriberg is my home town. I know the mountains. When I was growing up we were not allowed to climb Spirstock. I was a child of the Alps, you understand, and roamed safely the whole area, summer and winter, except Spirstock. It was forbidden."

"Why?"

"We were told there was some kind of creature there who would eat children. Sometimes you could hear it growl. Remember this was over fifty years ago. Bogey-men were commonly used to protect youngsters from danger. It probably prevented a number of deaths from avalanche. When you're young you're easily impressed. And there were some disappearances which drove the message home. I still shiver a little when I hear the name. Probably most Unteribergers of my generation feel the same.

"Did you know that there have been accidents there since they began the ski development?" Ruth told him what Tom had said that morning.

"I have heard about the development. Accidents—well they happen. Engineering in hostile environments is a hazardous business. There have been other deaths in other areas."

Ruth felt that the old man was trying to convince himself. "So it is not an unlucky mountain?" she said.

"Only for those who have come to grief but not unlucky in the way you mean. You are, like me, an historian. We look at evidence, weigh information and come to logical conclusions. Just because people are superstitious does not mean we should also become the same. It is interesting, nevertheless, how such beliefs might originate. Here we come back to your thesis. Where do the bogey-men come from? They occur in most cultures, thrive in primitive ones and are dying or dead in developed ones. Yet the Spirstock bogey-man was alive and well fifty years ago, which is not long historically. I believe they have traditionally been used to guard sacred sites. Some of these pagan practices were pretty fierce involving sacrificial rites and so on. There has been some evidence brought to light of the practice of evoking 'watchers' to protect the ancient sites. It has crossed my mind that these fearsome figures have survived in the subconscious. I have something here which may shed a little light." He rooted about among the books on the desk before finally selecting a volume and flicking through the pages. "This is not the Alps, of course, but the Andes. But archaeologists there seem to be uncovering a fascinating Inca sacrificial cult. Ah, here we are." He pushed the book across the desk. Two photographs faced her, one, the barren top of a snow-crusted mountain pegged out for a dig, the other a close-up of some artefacts—a seed pouch, a tiny gold llama and a carved human figure covered in tiny lines.

"I've seen this before," said Ruth.

Schneider smiled and nodded. "I know where. On the north wall of the church in Unteriberg, yes?"

Ruth felt chill in spite of the warmth of the room. She had been disturbed by the figure since she had first discovered it. There was something menacing about it. It was odd, too, that the lavishly illustrated and expensive guide-book she had bought in the town made no mention of it although everything else in the church was meticulously documented.

"But you must have known of it since you were a child."

"No, that is not so. I discovered it when I returned to Switzerland to take up my present post. I was researching, like you. I had not been inside the church before then."

Ruth's puzzlement showed on her face. "But you grew up there."

"As a Jew, my dear," he said.

Ruth stared.

"Is it so surprising?" said Herr Schneider, smiling.

"I'm sorry," said Ruth. "I didn't mean to be rude." Her mind whirled. Leah Frank. Ruth. "Things must have been very difficult for you when you were young."

"Not at all, not at all. My childhood was very happy. I was an only child and so I was always centre of attention." His face softened with pleasure at the recollection. "My father was a doctor, a very clever man. He took care that my mother did not spoil me too much. We had a comfortable house. I had friends. The Unteriberg valley was even more beautiful then, almost untouched by development."

"I was thinking of the war," said Ruth.

Herr Schneider's face clouded. "I left for America when I was still young. I have lived more of my life in the States than I have in Switzerland."

"But you were here in 1942," said Ruth.

Schneider looked startled. He focused on Ruth more directly than he had previously, his white eyebrows coming together guardedly.

"And how do you know that?" he said, sharply.

In answer, Ruth drew the photograph out of her document case and slid it across the desk. The old man studied it for a long time, his benign countenance stoney as he silently shook his head. Then he looked up angrily.

"Where did you get this? Who are you, some kind of journalist?"

"It was among my mother's things. She called herself Laura Francis but I think her real name was Leah Frank."

Herr Schneider sat back in his chair, closed his eyes and breathed out long and slowly. "My God," he whispered. He sat silently for a long time.

"That is you, isn't it?" asked Ruth.

Herr Schneider opened his eyes. They were brimming with tears. "So you are little Leah's daughter," he said in a low voice. "I could not have known. Your mother was only two when I last saw her. They wrote to me from London to tell me of her death. How did you find me? The solicitors were instructed not to inform you about me."

"So it is you in the picture? And my mother?"

Herr Schneider nodded.

"So you are Uncle Otto?"

"Is that what she called me?"

"It is something she said at the end when she was very ill. I found this letter, too, after she died. I think it was sent in error, like the photograph." Ruth fished out the copy. Herr Schneider took it but did not read it. He looked at Ruth.

"Such beauty," he said. "Your mother was beautiful too, I think?"

Ruth smiled at the old man. "Yes, she was," she said, simply. "I believe I have you to thank for my education, Herr Schneider. Perhaps I should call you 'Uncle Otto'?"

Herr Schneider kept shaking his head in disbelief, clutching the arms of his chair as if to grip reality. "Little Leah's daughter," he breathed in wonderment.

"So my name really is Ruth Frank? And I am your grand-niece?"

"Unless you have married, yes, you are Ruth Frank," said Schneider, a sparkle returning to his eyes. "But, no, you are not my grand-niece, although I would like to think so. Please, just call me Otto."

Ruth felt a pang of disappointment. She had learned to hide her envy at school when friends talked of going to stay with relatives or when hordes turned up for prize-givings and school plays. Since her mother's death she had felt rootless. She had unconsciously invested a great deal of hope in finding a blood relative. Schneider saw her face fall. He reached across the desk and laid his hand, palm up, in front of her. She hesitated a fraction, then placed her hand in his. His warm, dry fingers curled around hers. It made her feel secure.

"You have clearly taken trouble to find me," he said, gently. "I will not become invisible again. I feel as close to you as any real uncle could to his niece. I have no family and my greatest pleasure in life has been to help your mother and you."

"But why, if we're not related?"

Herr Schneider sighed. "It is a long story."

"Will you tell it me?"

Schneider thought deeply. There were some things about that bitter night that he would not tell Ruth, the blood, the rumours, Kurt's story. The nightmares created in his childhood need not be passed on. But she had a right to know her roots.

"Let me show you something." He felt inside his jacket and took out a wallet from which he extracted a yellow slip of paper protected by a plastic cover. On the paper, in angular German lettering, were penned the words, "Leah Frank, geb. d. 7. Oktober 1941, Reutlingen, Bayern. Vater, Jakob Frank, geb. d. 2. April 1905, Leipzig. Mutter, Sarah Frank, geb. d. 24. Januar 1906, Reutlingen. Bruder, Peter Frank, geb. d. 5. März 1936, Reutlingen".

"I carry this with me, always. This paper was hidden among your mother's clothes when I found her."

"You found her?"

Schneider sighed. "You were right when you said things were difficult during the war. Not so much for me. I was young, fourteen and foolhardy, but money was short and my parents were occasionally abused in the street. Slogans were daubed on our house too—anti-Jewish, you know. There are always those who will do this when the opportunity arrives. My father lost many of his patients and most of my friends dropped away. I was told to keep out of the way as much as possible until times changed, so I spent a lot of time in the house helping my father in the surgery or my mother in the kitchen." His face clouded. "I had one close friend who did not desert me. Kurt. His family disapproved but we used to meet secretly, as boys will. One night, in February, 1942, he told me that he had seen a German

Jewish family arrested in town the previous day—father, mother, young boy and baby girl. Apparently they had illegally crossed the border over the mountains and were to be taken back that night. When I returned home there was a bundle of rags on our doorstep. I knew straightaway what it was. I guessed that the mother, believing the child dead, had persuaded someone to deliver it to a Jewish family for an appropriate burial. Anyway, I brought her inside and gave her to my father. He examined her by the light of the fire. She was alive."

Schneider looked at Ruth listening intently, wide-eyed, to every word. The story sounded unconvincing to him. The details he was giving her were lies although the essentials were true. She need not know the full horror of that night. He continued the story, now with nothing more to conceal. "I saw the colour creeping back into her face and a tiny movement in her chest. I can see us now in the flickering firelight, my mother in tears, my father gently bathing the child in warm water, myself feeling serious and grown-up. We all knew it would be the start of danger and difficulty but my parents never considered anything but the need to protect the child. We knew enough about what was happening in Germany and elsewhere to know we had to get her out of the country once she had been nursed and fed back to health. It was too dangerous to keep her with us for long. At first, our social isolation helped to keep her hidden but your mother was not a child to keep quiet for long." Schneider chuckled. "I was given the job of keeping her distracted and entertained. Ay yai, she was a handful. What spirit! Anyway, my father made contact with people he knew in the Jewish community and eventually they were able to smuggle your mother away to England. I think it cost my father all his savings. He also made arrangements through a law-firm in London to support her with money as far as he could. The photograph that you have was taken by my father early one morning when no-one was about. It was a dangerous thing to do but he wanted to give your mother some evidence of her past. It accompanied her to England along with the information we had gained from this slip of paper."

"What happened to your parents?" asked Ruth.

"They both died soon after the war. My father gave me the address of the law-firm when he was dying and asked me to do what I could to help "Little Leah" as we always thought of her. When I went to America to study and take up an academic life there I kept up the contact. And now, here I am, an old man back in my homeland talking to little Leah's daughter." He took out a large handkerchief from his jacket pocket and noisily blew his nose.

"What happened to my grandparents and their son—my real uncle, I suppose? Were they taken back to Germany?" she asked.

"That was the story. Most people assumed they perished in the camps. In any event, they were never seen again."

Ruth shivered and her eyes glistened. "Poor, poor souls," she murmured. She looked at Schneider. "Thank you, Otto, for my mother's life," she said quietly. "And mine."

He was embarrassed . "Look," he said, "there is a good coffee house around the corner which also sells excellent gateaux. Allow me to take you there? Then you can tell me all about yourself and your mother and father. We must not brood too much upon the sadness of the past. Let the dead bury the dead, hm?"

✳ CHAPTER ELEVEN ✳

A hand tapped gently on the wooden slats of the trapdoor. "It's Dieter." The words filtered down in a whisper. "Are you ready?"

"Ready."

Dust danced in the lamplight as the trap was raised. Three hungry white faces looked up out of the darkness like chicks in a nest.

"Time to go," murmured Dieter. "There is rumour of another house-to-house soon."

Jakob helped his wife climb the first rungs of the wooden ladder until she could pass her child into the hands of the man above. He turned to lift his son through the hole but the little boy eluded his grasp and began the ascent himself.

"I can climb, Papa," he said proudly in his reedy voice.

Jakob followed closely, ready to hold him if necessary, his heart aching for the boy's fearlessness and vulnerability. "Well done, Peter," he said as the boy scrambled into the candlelit kitchen above. He followed. They stood around the hole in the floor, Sarah holding the baby in her arms, Peter hopping from one leg to the other and Jakob clutching the cloth bag which contained their meagre possessions. They watched Dieter close the trap and cover it with a rug. It felt as if he was sealing off a whole part of their lives, a route never to be retraced. They had cowered in the cellar for three weeks, loyal friends keeping them hidden from betrayal at terrible risk to themselves. Now it was time to head for the border. Peter was impatient to be gone. Being cooped up in a windowless room had been a sore trial for his youthful energy. Crossing the mountains would be an adventure. His father bit the ends of his prematurely grey moustache, knowing with the experience of adulthood that it might not be long before they would be thinking back on their incarceration in the cellar with longing.

The smell of soup drifted from the stove where Frieda stirred a large pan.

"Come to the table," she said. "We will eat together before you go and pray for better times." She ushered them around the rough pine board and ladled steaming, heavy green broth into their bowls. Hunks of black bread were piled onto a wooden plate. The candle-flames wavered as a grieving wind inserted cold fingers between the old walls.

"What will you do if... when you get across?"

Jakob glanced at his wife. She looked at him, her eyes wide with anxiety. He gave her a smile of encouragement.

"I will make contact with other emigres. I have heard that there are small communities all over Switzerland just waiting for the end of the madness before returning to their homeland."

He had heard no such thing. Dieter looked shamefaced.

"I'm sorry, Jakob," he said. "It is too dangerous for you to stay here any longer." He did not elaborate for whom the danger lay. The penalties for harbouring Jews were unthinkable.

"I know, my friend, I know," he said. "You have already done so much, helping to repair the shop when they smashed the windows, keeping us in food when we were made to close the business. It is a brave man who will stand by his friends when they are persecuted by everyone else." He placed his hand on Dieter's arm. "And now you risk your life. We cannot ask you to do so any longer. You have to think of Frieda and Ulla."

"I have put some food together for you," Frieda said in a tearful voice, "although God knows, it is not much."

There were shouts outside. Everyone froze. Dieter sprang to the window and peered from behind the curtain down the dark, snowy street.

"I don't know," he said. "I can't see. We cannot take any chances. You must go now."

Frieda embraced Sarah and kissed the baby and Peter. Jakob hugged Dieter then shook his hand in a tight grip. He ushered his family towards the door at the rear of the house. He had his hand on the latch when Dieter stopped him. He took hold of the star roughly sewn onto his overcoat and ripped it off. Then he did the same with Sarah and Peter.

"Pray God you will not need those where you are going," he said. He signalled to his wife to blow out the candles and turn out the lamp then he slowly eased open the door. Snow-laden fields spread away towards the foothills in the distance. The night sky was heavy with cloud, snow whipping across the land in the strong wind. The Franks pulled scarves over their heads, whispered their goodbyes and hurried across the creaking fields, heads bowed into the wind. Dieter fastened the latch behind them as the sound of urgent hammering and shouting began again, this time a little nearer to his door.

The first night's trek gave them all hope. Their limbs exulted in the freedom of movement after the weeks of hiding. Jakob had warned them not to speak until the town was many kilometres behind them in the dark. He wanted to avoid all buildings—villages, farms, roads—anywhere where there might be people. It was to be straight over the mountains, south-west to safety. Roads meant border guards, checkpoints, guns, dogs, but the mountains were vast and difficult to police. It should be easy to slip through the net at night. He reckoned on twenty kilometres per day. It would be frustratingly slow for him but he had to take into account the children and his wife's strength. Even so, they would cross the border in perhaps four or five days. If they could eke out the food there was enough to get them well into neutral territory. With these thoughts warming him as much as the blood pumping through his arteries he shepherded his family up the first range of hills, climbing to freedom. Little Peter plodded along happily, glad to be doing something. When his father asked him if he wanted to be carried for a while he shook his head.

"Well you tell me if you get tired and I'll give you a piggy-back."

Peter's eyes, wide and black in the gloom, looked solemnly at him. Then he put his finger to his lips and said, "Ssh."

Jakob smiled at his son. "I think we can talk now," he said, quietly. "We're a long way from people here." He turned to his wife. "How's Leah? Asleep? Let me carry her for a while." He took the warm bundle in its improvised sling and Sarah looped the tied blanket ends over his head. He looked down through the many folds of cloth to where the little white face lay. Her eyes were tightly shut. "That's right, my little one," he whispered. "You sleep. Gather your strength. It will be a better world for you to grow up in, I promise."

"How long shall we walk tonight?" Sarah asked him, taking Peter's hand.

"Are you tired?"

"No, my dear, not at all. I was thinking of Peter."

"I'm not tired," he said. "I can walk and walk. Look." He broke free of his mother's hand and strode ahead, swinging his arms like a soldier. His parents watched him fondly.

"I think we'll keep going as much as we can," Jakob said. "See, it's stopped snowing." A few stars were gleaming between the clouds. "We'll stop as soon as it becomes light and find shelter. It will be safer and warmer to sleep during the day." He took her hand. "God will protect us," he said as they headed into the wilderness.

He had miscalculated fatally. Dieter's map, spread out flat on his kitchen table, had made the journey look easy. It would have been better to have pushed the map from its four sides inwards and studied the result. Visualize the crumpled chaos enlarged thousands of times, add snow, ice and freezing temperatures and he would have gained some idea of what was facing them. Twenty kilometres a day might have been possible on a road but not among cliffs and ravines, over icy rock and through deep snow. After three days it became chillingly clear that their food would have to be severely rationed. A mere ten kilometres was exhausting, climbing up the steep lower pastures, through the trees, over windswept passes then down into the next valley. And although they might cover ten kilometres, they would only be three or four nearer their goal. The first few days were also a warning that, as yet, the mountains had barely shown their teeth. Each grey morning revealed another jagged barrier waiting for them, higher and colder than before. There was no respite in the weather. Snow, driven from the bitter sky, stung their eyes and dragged at their feet.

Days were spent in snow-holes, huddled for warmth, shivering and eking out their food. After two weeks, the grey-white scars of frost-bite made their appearance. Peter's young spirits were quite gone. He stumbled onwards like an automaton during the night or hung on his father's back when he could move no more. He said very little, never complained or whined. His wasted, scarred face looked like an old man's. The baby's breathing was laboured, she was fractious and reluctant to feed. Sarah was exhausted and desperate. Jakob had no idea how far they had come. He kept them heading south-west but whether they were over the border he did not know. All he knew was that if they did not find food and shelter soon, they would perish where they were.

They were in a high valley by a frozen lake. The pines which surrounded it had provided protection from the wind and Jakob had improvised a shelter behind a cluster of rocks using brushwood from the trees. It was afternoon and his wife and children were dozing and shivering, the baby cough-coughing pitifully. He looked to the south at another forbidding granite rampart. He turned to Sarah and found her watching him.

"We cannot climb further," she said, her voice thick in her throat. "You know that, Jakob. We need warmth."

"Yes, my dear, I know. I think we can follow this valley down. If we go lower we should find farm buildings where we can shelter, perhaps a barn with hay." He looked at his wife's thin face. "We must be over the border by now. We should move while there is daylight, find a warm place to sleep tonight and tomorrow I will find food." He tried to sound confident. "Do you think Peter can make it?"

Peter was curled up against his mother, his whole body shaking. He slowly nodded his head, his face expressionless.

It was almost dark when they stumbled on the hut. After so much climbing the descent had been even more painful, their weight thrown forward against weary knees and frostbitten toes. Sarah and Peter slumped into the snow as Jakob beat at the wooden bar that was wedged across the door, glued with ice. The heels of his hands were numb and each blow jolted through his body in his desperation. When it suddenly gave, he shoved the crude door open onto the darkness inside. There came the smell of sawn wood. He turned to his family. They lay where they had fallen, eyes closed, the snow blowing unheeded across their faces. The look of pain and endurance was gone, replaced by serenity, the sweet sleep of approaching death. Jakob lifted Leah from her mother's arms, carried her into the shed and lay her on the earthen floor. She was quite still. Then he gathered up Peter and brought him inside and finally Sarah. He was too weak to carry her and the effort of dragging her was almost too much for him. He felt giddy and faint. It was quiet and still inside, sheltered from the incessant moaning of the wind, but it was deadly cold. He looked around as his eyes became used to the gloom. Cut logs were stacked from floor to roof against two walls. Against the third wall there was a bench with a vice and, hooked onto nails driven into the wall, a bow-saw, a felling axe and a hand-axe. A shelf held chisels, wedges and other tools. But it was the lantern on the bench that caught Jakob's eye. He picked it up, shook it and was rewarded by a liquid sound from the base. Using his teeth, he removed his mittens and felt among his bundle for the precious matches. It became a race against the cold. His fingers were locked and useless, his hands, blunt and palsied instruments. It took him half an hour to light the lamp, half an hour of frustrating agony as he found ways of using his knuckles and his teeth to raise the glass, strike the match and ignite the wick whilst seeing all he cared for in the world slipping away. He endured the torture of returning blood as he held his hands to the warm glass, then desperately built a fire on the earth floor. As the shavings crackled and spat and he added slivers, then sticks, Sarah's eyes flickered open.

"Jakob? Jakob? What happened? Where are we?"

"Sh, sh, my dear, we're safe for tonight and we'll be warm." He took her hands and gently removed her mittens, holding her ice-cold flesh in his warm fingers. "Can you sit? Come closer to the fire."

"The baby!" she wailed, looking wildly about her.

"Gently, gently, my love. Here she is, quite safe but very hungry." He undid his coat where he had tucked the bundle of rags to share his warmth and the increasing heat from the fire. "When her Mutti is quite warm she would like to be fed." A thin cry came from the depths of his coat. "See? I will look after Peter." He passed the child to Sarah, removed his coat and spread it in front of the fire. "Here you go, young man," he said tremblingly as he lifted the boy close to the warmth and laid him gently down, tucking his scarf under his head for a pillow. "Come on, Peter," he whispered. "Fight a little longer. A little longer, my son."

Jakob watched throughout the night, keeping his family alive by will alone. Peter's groans and Leah's cries came as music after those terrible moments of dead silence. A snow-shovel enabled him to create warm melt-water to drink. They fell into fitful sleep in the early hours, Jakob intending to leave at first light and find food, whatever the risk.

He was woken by the snort of a horse and the jingle of harness bells. He sat up, faint with hunger, and listened. There were movements in the snow outside, then came a volley of deep barks at the door followed by a sharp command, "Sei still!" Someone was standing there puzzling over the foot-marks and the dislodged door slat. A voice called, "Wer ist da? Raus!"

The door was kicked open and Jakob was blinded by a flood of light. There appeared, against a dazzle of snow-reflected sunshine, the silhouette of a man gripping a large dog by the collar. After weeks of living in darkness his eyes felt bruised by the onslaught. He raised his arm to shield them and the dog leapt to its hind legs, lunging towards him and barking hysteri-cally, half throttled by its collar. The man yanked it down to its four legs where it continued to growl and pull, its eyes bulging. He dragged it away from the door opening.

"Out!" he ordered.

Jakob tried to stand. He turned himself onto his knees then levered himself into a half crouch. Still shading his eyes, he staggered to the door and used the frame to haul himself upright.

"Help us," he croaked before sliding back to his knees.

Anton Bauer looked in amazement at the wasted figure crumpled at his feet. There came a whimper from inside his wood store. He peered inside and met two pairs of eyes staring at him in terror. Two figures lay on the floor, apparently unable to move. The whimper came from a bundle clutched in the arms of the one who, Bauer could now see, was a woman.

Bauer was a simple man. His family had grazed goats on these upper pastures for generations, wresting a poor living from the hostile terrain. Now the mountains had provided him with a winter windfall. He was not stupid. He read newspapers. It was clear to him who these people were. The question was, how to turn the situation into profit. He stroked the stubble on his wind-burned face, seeing desperation in the faces before him, calculating.

Everybody knew that Jews carried gold. These would pay highly for his help. The priority was to keep them alive. He would take them back to the farmhouse, Lotte could feed them and he would send Max to town to fetch the Polizeimeister. Hermann would be grateful for being informed first, generously grateful. It was also the time of year to sell him another goat, for which he always paid too much. This could be a profitable day all round.

"Can you walk?" he asked Jakob who had managed to get to his feet.

"A little, but you see how my family is." He gestured painfully.

"So. You get in the cart. I will help with the rest."

"Many thanks, many thanks," whispered Jakob." We need food."

"Yes, yes, soon. In the cart with you."

Jakob waited until Bauer had raised Sarah to her feet. She could not walk. He picked her up, still clutching Leah, and carried her to the sleigh, Jakob watching every movement. He waited until Peter was lifted by the burly farmer and placed next to his mother. Then shuffling warily past the dog which lay in the snow at its master's command, he slowly climbed in himself, waving away the assistance offered. He did not want his family to appear totally helpless. There was vulnerability in weakness as he well knew.

ICE

Harness bells jingled cheerfully, the shining mountains were sharp cut-outs against the blue sky as Bauer urged his tough little pony along the hard-packed track. He whistled as the runners swished beneath him. The dog ran alongside, its pink tongue lolling. In the cart, Jakob wrapped his arms around his dying family and prayed. The indifferent sun, now high in the sky, warmed them but their life force had ebbed very low. When the sled swept up to a low wooden building, crudely but sturdily constructed, Jakob was unconscious. He was unaware of being lugged under icicle-hung eaves into a dark, smoky room, warm with the smell of animals. He came-to from a dream of his childhood. Mutti was serving breakfast in their cosy kitchen and he was teasing his sister. Papa told him to leave her alone and eat his food. There was the flicker of fire-light across his eyes and a meaty scent wafting under his nose.

"Eat, now. There. That's good, mm?"

A spoon was in his mouth and thin, warm liquid ran down his throat. He opened his eyes wide, memory flooding back, gasped and choked.

"Gently, gently," a woman's voice was saying. "Look." She pointed at the shapes of Sarah and Peter lying in front of the fire, breathing easily. "They have eaten and are sleeping. Now it is your turn."

"Don't give him too much," a man's voice said. He recognized it as the man who had found them in the hut. His eyes focused and he saw Bauer silhouetted against a low window, staring out. "Max will soon be back with Hermann."

"I know, I know," the female voice replied, close to Jakob's head. He realized she was supporting him, one strong arm around his shoulders, the other dipping a spoon into a bowl of clear soup. "Haven't I fed enough young goats to know how? Easy, Easy," she said to Jakob who was trying to grasp the spoon. "Too much too soon is as bad as too little. You came over the mountains?" She drew in her breath. "You are lucky to be alive. And your wife, too. With the baby. Pretty little thing," she said, glancing over at Leah, her voice softening. "But she has had her mother's milk. Ah, but your boy. So much trying to be a man. He says nothing, no complaints. A son to be proud of," she added wistfully, all the while lifting spoonfuls of broth to Jakob's lips. "Things must have been terrible for you to risk the mountains in winter. But you are safe now. You must rest and eat, rest and eat."

"Be quiet, woman. You talk too much," growled Bauer, turning from the window. Here is Max with Hermann. Leave him now. Prepare a drink for the Polizeimeister."

The door was pushed open and a burly man, impressive in silver-buttoned greatcoat, helmet and leather boots was ushered in. His stooped shoulders seemed to feel the weight of the low ceiling, and he took the offered chair quickly, removing his official hat as he sat down and smoothed his hair flat with one large, meaty hand.

"Take Polizmeister Brucke's hat, Max," Bauer urged his son who was standing behind the policeman with his mouth open. He did so and stood with it like an offering in his outstretched hands, his eyes flickering between the smart, uniformed figure seated in the household's best chair and the sorry wretches now slumped in the corner of the room who were eyeing the silver buttons and insignia of rank with deep fear.

"Well go on, hang it up behind the door. And when you've done that you can go outside and see to the horse." He shook his head as Max slouched out and gave the policeman the conspiratorial glance of parents with useless children. "Lotte! Where is that wine for the Polizeimeister?"

Chief Brucke had not taken his eyes off the Frank family since he had entered the room. He absently took the mug of rough wine from Frau Bauer and seemed to be calculating. He was a young man but his stocky build and heavy, blue jowls made him appear older. He had risen quickly through the ranks, it was said more through his connections in Masonic circles than ability, but he had a terrier-like tenacity combined with a reputation for violence which made him feared and respected, if not liked, both amongst his colleagues and the community. He knew Bauer well, as he did all the local people, being one of them, born and educated in Unteriberg. He always paid one visit each year to the Bauer farm to pay for the kid or the lamb which he said was to be donated to one of the many charities that the police-force supported. He thrust his hand forward suddenly. "Papers!" he barked.

Jakob Frank submissively handed over the dog-eared sheets which he had unearthed from his rags, bowing his head so as not to meet the eyes of the officer, a practice he had perfected in Germany and which had saved him from many blows. Brucke glanced briefly at them then thrust them into his tunic pocket, turning to Bauer appraisingly.

"They were in your hut, you say. You know what they are, of course."

Bauer played dumb. He had learned from a brutal father that those in authority do not like knowledge among their underlings. "No, sir. Lotte and me were just saying, it's a mystery where they came from."

The policeman looked at him thoughtfully. He did not trust this farmer. He might be ignorant but he was of peasant stock and that meant cunning. It was going to cost money if he were to deal safely with what fate had offered him. He cleared his throat.

"Well, Bauer. You did right to call me. They are of little importance but will have to be processed by the authorities. Vagrants usually mean crime. They will come with me, now." He stood up, using his bulk to impress his power. "We do not want our canton to become a haven for scavengers so it would be best if you said nothing about this. To anyone, you understand. We do not want rumours to encourage others." He thrust a hand into his trouser pocket and when he pulled it out again there was the crackle of money. "We are grateful for your public-spiritedness, Bauer. For your trouble."

Bauer looked at the grubby notes. Of little importance indeed. Bargaining time.

"You can trust me, Herr Polizeimeister, as you know. However, I worry about my son, Max. You know what a loose tongue he has."

Brucke gave him a black look and fished out some further pieces of crumpled paper. Bauer stuffed them into his shirt pocket with a grin. "I will see that he is discreet, sir. About the goat? It has been a harsh winter so prices are high but I am sure we can come to an arrangement."

He realized as he spoke that he had overstepped the mark. The policeman's voice was cold.

"Hear me, Bauer. Do not begin to think that I am in any way in your debt. I could have you and your son in army uniform by tomorrow, farmers or no. Understand?" Bauer's grin vanished. "And you may feed your high-priced goat to the crows." He spoke to the wretched family who had been following this exchange in bewilderment. "Come," he said sharply. "Into the wagon with you."

They slowly climbed to their feet and shuffled to the door, Peter glancing back with longing at the warm embers in the fireplace, Jakob whispering encouragement to them.

"Nearly at the end of our journey," he murmured. "Soon our struggles will be over."

As Sarah passed Lotte she felt a hand slip a flat loaf of bread into her shawl. She looked at the rough-featured woman in gratitude but Lotte, her eyes bright with tears, looked frightened and pressed a finger to her lips. Bauer, who had been outside to talk to his son, re-entered the room. He looked at his wife with suspicion but said nothing, still pleased with his morning's work. He watched the Franks roughly bundled into the wagon and driven off by his oafish son, the policeman by his side. He felt the same satisfaction he would have enjoyed at seeing his livestock sold for slaughter at an unexpectedly high price.

It was late evening by the time the policeman had contacted all the Brothers and arranged the Gathering. Unteriberg lay dark and hushed under thick snow, the clock chimes muffled and echoless. The Franks had been hurried into a monastery outbuilding, unseen by anyone except Max who was so scared of his father and even more terrified of the Polizmeister that Brucke felt assured of his silence. Jakob wondered uneasily what lay in store for them even as he continued to offer comfort and hope. He did not like the furtive way they had been shoved into this freezing outhouse. He had been prepared to face uniforms, offices, questions, abuse, but in some kind of official setting, even a jail cell. That would have felt safer. The way the policeman had not asked him any questions was sinister, too. He tried the old wooden door which looked rickety but it was firmly locked and stoutly barred. He cradled his family in his arms to give what little warmth he had against the bitter cold. Peter had reverted to the trance-like state of the last few days as if he had closed down all systems to preserve his fluttering heart-beat. Sarah clutched the baby as if she could keep it alive by physical force, all the while knowing the creeping chill was sucking out both their lives.

Kurt Muller was sitting on a bench in a side-chapel of the monastery church when he heard the door open. He had just finished his cleaning and was stretching his back for a few minutes before closing up to go and meet his friend Otto outside. He had come to know this dusty cavern intimately since his father, irritated by his idleness, had got him the job. At first he had hated the drudgery of dusting and polishing, at thirteen years old preferring to hang around with friends, but he had come to like the silence, rarely being disturbed, his hours outside the times when the monks chanted their liturgies. So he was surprised by this late visit. He leaned forward to peer around the stonework then drew back sharply. He had only glimpsed for a fraction of time the black hoods and robes but he knew, like any Unteriberger would know, that he should not be here. These were not monks. This was the Brotherhood whose hidden rites and practices were said to be older than the church itself. They should not be here. He should not be here. No-one outside the sect was allowed to witness their rituals. It was said they protected the town although no-one could say exactly how. It was not something you gossiped about, if you knew what was good for you. Kurt breathed shallowly trying to gulp back his white breath before it betrayed him.

He could hear a deep murmuring and the scrape of dragging feet. His fear was replaced by a burning curiosity. Now he would see something no-one outside the Brotherhood had seen. He cautiously bent forward again. Five cowled figures were pushing three ragged individuals, two adults and a child, towards an archway in the north wall. Beyond the arch came the blink candle-light.. Kurt recognized the gated doorway below the little carved figure on the wall, a doorway he had never seen open before. Now visible was a small cell containing a stone table upon which lay an ornately-carved bone-coloured casket. The lid was open. A sixth figure was standing in front of the table holding aloft something small the colour of old leather, something bent like a claw. Words were being intoned in a language Kurt did not know but in a voice he did know as that of the Polizeimeister. He shivered. There followed the sounds of imploring then a heart-rending cry. Something that looked like a small bundle of old clothes was wrenched away from one of the ragged figures. He heard a voice mutter, "This one's dead." It was thrown onto a bench and left as the whole gathering entered the cell and the door was closed. The screams that then sliced through the oak timbers and bounced off the stonework towards where he crouched would echo down the years of the rest of Kurt's life. He sprang from his niche and scurried down the aisle to the front doors, slipping out into the cold, welcome dark. He stood in the shadow of the clock tower, shaking. He felt he had been touched by the evil that somehow he had known lay at the heart of his home town. There was always one day in winter when no-one went near the church, when children were kept indoors and shutters were closed. Word was quietly passed from mouth to mouth, no-one knowing its origin. It was always a day of dark looks and hushing up. But there had been no word yet this winter. At least, none that had reached him. He peered down at the high street, empty and silent, the shuttered houses darkly hunched against each other, sickly greenish moonlight reflecting off the snowy roofs. Where was Otto? He should have been here by now. Kurt began to feel very afraid.

There was movement in the entrance porch. A cloaked figure said quietly to someone inside, "I'll get rid of this. Jewish brat. It's no use to us," and then the hooded shape was passing within inches of Kurt pressed against the ancient stonework of the tower. It clutched the bundle that Kurt had seen thrown down on the bench inside. He held his breath but the man was intent on his purpose. Against the wall of the monastery outbuildings was a log pile. Working from the back of the pile where wood had lain undisturbed and rotting for years, he lifted out piece after piece until he had created a deep hole inside. He dropped the bundle into the hole and threw chunks of wood after it, arranging the ones at the top to hide the disturbance. Then he swiftly made his way back inside the church, brushing dirt from his hands as he passed Kurt once more. The voice had chilled Kurt even deeper. It was a voice that had taught him for many years in the town school.

"Kurt!" someone hissed. His heart pounded. He was ready to run for his life. "It's me, Otto."

The small figure of his friend detached itself from the gatepost by the courtyard and ran across the cobbles to where he was hiding. Otto's eyes were wide and scared.

"I came to get you. The word's out. You shouldn't be here," he hissed. "I had to sneak out of the house. What's happening? "

"Something bad. We've got to get away from this place." But as he spoke, the doors opened again and they both crouched back into the gloom, unwilling spectators to a tragedy that was being played out towards its final act. The sable-clad six emerged and stared, as Kurt had done, down at the silent town. They emanated cold command. Kurt, convinced that murder had been committed in the church, was relieved to see the wretched trio were still alive. Just. They were dragged outside, feet trailing, down the flight of steps to where they dropped on the cobblestones. Kurt saw Brucke (he recognized him as the tallest figure) direct someone to the side of the church from where he emerged moments later leading a small pony hitched to a cart. The family were hauled up off the ground and into the cart, the young boy flung in easily as if he weighed nothing, the father too weak to come to his or his wife's assistance. They lay on the floor of the wagon, the shrouded men climbed onto the sides, one took the reins and the cart creaked away towards the trails that led up to Spirstock, the gigantic mountain that watched over the town. Spots of blood were black against the snow as a maimed hand hung over the tail of the cart.

Kurt and Otto looked at each other, eyes wide with horror.

"We've got to get home," Otto hissed urgently. "We'll be missed. Were you in there? What happened?"

Kurt shook his head. He discovered he was weeping. "I don't know. They hurt those poor people. I don't know why."

"Did they see you?"

Kurt shook his head. He was slumped on the ground, head in hands, his childhood over. Otto tugged at him.

"Come on, Kurt. They might be back. We've got to go."

Kurt rose wearily to his feet. He knew they would not be back, not just then, not in the guise in which they had left. He also felt certain that three were never coming back. "Listen, Otto," he said, "we weren't here, tonight. We saw nothing. We don't talk about it."

"Yes, I agree, but just, let's go. I'm scared." Otto peered about him, half-expecting a black apparition to manifest itself out of the shadows. Snow fell, masking foot-marks, tracks and the spattered trail of bloodstains that led to the church doors. All was still and hushed. The two boys were creeping across the courtyard when a tiny cry froze them in their tracks.

"Did you hear that?" Otto looked into the gloom from where the cry had come.

"An owl," muttered Kurt. "Or something. Does it matter? Come on."

But the cry came again and Otto knew that it did matter, that it was no owl. Kurt wished he had not heard it, wished he could be safe in bed, at home, wished he did not have to make this awful choice. The sound would go away. Eventually. But something told him that, if he ignored it now, that little cry would never cease to ring in his ears.

"Listen to me, Otto. I do know what it is. It's a baby." Otto's breathing stopped. "And I know where it is." He felt he had aged over the last half hour. "It's in the woodpile. They thought it was dead. They called it a Jewish brat. What can we do?"

"We can't leave it!"

"But what can we do with it?"

"I don't know, I don't know. But we can't leave it to die, can we?"

Kurt had known that that was the truth of it when he first heard the sign of life. But he was very frightened. They could both so easily be in deadly trouble. His friendship with Otto was already disapproved of by his parents when they had felt it expedient for their business to cut any ties with Jewish families. The boys' closeness was stronger than any parental pressure but they had learned to be discreet. But now Kurt was a witness to brutality and possibly murder involving the chief of police, the schoolmaster and others and here he was contemplating rescuing and hiding a Jewish refugee. He was panicked into paralysis.

Fortunately, Otto, who had seen less of the night's work, was aware of the urgency of the situation. He shook Kurt.

"Where is it, Kurt? Come on, show me. It won't live long in this cold if we don't do something quick."

Kurt led him to the woodpile and began removing the logs at the back. Then he reached inside and drew out the ragged bundle which was now ominously still and silent and passed it to Otto. He cradled it in the crook of his arm and gingerly unwrapped the rags where, he knew by the weight, the child's head would be. The two boys peered down at the tiny features, still and blue in the moonlight.

"We're too late," whispered Otto.

"Put it back, then and let's get away from here."

"We can't do that!"

"Why not? It's dead, isn't it? There's nothing we can do."

But Otto knew that he could not do that. In spite of his youth he was sensitive to the need for respect towards this tiny fragment. This was not a piece of rubbish to be dumped. He opened his jacket and held the child against his chest, cocooning it in the flaps of his coat.

"My father will know what to do. Don't worry, Kurt, you can forget about it. My father is very discreet. We will give it a decent burial, say the right words from our faith. No-one will know. Go home."

Kurt, relieved, shuffled off home. He kept close to the walls, aware of being alone and knowing that, whatever Otto had said, he would never forget about it. Otto threaded his way home through the back streets, head down against the swirling flakes. He knew he was bringing home trouble but his love and admiration for his father as a man of compassion and principle made him certain that he was doing the right thing. He felt the weight of the baby gently rocking in his grasp as he hurried along, his blood, pacing with warmth and life, wrapping her round.

❋ CHAPTER TWELVE ❋

Fasching was to be chimed-in during the dead hours to mark the Lenten approach to Easter. An evening of carnival, timed to offset the bitterness of the crucifixion, would provide colour, light and comfort ahead of the agonies of death and resurrection. Fluorescent posters, glowing with distractions, flapped damply on the town's lamp-posts. Shop windows were full of masks, costumes and blizzards of confetti. The gentle snow-field behind the monastery was chopped out of the night by shimmering floodlights. Catering vans steamed richly, flavouring the refrigerated air with onions and wurst, spicing it with glühwein. Deedly-deedly, wafting from the speaker horns erratically wired to fence posts, tinkled in the vast air and faded up the hills, dying in the blackness of Spirstock, Unteriberg's eternal backdrop. The mountain was to be the setting of the evening's finale, a dark canvas down which would sweep a stroke of fire, a swish of skiers bearing flambeaux, glissading from summit to base.

Marco took in the clustered crowds with dark pleasure, his nostrils flaring over the wiry curl of his moustache. He smelled money. It came rustling and chinking over the counter of his mobile bar as holidaymakers, bulging with furs and funds, demanded schnapps and punch to light up their fingers and toes. The gently-sloping hillside also produced another cash-crop as a permanent queue of thrill-seekers paid at his concession for ski-bikes or inner-tubes and a tow to the hilltop. Their yells of fearful laughter as they swept or bounced their way to the foot of the slope urged others to join the line. But this was only loose change. Spirstock was the jackpot. He had shovelled money out of his disco and dumped it onto those frowning slopes in a gambler's bid for riches. By next season the mountain would be avalanching wealth in a torrent powerful enough to satisfy Marco's avarice. If all went well. But something was germinating in the black shadows of his unconscious. He had begun to fear the mountain's dark reputation. There had been too many accidents. The most recent would have stopped all work had he not been able to use his bankroll to beat and bribe the authorities to submit to his will. He could not afford to fail. He had bled his club almost fatally to give vitality to his investment and now, without an income as a ski-instructor, he had to send an infusion of confidence into the venture. Without the approval of the local ski-school he had hired a professional display team to make the torchlit procession. It would focus positively on the lucrative possibilities of the new ski area. An unexpected shudder shook his body and he grabbed the schnapps bottle from the surprised hands of his barman and poured himself a fierce shot.

A mummy, bandaged like a first-aid victim, stomped through the hotel foyer, arm-in-arm with a Bacofoil astronaut and a feathered, shoe-polished Indian. Cheers and applause greeted them in the normally staid bar of the Ledermann, now a Disneyland of pirates and princesses, werewolves and witches priming themselves for further mayhem in the icy streets. Tom pulled Ruth's coat across her shoulders. He wanted to touch her, old-fashioned courtesy merely an excuse. She smiled at him, understanding.

"Thanks," she said, kissing him on the lips, taking his hand. Their fingers warmly interlaced, snug as cogwheels, their contours excitingly new yet becoming lovingly familiar. Since their first night together they had been suspended in a bubble of self absorption like frozen figures in a souvenir snow-storm, unable to look away from each other, the world beyond misty and distant. Left alone, unreachable, drawn closer by confidences, they breathed each other in like life and embraced each other's loss, all else abandoned. But now it was time to rejoin the carnival.

The high street had been reclaimed for pedestrians, the bullying motors, for once, intimidated into the back streets.

ICE

Insurrection was in the air. Ruth and Tom scented its intoxication as they wedged themselves into the rowdy river which, squeezed between the banks of buildings, flowed slowly uphill towards the lights of the monastery fields. Where sprays of confetti lay on the trodden snow, pink dye had leached out in splatters like the sites of shootings.

A wail of wild jazz infiltrated the pompous marching bands battling through the crowds. Accordions blended seamlessly, at home in a squeeze. Ruth, one arm tightly linked through Tom's, was startled to find her other arm taken by a very moth-eaten bear. A blowsy Goldilocks had claimed Tom. Instantly, like cells dividing, the chain lengthened, becoming a grotesque bracelet of fairy-tale figures, mostly grim. A bottle wove down the line, emptying on its way, fuelling a dervish dance which wheeled out a space, Tom and Ruth at its helpless hub, until it whirled apart in giddy laughter, leaving them dizzy.

"It doesn't seem like the Swiss, this," Tom said breathlessly, adding, for the melody, "miss."

Ruth smiled and shrugged. "Misrule," she said. "You have to take the lid off sometimes. 'People mutht be amuth'd.'"

They gave themselves up to the turgid current and were carried slowly among the colourful flotsam of the carnival crowd to be swirled together onto the snowfield behind the monastery. With hands snugged around hot glasses of fragrant glühwein, they waited to witness the torchlit trail trace its way from the summit of Spirstock down into their midst. As the moment approached, the floodlights blinked out and left the arena lit only by an icy moon and the stars glittering through the clear, cold reaches of space. Tom and Ruth saw the shadowy fields bathed in a silky glow, the black block of mountain etched against a speckled sky. Arm-in-arm they wedged themselves into the crowd, the noise and chatter dying. The engine for the ski-bike tow-lift whined into silence and the jolly accordion tunes clicked off the loudspeakers.

There came a pause. White breath wreathed upwards and chilled to invisibility. Children's thin voices urged to be lifted to see better. Then an excited shout, "There they are!" and, high in the sky, a point of red fire appeared, then another and another until Spirstock appeared to be wearing a scarlet coronet. The illusion altered as the string of light began to move, a scarlet thread drawn across a black backcloth, one way and then the other, weaving graceful patterns against the dark. The onlookers began to gabble again, their occasional "ooh!"s and "aah!"s sounding like a firework party. At one point the red line trailed vertically downward then divided into two and came together again to create a circle of fire.

Ruth's eyes sparkled as she clutched Tom's arm. "I love anything like this," she whispered. "It's the silliness that's so wonderful. It doesn't make anything, it doesn't achieve anything but it looks pretty."

"I suppose it's all publicity," Tom replied. "It'll bring the money in eventually."

She punched him on the arm.

"Stop being a businessman, you. Not everything needs a point. Flying kites. It's just nice to do."

Tom put an arm around her shoulders and pressed his lips to her ear.

"I love you, you know," he murmured. "What are we going to do when it's time to go back home?"

"You're doing it again," Ruth smiled. "It'll be targets and deadlines next. Come on, just enjoy the moment. The future will sort itself out when it needs to."

And Tom, who had always liked to be organized, who needed the reassurance of a plan of action, was completely happy. She had that effect on him, gave him confidence that all would be well.

The fire-snake reached the foot of the mountain and threaded through the pines that fringed the lower slopes. Lights flickered like eyes in and out of the trees, sometimes blinking out then glitteringly ignited once more. As the skiers reached the snowfields of the foothills, the crowd could make out the figures holding torches, dipping and rising to the contours of the ground, completely at ease as they sped over the grey snow. Those in the crowd for whom this holiday was their first ski experience and who had been battling to master the tricky element whilst burdened with unfamiliar equipment, marvelled at the careless grace of these experts who without any poles for support, were skimming effortlessly towards them. An area had been marked out with staves and tape and the torchbearers swept into it amid whoops and cheers from the crowd. The leader skidded to a spectacular, snow-spraying halt, his cohort followed to create a fiery, smoking huddle with torches held aloft. Then the floodlights burst on and the crowd applauded the entertainers who were slapping each other on the back, taking off their hats and punching the air, all talking at once. Tom watched someone from the Eisbar walk up to the leader of the skiers and shake him by the hand and realized it was Marco. Invisible in the crowd, he didn't wish to risk another confrontation so he and Ruth slipped towards the boundary of the carnival area on the edge of darkness. Here they embraced, holding on to what they had found, strong against the Marcos of this world. Behind them, two skiers, flambeaux extinguished, were deep in anxious conversation and staring out into the darkness towards the mountain.

An hour earlier they had formed up for the descent. The mountain was unfamiliar, they had been drafted in by a young entrepreneur to do the run and they were being paid well to do it but many felt it was still not enough. The piste was not easy as they had found out that afternoon on their training run and although expert, they had had to concentrate hard. Now, in the dark, it was going to be more difficult. New snow on new, untested trails. The night was freezing hard so there were bound to be patches of ice. Without ski-poles and with a torch to hold aloft, it was a real test of their skills. Some had also expressed their dislike of the place. When they slid from the chairs which had hauled them to the top station, many felt an increase of the afternoon atmosphere—hostility, a sense they should not be there. Vague unease in the daylight had become, among the flickering shadows, a palpable threat. The black rock around which the new buildings were being structured lowered over them as they lined up on the new piste. Their voices were hushed, and more than one looked over his shoulder in an involuntary nervous gesture. There was a lot of tapping of boot against binding to release crusted ice blocking the mechanism.

The leader wanted to be off. He would feel better once under way, picking his route and concentrating on the skiing, rather than standing around here in the icy wind as it called through crevices in the rock and whined round half-completed buildings. He checked his watch. The timing of the run had been agreed with his sponsor and it was crucial they arrive promptly to impress the carnival crowd down in the village. As the seconds ticked away he checked the team.

"OK,ladies and gentlemen. Two minutes. All torches lit? Good. Remember, ski in the tracks of whoever is in front of you and keep close. Turn where they turn and try to keep the distance between you at all times exactly the same. You know the routine for the split. You've got your numbers. We do that on the lower slopes where the gradient is less so it should be straightforward. Any problems?"

He turned to go when a voice said, "Hold it. Ice in the binding."

"Give it a good kicking."

The skier at the end of the line had his skis off and was booting the bindings enthusiastically, trying to loosen the chunk of ice wedged under the compact block of springs, screws and levers. One ski clicked satisfyingly into place but when he stamped into the other binding his boot lifted out again. The leader was impatient.

"Hurry it up, Karl. We've already missed the start time. The bastard who's paying our wages looks the sort to demand penalties."

But the boot would not bind.

"Look, go on. I'm nearly there. I'll catch you." He had a small screwdriver and was poking at the jammed works.

The team leader checked his watch again, waited for a few more moments then said, "OK, we're off," swung his points down the fall line and slipped away in rapid acceleration, the rest following at precise intervals. Karl watched their lights shrink. They would stay visible for a long time on the open face of this mountain. He bent to his task again but the ice would not budge. He needed something solid to steady the jammed ski. He took off the other and stumped back to the rock face which dominated the top station. He leaned the skis against the icy granite and picked at the blocked binding. Now that the dots of light from his companions were far away down the slope and getting smaller all the time, he felt isolated. It was cold, the bitter wind steadily increasing, its wail rising in pitch. It dragged a cloud across the moon and turned the half-light into gloom. He pulled a torch from his patchwork of zipped pockets and stabbed the beam at his ski. Instantly, the crude figure scratched into the rock face sprang out at him like a slap in the face. He gasped and stepped back. The straight lines of the face, eyes horizontal slits, nose a vertical dash and the mouth, a straight gash stitched by vertical strokes gave it a cold, pitiless expression. And he sensed something was happening. He knew he should not be here. Something wanted him gone. Now.

He was already too late. As the last piece of ice rattled out of the binding there came a noise, the thin scrape of claw on stone. He flung both skis to the ground and tried to step into them but in his haste and panic his boots were not aligned properly and the heels slid out sideways. It was then that he saw, crawling towards him over the rock, the huge, black figure, leathery and reptilian. The skier dropped his torch, frozen by its slow, purposeful approach. As it reached the edge of the rock, it leaned its head towards him, its round head with the slitted lids and stitched lips, sensing his presence. Then the slits opened to disclose yellow eyes. And yellow teeth. Row upon row.

❋ CHAPTER THIRTEEN ❋

The bells began in the blackness. Four a.m. precisely. Swiss time. Not that Tom and Ruth knew the hour that they were mercilessly rung out of sleep, the clangs booming up from underneath their balcony. They had only slept a few hours. Their late night at the carnival had been followed by languorous love-making in Tom's room. Loth to divide their warm nakedness, their position every night since that first, miraculous realization, was as one body, flesh to flesh, arms locked, all safe. They stared into the dark.

"What is it?" whispered Ruth.

"I think it's the signal for the start of Fasching," Tom replied. "Let's look."

They scrambled to their feet. Tom wrapped the duvet around himself and a giggling Ruth, and tiptoed to the window. When he levered open the French doors they gasped at the assault of frozen air and chaotic noise. The bells made a sound like a physical presence, a deep, monotonous percussion, hypnotic and ominous. It came from a procession of apparently hunch-backed dwarves marching in slow time down the street, plodding purposefully and menacingly at matching pace. As Tom and Ruth stared and shivered, they realized that they were seeing men in traditional costume, foreshortened by perspective and each hunchbacked by a giant cow-bell on his back. They leant forward to balance the weight and each bobbing step produced a teeth-chattering boom. The sound shivered between the tall buildings of the narrow street, vibrating the air and rattling the windows. People appeared on balconies up and down the street, many with hands over their ears. The procession crawled down the road like a grey lizard sniffing its way, buildings shuddering with the noise.

ICE

"I could understand them ringing the monastery bells," Tom said, close to Ruth's ear, "but this is something else!"

"It's pagan," said Ruth, wide-eyed. "Like the Chinese and their fire-crackers. They're scaring away evil spirits."

They held each other as the bells passed below them and down the street, the noise fading and deepening in the distance. They stayed on the balcony and looked out over the little town illuminated by moonlight and a speckle of lighted windows. There were still shadowy figures out in the streets, late-night revellers wringing out the last drops of excitement from the carnival, costumes the worse for wear. Tom and Ruth climbed back into their big, boxy bed, shivering as the tolling bells traced the streets of the town and drove out the demons.

"I know a great way to warm up," said Tom.

So breakfast had been late and lingering and they were still in the dining-room mid-morning, sipping fragrant coffee from a jug kept generously replenished by Herr Brucke. Many guests were doing the same, shadowy eyes and yawns bearing witness to the festivity of the night before. Ruth noticed Caroline and her parents. There had been some kind of transformation in Caroline. Instead of a silent, sulky child there was an animated young lady chatting freely with her mother who, instead of looking at her suspiciously, was listening to her daughter with a smile. More importantly, she was looking at her daughter's face as if seeing it for the first time. Because Caroline looked beautiful. And Mr Bryon, quietly doing the crossword in his English paper, kept glancing at them , also with a little smile on his face. Ruth was surprised. She had seen Caroline with Rudi the night before up on the snowfield, their arms around each other. It had been close on midnight and her parents were nowhere to be seen. It had crossed her mind at the time that Caroline was in for some trouble on her return. But apparently not.

Mrs Bryon crossed the room towards Ruth, noticeable in her white sweater with its pink letter H on the front. Mr Bryon wore a G. Somewhere, at the bottom of a suitcase, Ruth knew there would be one with a C. Today Caroline was in T-shirt and jeans.

"Have you any milk to spare? Mrs Bryon enquired. "We've just run out and I don't like to keep bothering Mr Brucke. He seems run off his feet, doesn't he?"

Tom handed over the jug. "Help yourself."

"Did you enjoy the carnival?" Ruth asked.

"Oh, yes. We weren't going to miss the torchlight skiing. Were you there? Wasn't it wonderful? We took lots of snaps." She looked at Tom and blushed a little. "I have been wanting to speak to you, Mr—er—"

"Shepherd."

"Mr Shepherd. I was short with you the other day and I should not have been. I'm sorry. I'm sure you understand. We do worry about our Caroline but I should not have been so rude. No, no," (as Tom was protesting,) "I was. But, you were right, this Rudi is a nice boy. He spoke to us last night and he brought our Caroline back at the time we asked him. He's making her holiday, I can see that."

Tom saw that this had cost Mrs Bryon an effort and he was touched, even though it had been unnecessary. "Look," he said, "instead of pinching our milk why don't you bring your coffee over here and join us?"

"Well, I don't know—" Mrs Bryon began hesitantly.

"Please do," Ruth put in. "I would like to talk to Caroline. Were you woken by the bells this morning?"

Mrs Bryon relaxed. Her stiff fussiness and narrow sense of propriety evaporated. Behind her formidable bulk she was anxious and under-confident, especially outside the tight family circle. Her essentially kindly nature responded to the ease and naturalness with which Ruth had made friends with her daughter and she had found herself breaking old boundaries and enjoying new horizons this holiday. The tight routines she and George lived by had become a strait-jacket. Her daughter's gentle rebellion had begun to free her too.

"Well, thank you," she said. "I'll bring them over."

With a good deal of chair scraping and table bumping Mr Bryon levered himself and his crossword from the chair, scooped up his coffee and stumped stiffly across. Caroline stepped lightly in his wake. He stood by Tom and Ruth's table, breathing wheezily, smiling jovially.

"Good morning, good morning," he said in his hand-rubbing, avuncular way. "Most kind of you. I think we're all glad of a slow start this morning. Late nights on top of skiing beginning to take its toll. You 'downhill only' people don't know the meaning of exercise when it comes to skiing." He beamed to show he was being comical. "And talking of 'taking its toll', did you hear the bells last night?"

Still in crossword mode, thought Tom. "Yes," he said. "Ruth was talking about it to your wife. I'm sorry, I don't think we've ever introduced ourselves—Tom and Ruth."

"George and Hilda."

They shook hands with English formality.

"Yes, the bells," Tom continued. "Must've woken the whole town. Let's hope they chased out the demons."

"Is that what they're about?" Caroline asked as she slipped her chair next to Ruth.

"Probably, originally, although today it's just part of the carnival," Ruth replied.

"Didn't feel like a carnival when we watched it from our balcony, did it?" said Tom looking at Ruth. "Grimmer than that. Did you get up to look?" he asked Mrs Bryon, aware of the flash of curiosity on her face as she tried to work out their relationship.

"Certainly not," she said with a flash of her old pomposity, but then with a sudden change of tone she confided, "but I was awake anyway. They woke George up, though. Thank goodness."

Ruth and Tom looked at her in surprise.

"He snores," she said simply.

Tom laughed, Ruth smiled and even Caroline giggled. Mrs Bryon was not trying to be amusing but she basked in the unfamiliar role of entertainer. George took it with equanimity. His shoulders were broad.

"Olly's crowd stayed out to watch it," Caroline volunteered. "That's what Rudi said." She blushed.

"How were the ski-bikes?" Ruth asked.

Caroline's eyes gleamed. "Wicked!" she said. Tom caught Mrs Bryon's eye and they smiled a conspiratorial smile. "Mega fast, no brakes. Awesome! Rudi'll tell you. He said he'd come over this morning."

As she spoke, the door to the dining room opened. Caroline looked up eagerly. A young, uniformed policeman stood there next to an older man in a grey overcoat. They surveyed the room. Herr Brucke, behind them, pushed between and addressed everyone. He looked haunted.

"Ladies and gentlemen," he began hoarsely, "please remain seated for a few moments. These..." he gestured weakly at the impassive figures behind him, "wish to say something." He left off helplessly.

The older man stepped forward, clasped his hands behind his back and smiled easily at the serious faces looking back. His colleague remained by the door, impassive.

"I am sorry to disturb you," he began urbanely. "This will only take a few moments I am sure. I am Detective Inspector Beck from the Zürich police. I am investigating a crime which occurred here in Unteriberg late last night. We need to speak to everyone who was in the vicinity of the church any time between three and four this morning. My team is asking everyone this question so please do not feel you are suspected of anything." He smiled ingratiatingly. "But it is vital we gather information."

He paused. There was a buzz of talk around the room, much shrugging and shaking of heads. Someone asked, "What sort of crime?" Beck, expecting the question, ignored it.

"My colleague and I will be in the Adler Lounge next to reception for the rest of the morning. If anyone did see or hear anything at that time in that area please let us know." He turned and strode out through the doorway, his colleague following, but not before he had beckoned with a crooked finger at Herr Brucke.

The room once more burst into excited chatter. At the far side of the dining-room, three people left their table and crossed over to join Tom, Ruth, and the Bryons. Dot, Kath, and Geoffrey had been sipping late coffees like everyone else. Tom and Ruth had given them a muted wave as they ate their breakfast, receiving sleepy smiles in return. Now they were reanimated, eyes sparkling.

"Hi, can we join you?" Dot asked, dragging spare chairs into the widening circle. "What's been going on? Did you see anything last night? Geoff's been out for a paper today—he says there's cops all over the place." She put her hand on his as she spoke.

"Yes," he said. "Police cars in the street, policemen knocking on doors. I've never seen anything like it. Unteriberg is usually so quiet."

"It's something serious," Tom said, "or they wouldn't be making all this fuss. Isn't there a bank near the church? Maybe someone broke in. Swiss banks are rolling in it, they say."

"Swiss-rolling," put in Kath with a giggle. "But Kristian says these days money is not so plentiful. He told us his company really struggled to get the finance together for Spirstock and there are rumours that the main investor is dodgy. You know who that is, don't you, Tom?"

"Yes. Kreiz. I haven't seen Kristian for some time—not since the accident to the surveyor. I thought everything had been on hold since then—I've been waiting for a call. When did you see him?"

"Last night," smiled Kath, looking smug. "He came over for the carnival. I'm surprised you didn't see us—although you were a bit preoccupied when I saw you." She gave him a roguish look.

As if their table had a magnetic field, Dot had just finished speaking when Olly, Sharon and Rudi came through the doors and were sucked towards them like iron-filings. Two minutes later they were followed by Alec. Not just chairs but tables had to be rearranged. Alec called through the kitchen doors for more coffee then faced the gathering, full of news.

"So, what's the story?" asked Tom.

Alec's boyish features were full of concern. This week had been a nightmare—a death, a disappearance, a serious accident, fights, complaints and now this. It was as if some malevolent force had been unleashed. Everyone's job was on the line. But all this came second to the horror of what he had been told.

"There'll be no skiing for a day or two," he said. "There's been a murder."

Rudi looked up. He had been chatting quietly to Caroline. "What?" he said.

"Someone was killed last night? Haven't you seen the police?"

Olly broke in. "No. We've been out of it since last night. Rudi crashed on our floor in the chalet and we came straight over here for a caffeine shot. I haven't got my eyes in focus yet."

"They found a body by the church last night. It's one of the skiers in the torchlight procession. I've been talking to the local ski-school. They've spoken to some of the display team who were brought in from outside. One of their group was late starting the run and when they eventually got down the mountain, he wasn't with them. They sent a search party back up the trail but he'd disappeared. He turned up dead in Unteriberg."

"How?"

"Broken neck. Throat cut. Very nasty."

Mrs Bryon shifted uneasily in her seat. "Perhaps we ought to go," she murmured to her husband, her eyes signalling towards Caroline. She half-rose, expecting her entourage to follow but Caroline smiled quietly, put her hand in Rudi's and said, "I'll stay, mum. You and dad go if you want."

Her mother looked confused. She began to sit down again but her husband took her by the elbow.

"Come along, Hilda," he said. "As we are not skiing today, I'll take you for lunch at the mountain restaurant." He smiled at the group. "We'll no doubt hear all the latest news tonight. See you for dinner at seven, Caroline, love. All right?" As he gently propelled his wife out of the room, he could be heard saying, "Now Hilda, I'm sure these young folk can get by without us."

Caroline felt both relieved and guilty. Each day shifted the ground in her relationship with her parents, a movement that left her feeling stronger yet less secure. She knew that her quiet bid for freedom hurt her mother more than her father. It was taking huge efforts of self-control by her mother to avoid an explosion of emotion. Her father's tact and surprising wisdom also filled her with contrition and affection. She would ask specially to go trail skiing with them tomorrow. Perhaps Rudi could come along. As she watched her parents go, she saw Shelley arrive, eager-eyed and bursting with news and self-importance. She came over to the table to hold court, a trump card about to be played. She had ingratiated herself into the local ski-school over the season and had made a string of conquests over the handsome young men doing their ski work between National Service and University. In spite of their glamour—the scarlet jackets, the new, state-of-the-art equipment, their brilliance on the slopes—they were often quiet, shy, family boys, out of their depths with someone like blonde, vivacious Shelly. She simply took them apart, much to the resentment of the two female instructors.

Shelley loved an audience. She flicked back her pale hair in a well-practised gesture and made the waiting faces wait further. Then she leaned forward dramatically and said, "I suppose you've heard about the murder. Well, I found the body."

She enjoyed the stares for a moment, then added, "Well, actually, it was Jürgen who discovered that it was a body. You know Jürgen—one of the Unteriberg ski instructors? We went to a night-club in Zürich after the carnival. When we got back at about five o'clock, we left his car parked up just by the monastery. There was this bloke lying on his back, spread-eagled in the fountain. There was no-one else about. I thought he was drunk but it was odd because he was in his ski gear. I said to Jürgen, "God, what a state!" and tried to stop him going over but he said he would freeze to death if we just left him. That's funny, now I think of it. So we went over." She paused. "I could see straight away he was dead. His eyes were open, his head bent back over the lip of the fountain—I mean, back further than it should be—and his throat was just a gaping hole. His ski-gear looked torn. Jürgen called the police. We've been at the police-station ever since. Alec, we're to tell the clients that there will be disruption to the ski programme today. The instructors are being questioned."

"Done it," said Alec.

"Did you see anyone?" asked Tom. "You know, before you saw the body?"

"Nope. Everywhere was deserted. Not a soul around. It must've been about five o'clock this morning. It was certainly after the parade and that finishes around four. The police are asking the same question but I think everyone was in bed by then."

Rudi, who had been looking agitated as Shelley came to the end of her story, turned and whispered to Olly and Sharon.

"Did you say about 4:30?" asked Olly.

"That's right."

"And the police want to talk to anyone who saw anything in the region of the church?"

"Apparently."

"Jeez!" Olly's breath whistled out.

"What? What's the matter?" Caroline asked.

"We were there at 4:30. Me, Shaz and Rudi. Our crowd had been to Marco's—he had a special late-night licence for after the carnival. We watched the procession. Then we three just went for a wander—a bit pissed, really. But we saw somebody."

"Who?" asked Tom.

"Someone in a costume. Big guy. Just a glimpse but we all saw him. We assumed just another late-nighter still wearing his costume, a bit boozed-up like us. He lurched off behind one of the outbuildings by the monastery."

"You'll have to tell the police," Ruth said urgently. "They're in the reception lounge now. Did you see him clearly?"

"Not really," said Sharon. "We weren't seeing anything very clearly, mind. But we thought he was in a sort of monster costume. You know, Frankenstein. It looked leathery anyway and the guy seemed to be moving in character—you know, a sort of staggering movement—which may have been the hooch, of course. But it looked like he was dragging something, didn't it? We thought it was a sledge."

There was silence.

Olly spoke. "The costume. It had stitches. That's what made us think of Frankenstein."

ICE

There was a crash behind them. Herr Brucke had been standing unnoticed with a tray of fresh coffee, listening to what was being said. The tray had slipped from his grasp. Shattered pottery and hot coffee exploded on the tiled floor. He ignored it and stared at Olly and Rudi fearfully. He looked ready to collapse. Tom stood, took his arm and pulled a chair under him into which he dropped, a dead weight, head bowed.

"So," he whispered. "it has been in the town."

"Are you all right, Herr Brucke?" Tom urged, aware that he wasn't but wanting him to focus. "You had a bit of a turn there, I think."

Ruth, who had been thoughtful since Olly mentioned the stitches, left for the kitchen, returning with a glass of water which she placed in front of the stricken hotelier. Tom tried to loosen his collar but his hand was weakly pushed away. He raised his head to look at Olly and Rudi but dropped it again. It was as if he was afraid to look.

Rudi pulled his chair next to Brucke and spoke quietly to him. Brucke shook his head repeatedly, muttering a reply.

Rudi turned to Caroline. "He's terrified. He fears the man in the costume. He says it is 'The Leatherman.'"

Dot whispered to Kath, "He's having a breakdown. I think it's overwork." Ruth overhearing, shook her head.

"I don't think so," she said.

Brucke looked at the faces watching him. "It is not a man," he said clearly.

Olly laughed abruptly but was stopped by the glare of Brucke's eyes.

"Oh, come on," he said. "I saw him. It was a big bloke in a monster costume. You saw him too, Shaz."

"Course it was," she said. "You sure you weren't at the schnapps last night, Mr Brucke? You haven't woken up yet, you're still dreaming. Go and make us another pot of coffee and have some yourself. That'll clear your head of ghoulies and ghosties and long-legged beasties…"

"And things that go bump in the night," concluded Olly.

Their smiles and chuckles infuriated the hotelier.

"Listen to me!" he hissed. "You people, you know nothing! Nothing! It is here. It is always here. We leave it alone. There are places we do not go. Places to be left alone. It keeps us safe. And now we have the warnings. The keeper is out. And killing."

"Have you heard of this, Rudi?" asked Ruth. "You're from Umteriberg."

"No, I am not born here. My family came here from Bern when I was six. But I hear of this "Ledermann" in school from local kids. Stories." He laughed dismissively, a towny pitying the simple locals.

Brucke gave him a dark stare. "They would tell you nothing. Outsider. The mountain must be left alone. Alone. It was made to guard it."

"What was?" asked Ruth.

"Der Ledermann. Made to watch and wait. Until disturbed. Folk die on Spirstock."

It hit Tom hard. He was trying to keep a common sense view of what Brucke was saying. The man was clearly unhinged, but his fantasy was disturbing. He thought of Anita. Ruth slipped her hand into his.

Geoffrey, who had listened like everyone else with incredulity, chipped in with his dry, solicitor's logic.

"The man last night, the skier. He didn't die on the mountain. He died in Unteriberg."

"No, he died on Spirstock," came Brucke's remorseless tones. "He was brought here. As a warning. It must be placated. My father knows these things."

Ruth thought of the shrunken figure in the wheelchair she had glimpsed in the corner of the kitchen. Face as frightened as his son's. There was also something niggling her about Brucke's account. It was that word, "made". Did he mean "made" as in "compelled" or "made" as in "constructed"? And how do you make a watcher?

"Have you told all this bollocks to the police?" asked Olly, bluntly.

Brucke looked at him contemptously. "They are from Zürich. They would not understand."

Ruth was thinking. Stitches. Her tattooed man in the notebook. Not tattoos. Stitches. A made man. Leathery.

"Olly," she said. "You said this costume was covered in marks like stitches?"

"Yes, a Frankenstein costume. You've seen the fancy-dress in the shops. There were plenty of witches and Draculas and skeletons out last night as well as Mickey Mouses and fairies. I can't believe the fuss you're all making."

"Was it something like this?" Ruth asked. She had been fishing in her bag and produced a file. In it was the sketch she had done of the engraving in the church.

Herr Brucke sucked in his breath sharply. Olly's face showed recognition. He passed the sketch to Sharon and Rudi.

"That's the fella," he said in surprise. "Where d'you get this?" He concentrated on bringing back to mind the shadowy shape they had glimpsed by the monastery. Now that he had the sketch he could see it was a simplified version of what was in his mind. It had been by the side of the church where an alley ran to the monastery buildings at the rear. And something struck him that had not registered before. There were tall windows in the church and the figure's head had been level with the tops. Which would make it about eight feet tall.

"It's scratched on a wall inside the church," Ruth said.

"It's also on a rock near the summit of Spirstock," added Tom. "Kristian Weller and myself have seen it."

"Well, that'll be it then, won't it. Somebody was using a bit of local folklore for their costume," Olly said complacently. "Quite imaginative, really."

"Perhaps," said Ruth.

"You'd better tell the police," said Alec. "Whatever you saw was certainly in the vicinity of a mutilated body. They'll want to know."

Olly, Sharon and Rudi stood up. "The reception lounge, yeah?" asked Olly. "Right. But I'm not mentioning any of this Ledermann crap," he added as a parting shot.

Herr Brucke seemed a little calmer when they had left. He spoke to the remaining group.

"You think I'm crazy." He touched his temples in the universal gesture. "But listen. For your own good, for the good of others, for the good of the town. I have known of this thing since a child. All local children are told of it as soon as they are old enough to understand. My father told me. We were to keep away from Spirstock. It is the place where this creature lives. In the past, groups of important villagers were given the task of ensuring it remained undisturbed. My father is the only survivor of this group. During the war years he was police chief and he was one of the chosen. Each year there was a special ceremony—I do not know what they did, he was sworn to secrecy, could not even tell his own son—which kept everything safe. If it is disturbed, there are deaths. The last time the Ledermann was seen was just before the war. Some archaeologists had discovered evidence of an ancient ritual site on Spirstock and were excavating. There are records in Zürich university of them sighting a large creature. They all died in an avalanche, as did thirty local people when the ice reached the edges of the town. Since then, Spirstock has been left alone. But people forget, the rituals die. They say it is all old-fashioned nonsense. Avalanches are controllable, there is money to be made. So, once more, Spirstock is violated and the deaths have begun again." He stopped, then resumed. "I tell you this so that you can halt the development. Herr Shepherd, you want to bring skiers to Spirstock. You must not. Tell your associates it is dangerous. More dangerous than you know." He stood up. "I go and help my father now. He is frail and this has upset him. I am sorry this has happened but you must believe what I tell you." He got to his feet and shuffled towards the kitchen.

Tom looked at Ruth. "What do you think?" he asked. "One thing is for sure. This is an unlucky mountain. I think this latest incident may well be the end of the Spirstock development anyway. Something doesn't seem to want us there. But a watcher? A bit far-fetched don't you think?"

Ruth was thoughtful. "It's not unknown," she said. "I've studied ancient rituals and there are instances of spirits being conjured to act as guardians of sacred sites. And mountain tops are favourite places—remote, near the Gods. There are

ICE

examples in the Andes, the Himalayas—why not the Alps? But I'm puzzled by what Brucke said about this 'made' figure. I think he meant it was constructed. Those marks that I thought of as tattoos. Olly said it—stitches. As if it was sewn together. All the other 'guardians' I have read about appear to have been conjured out of the spirit world. This seems too solid, too real. Too like Frankenstein's monster."

Shelley and Alec, who had been quietly conversing, now stood.

"We'll leave you to your detective work," Alec said. "We have to call at the other hotels to see the rest of our clients. Remember, no ski lessons today I'm afraid, but I've spoken to the company and they'll organize a free extra evening activity for you, as a compensation. Come on, Shell."

"I think we will take our leave, too," said Geoffrey. "It is all rather a shock, this dreadful business."

"But nothing we can do anything about," said Kath sensibly. "And nothing to do with us either," she concluded. "So let's go and find that café where Kristian said he'd be and have lunch. I'm starving." She linked her arms through Geoffrey's and Dot's and frog-marched them outside in a burst of normality that exorcised the dark images evoked by the night's events.

Tom called to Dot, "Ask Kristian to give me a call, would you?" and was given a thumbs-up as she disappeared through the door.

"Shelley seems to have taken it in her stride considering she actually saw the body," Ruth commented.

"She's a rep.," said Tom. "Tough as old ski-boots." What was it about Shelley that was niggling him? Something recent. Something Ruth had said. Something he'd seen. It came to him. He turned to Ruth. "You know you said this 'thing' was far too like Frankenstein's monster to be credible? What if it was the other way round? What if it was the monster who was like this creature?"

"What?"

"Shelley? Frankenstein? The writer. Mary Shelley. It was Shelley who reminded me. And there's something else. I've seen that name recently. It's in the church. In the visitor's book."

160

Ruth stared at him. "Are you saying that Mary Shelley visited Unteriberg?"

"Perhaps. When I first visited the church I signed the book then flicked back through the entries. I was looking for… well, it doesn't matter what, and I started looking through the older volumes. They go back about a hundred and fifty years. This place was probably a stop for those on the 'Grand Tour'. The name caught my eye—Mary Shelley—I forget the date—early 1800s, I think. I didn't register at the time why the name had caught my eye but now I know. Anita had been teaching the book and we had a dog-eared copy at home, covered in notes. I think the writer must've been here!"

"We can't know that," Ruth said slowly. "It's not an uncommon name. And even if she did visit here, so what?"

"Don't you see? Where did she get the idea from—a constructed man? Unless she heard of this local legend and used it in her book."

Caroline, who had been listening now broke in. "That's my exam text! I'm doing it now. And she did visit Europe—with her husband and some other writers. It said in the introduction that she wrote the story while she was on the continent—it was a kind of horror-story competition they created and hers was best. It was done as a bit of fun, really, but when she got back to England her husband persuaded her to expand the story and get it published. I've got a copy with me 'cause I'm supposed to be revising. It's in my room. I'll get it. Back in a sec. Come on, Rudi." She took his hand and pulled him out of the room.

"So, what do you think?"

Ruth shivered. "I don't know," she said. "I don't want to think too closely about it." She took Tom's hand. "I'm scared that your wife's disappearance, Brucke's brother-in-law and this skier are all connected in some way. And maybe my grandparents. I think Brucke is telling the truth as he sees it. There clearly is some remnant of a cult lingering here—it's why I came here to study. But Brucke has been brainwashed since childhood to believe this Ledermann story. Early influences go very deep."

Caroline and Rudi burst through the doors, Caroline flapping a tattered paperback.

"Found it! She wrote the first draft somewhere near Geneva in 1816."

"That's not very far from here. She could have visited," said Tom.

"You may be right," said Ruth. "Perhaps she did construct her monster from the local folk tale. But even so, we are still looking at a fiction. Even if there was originally some kind of creature made to guard the site, it's not a living entity as Brucke seems to believe. But the deaths and the accidents are real. And there is nearly always something else associated with these powerful sites of pagan worship. Sacrifice. Animal and human. Appeasing the angered spirits. The greater the anger, the bigger the sacrifice required. And you can be sure Brucke is not the only one who is familiar with all this stuff. I think there may be a psychopath on the loose."

❀ CHAPTER FOURTEEN ❀

Beck and his colleague stared at the deluded couple who had just expounded their bizarre theory. The inspector leant back in the comfortable armchair he had commandeered, his overcoat draped carefully over the arm. The younger policeman was on an upright chair, notepad on knee, scribbling down Ruth and Tom's imaginings. His face was impassive. He had not been in the job long but knew to expect some crazy stuff from the general public. It was his job to listen. They did have a murder to investigate and it was his first.

Not for the inspector, though. He brought the tips of his fingers together judicially and gazed at his informants. They seemed sensible people, not overly-imaginative or stupid. They had presented their thoughts hesitantly, fully aware how far-fetched they sounded. It was something to add to the first real lead they had, the sighting of someone in the area where the body was found at around the right time. He had talked at length with the three witnesses and officers were following his instructions to interview all suppliers of fancy-dress. The trouble was, on their own admissions, the young people had all been drinking steadily for most of the night. Beck believed they had seen someone but it was a large jump from a man in a costume to a psychotic murderer and ritual sacrifice. He would have dismissed the whole thing were it not for the manner of the death. He had seen many murder victims in his career but never one mutilated in this way. It was as if a wild animal had been at. He knew that the killing could have taken place on the mountain and the body brought to Unteriberg for some reason. Mountain police had been inspecting the dead man's route down Spirstock since first light but snowfall through the night had covered all.

"So, Fräulein Francis. You think that this murder has something to do with a cult based here in Unteriberg, a case of an 'old wives' tale' being taken seriously by some deranged person who does not like the ski development. He dresses in a costume and slaughters a visiting member of a ski display team. Oh, and it is also something to do with other deaths and disappearances going back years. That is what you are telling me, yes?"

Ruth sighed. "No, not really. I don't know. It's just that some of these things do seem to connect. We thought you ought to know, that's all."

"But no-one else has said anything to me about it, no-one locally."

"But they won't, will they?" Tom interrupted. "We told Herr Brucke to talk to you about it but he wouldn't. He knows he will not be believed. Actually, I don't think he would care whether you believed him or not. He just wants the mountain left alone."

"Perhaps you think he was the mad person in the costume?" Beck said with a smile. "I checked. He was serving drinks here all night to carnival-goers."

"No, I never thought for a moment of Herr Brucke as a suspect," said Ruth. "He was more horrified than us. But if you want to know about the cult you should speak to him. Or his father. According to Brucke, his father was specially chosen from the village to be responsible for maintaining the rituals. His father has been deeply affected by the discovery of the body."

Beck pursed his lips. Privately he thought the whole thing nonsense. This attractive young lady had filled her head with odds and ends of local lore, added it to her historical research and made a monster. On the other hand, they had come forward to help and he knew from past experience that you ignore information, however unlikely, at your peril. But he did not intend to spend any more of his own time on it. This bit of the investigation he would pass to his sergeant while he went to speak to the pathologist.

"Well. Thank you both for your concern. I shall leave Meier to follow up." He stood. "Be assured, we won't leave your 'stone unturned'." He spoke quietly to the sergeant as he left the room. "I shall send Brucke and the old man to you, Meier. Just clear this up quickly. I don't want distractions, OK?"

Gunther Meier was delighted. It might be a wild-goose chase but at least he was being put in charge of it. That was a kind of vote-of-confidence. He watched Beck usher the two English people out of the room, flicked over a new sheet on his notepad and clicked his pen. He tried various voices in order to find the authoritative one he desired. He still sounded unsure of himself. His career in the force had not been as meteoric as his mother had predicted but perhaps, if he made a good job of this, Beck might place a word in the right quarter. He waited nervously for the Bruckes to arrive.

An hour later he admitted defeat. The younger Brucke had refused to corroborate anything the two English people had said. He claimed he had no idea what they were talking about, that the woman had a vivid imagination and, because the man was a tourist manager, he probably only wanted publicity. Brucke seemed amused by their stories and claimed he found it hard to believe that the police should take them seriously. He denied speaking about cults or anything else. He sounded reasonable and sensible but Meier sensed he was lying. It was something you learned quickly in the police.

The other concern was the old man. It was obvious the moment he was wheeled in that he was incapable of answering questions. He sat shrunken in his chair, scrawny, liver-spotted hands nervously picking at the rug over his knees. As Meier spoke to the son, the father maintained a constant mumbling, an endless monotonous ramble, head nodding on its scraggy neck, watery eyes constantly on the move, checking around the room again and again. At first Meier tried to ignore the muttering, the wheezing and coughing, the champing jaws but his attention was caught by repeated words and phrases. He also gained the impression that whenever the old man's words began to be audible, the son spoke louder. It became clear to the young policeman that old Brucke was obsessed and frightened. He scribbled down what he could. Brucke wanted to get back to his kitchen and Meier saw no reason to keep them both any longer. He thanked them and let them go, the son manoeuvring the heavy wheelchair through the doors, all the while shushing his father's mutterings and whinings. When they had gone, Meier checked his notes and thought. Then he tucked his pad into his tunic, picked up his cap and made for the dining-room.

Tom and Ruth were at their table, thinking about what to do next. There was no-one else in the room. Brucke had hurriedly wheeled his father through to the sanctuary of the kitchen, favouring them with a dark look as he passed their table. Meier entered crisply, pulled out a chair and sat down, crossing one leg over the other. He studied the two English people carefully. They did not look like the usual inadequates who came up with this sort of stuff. Something was not right, he could feel it.

"I spoke to father and son—" he began, and paused.

"And?" prompted Tom.

"I do not understand. He says there is no secret group in Unteriberg, no beast, no Ledermann."

"But he—"

"And he has not spoken to you. He says."

Ruth and Tom eyed each other. Ruth nodded.

"I'm not surprised. Whatever is going on, real or only in his head, he sees as secret. He told us because he thinks Tom is helping to develop Spirstock and he saw my sketchbook."

"But you think we are making it up, don't you?" Tom said. "That's all right. I don't know what we think, anyway. It's bits and pieces. It's just that some things appear to fit together. Somehow. But I guess the police need more than that."

He stood up and reached to take Ruth's hand but Meier put a hand on his arm.

"Please, Mr Shepherd. Sit down again. I did not say I did not believe you but it is not a matter of belief. I need evidence. Tell me, Miss—" He checked his notes. "Francis. What were these drawings you mentioned?"

In reply, Ruth took out her file and showed the young officer.

"Olly—the student, and Sharon—and Rudi, too, they told us that the figure they saw, the one they told you about, looked like this. They said it was a fancy-dress costume but it looked like this. With the dotted lines." Ruth pointed.

The policeman grunted. "They also say it was dark, they were drunk, and what they saw was half-hidden."

Ruth shrugged.

"Where did you see this? To make the drawing?"

"Inside the church. Quite an obscure spot but there, nevertheless." Ruth wondered about the interest. She thought their input had been discounted.

"Could you show it to me, please?"

"Of course," said Ruth. "I don't know what it can tell you. Did Herr Brucke really deny any knowledge?"

"Oh, yes, clearly. But the old man said some odd things that I would like to follow up." He pulled out his notebook and scanned through the jottings. "When I asked Brucke about the figure by the church he said it must have been a drunk in costume. I did not hear clearly what the old man was mumbling about in the background but I heard the word 'Kapelle' a number of times and 'Brudergruppe'. Do you know what he meant?"

Ruth shook her head. "There is no chapel as far as I know. The 'Brotherhood' is probably this group that Brucke mentioned—those responsible for maintaining rituals. I suppose it was something like the Masons. Apparently his father is the last surviving member of it. I presume it died off as the older people passed away. Youngsters today would think it laughable."

"There was something else. He spat out something about 'Juden'. His son was trying to wheel him out but I thought he said, 'Give it more Jews.'"

Ruth went pale and looked at Tom, wide-eyed. Meier watched.

"You know what this means?"

"An old tragedy, I think," Ruth murmured. "I think we ought to go to the church now. There are answers there."

They collected coats and joined Meier in the foyer. They left the front door of the hotel and Tom looked up at the wrought-iron sign with its jolly figure in lederhosen and Alpine hat. He pointed to it and raised his eyebrows at Ruth. A mild rain was falling, turning the pavements to slush. Water trickled down the sign and hung in beads along the bottom before dropping steadily to the ground.

"Things change," Ruth whispered to Tom as she tucked her arm in his and they set off up the street towards the church, now looming mistily through the damp air, the afternoon clock chimes clogged and muffled. The snow on the fields was grey and pock-marked, paths beginning to show as muddy brown patches.

"Maybe it was best to close the lifts today, anyway," said Tom. "I wouldn't fancy skiing in this slush. Have you noticed how warm it is?"

Ruth nodded and pulled up her jacket collar. The mild, cloudy damp chilled her more than any clear, ice-cold day. She felt drawn to the church yet reluctant to enter. Her recent knowledge was announcing itself with alarm bells..

Meier led them into the gloomy interior, his energetic footsteps clicking on the marble floor and cutting through the hush. Incense swirls echoed the misty outside. Quiet figures knelt in prayer. Idling tourists glanced towards Meier's uniformed figure. He glanced around and approached a figure in brown who was replacing a candle next to an ornate reliquary. There was a brief, murmured conversation then he returned to Ruth and Tom, now standing in an obscure corner of the church. He stared over their shoulders at the wall where they were looking. The lines, worn and faded almost to nothing still had power. This scratched figure had a malevolence that made him shiver. It stared back.

"So this is it," he breathed.

"This is it," Ruth echoed. She felt the same disquiet as Meier. Tom was more intrigued than disturbed. It was identical to the figure on Spirstock—even down to the four-fingered right hand. It clearly was not casual graffiti. There was a connection.

He stretched out his hand and traced along the faded lines, the stone cold under his fingers.

Meier looked around. There were no annexes, no side-chapels, not even a niche in the blank walls.

"Well, there's nothing here," he said. "The Abbott is coming to speak to us. He might shed some light."

Tom and Ruth were expecting to see an elderly, solemn person who would fit their preconceptions of monastic life, so were rather taken aback by the sprightly young man who strode up to them, his sandalled feet slapping vigorously on the floor, robes flapping in the wind of his movement. He shook hands briskly with them all, black eyes sparkling with goodwill and intelligence.

"Good, afternoon, good afternoon," he said. "Welcome to the church. Brother Martin tells me you wish to speak to me. I assume it is about last night's dreadful occurrence. Please, come," he said, beckoning. "We will be more comfortable in my office, I think, and we will not disturb the congregation. Follow me, follow me. Cold, eh? But not as cold as it has been." He kept up a cheerful chatter as he led them along corridors and up stairs. "I think it is the föhn. You know this, hm?" He turned to the two English people. "It can arrive suddenly, this warm wind. Not so good for the skiing, of course. You ski, I see," he said, taking in their clothes. He sighed. "I only wish that our visitors would queue for our church services as eagerly as they queue for the ski-lifts." Then he smiled. "I am only joking, you know. People worship in many ways and loving the beauty of God's creation is one. Ah, here we are."

They arrived at an arched, oak door. The Abbott pushed it open and gestured them inside. If they were expecting a spartan cell they were disappointed. A modern office greeted them with filing cabinets, computer, desk and chair, central heating and fluorescent lighting. The Abbott noted their surprise as he invited them to sit.

"Medieval times were long ago, you know," he said with a smile. "Today's church has to be modern like everything else. I look after a large, complex organization so I use modern methods. People still think we use quill pens and copy every-thing by hand. So, how can I help you?"

Meier cleared his throat. "Well, er..." He stopped, unsure how to address an abbott. "Well, sir," he chose. "As you will have been told, the murder victim last night was discovered lying in the church fountain."

"Yes, yes. Dreadful business, dreadful. We had a police visit earlier. As you know we perform our offices throughout the night but there was no disturbance here. I told them that this morning."

"Yes, I'm sorry to disturb your routine again, sir, but some information has since emerged which I thought you might be able to help us with. It may have nothing to do with the crime but we must investigate all lines of inquiry. I am sure you understand."

"Of course, sergeant, of course."

"There have been rumours of a cult whose origin may be in this church. This lady has been helping us with some historical background."

"A cult, you say? What kind of cult?"

Ruth interrupted. "We don't know. We don't even know if what we have been told is true. I am working on a paper for Oxford University looking at the foundation of Christian churches on pagan sites. Which is why I'm here."

"Yes, well, that is well-known," the Abbott responded. "The early saints demonstrated the power of their new religion by constructing cells on pagan, sacred sites. St Bulov, here, you may know, lived by a sacred spring, the one that feeds our fountain. They may have been primitive but they were not stupid. Eclipse the local beliefs and you have your converts." He smiled. "Practical, too. Fresh, running water. But a cult? Do you mean now? Connected with last night?"

"We don't know," Meier said. "Our information is that there was a cult here, a violent cult. Now, if it is true, it has certainly not been active for half-a-century. But, as police, we come across people, confused people usually, sometimes mentally ill people, who latch on to these things to give meaning to their lives. Occasionally they use them as licence to commit crimes.

So we need to know more. It might help us create a picture of whoever committed last night's crime."

The Abbott listened intently and with concern then shook his head. "I think someone has been telling you tales, sergeant" he said. "I have heard nothing of this. I studied the history of this foundation when I was appointed here a year ago. We have an extensive library with manuscripts going back a thousand years and more. There is no mention of anything similar to what you are suggesting."

"It might have been kept secret," Tom said. "Even from the church. A parallel form of worship?"

The Abbott looked sceptical. "I cannot see how that could be. Someone in the church would know."

Ruth produced the drawing she had brought and slid it across the desk. "Do you know this?" she asked.

The Abbott raised his eyebrows. "I know where it is, if that is what you are asking. I have spent my life in churches. Graffiti like this occurs in most."

"Like this?" asked Tom, dubiously.

"Well, perhaps not exactly like this, but crude drawings, initials, dates. Odd symbols. They occur everywhere there is a surface to mark. Any monument that is visited will have graffiti. You must know this."

Meier nodded. "I'm sure you're right, sir. So, nothing in your studies about secret practices?"

"No, sergeant, nothing. This sort of gossip damages our reputation. We try to be a force for good in the modern world. Here, younger men are encouraged into the order, men in touch with the present. Dragging history around with us can be a burden. Our brothers are quite youthful compared with other foundations. Most of our older brethren asked to move when I was appointed and they saw the changes I proposed. We have to accept that their day is past."

Meier rose and shook the Abbott's hand. "Thank you," he said. "Rumours are always tricky but, as I said, they have to be followed up. We've taken enough of your time. Thank you once again."

Ruth and Tom stood. As they were ushered through the door, Tom turned to the Abbott. "You said most of the older members of the order have left. Does that mean some remain?" He turned to Ruth and Meier and murmured, "It might be interesting to talk to them. This guy hasn't been here all that long."

"There is only one member of the old order remaining," said the Abbott. "But I would rather he was not questioned. Gregor is elderly and frail. He was taken ill last night during Lauds. He is recovering in the infirmary."

"What kind of illness?" asked Meier.

"He had some kind of seizure. He is in his nineties so one has to expect frailty. He did remarkably well to make the night service. It wasn't required of him but he insisted." The Abbott smiled indulgently. "Brother Gregor is a stubborn man. He chose to stay here to battle against the changes I have put in place. We have had some mighty arguments. But we respect each other. He was calm when I visited him early this morning."

"I want a word with him, even so," Meier said. "I will try to disturb him as little as possible."

The Abbott looked unhappy but shrugged. "If you must," he said. "But please respect his age and infirmity. Follow me."

They set off again along the labyrinthine corridors which enveloped the church. Stopping by a door with a faded green cross stencilled in its centre the Abbott put his finger to his lips and gently pushed it open. The chamber revealed better fitted their expectations of a monastic dormitory. Wood beamed roof and whitewashed walls were unadorned except for a large crucifix. Arched windows projected shafts of grey light down to the floor. There were six metal-framed beds but only one was occupied, the one below the cross. A gowned figure seated by the bed sprang up as they entered and hurried towards the Abbott.

"I was about to send for you!" the monk said urgently. "I think he's had another attack."

"Has the doctor called?" asked the Abbott as he strode towards the figure tightly wrapped in crisp white bed-clothes.

Its skull-like head lolled restlessly from side to side on the pillow, sunken eyes glancing at the crucifix then away again. The Abbott sat by the bed and placed his hand on the feverish forehead.

"Gregor? Gregor? Can you hear me? It's Father Anthony. Now be calm, be calm." His voice was gentle and soothing, hypnotic in its tranquility. "That's right. Rest. Rest. There is nothing to fear, nothing at all. Be at peace, brother. At peace."

Slowly, the restless rolling of the head ceased, the shallow breathing deepened and steadied. Father Anthony gently wiped the hot brow. "Did the doctor call?" he asked. The attendant monk nodded.

"This morning, as soon as we could reach him. He gave Gregor some sedatives and he slept the morning through. I relieved Brother Francis only a few moments ago and he was fine. Awake but calm."

"So why the change?"

The monk looked anxious. "I was only talking to him, Father. He had been asleep when we had all the drama with the police, so he knew nothing of it. I thought he might want to know the news but when I told him what had happened he seemed to have another fit."

Gregor began to murmur again and move restlessly in his bed. His eyes flickered open and his glance searched the corners of the room. An emaciated hand emerged from the bedclothes and clutched the Abbott's arm and a faint, raspy voice importuned, "Hear my confession."

Father Anthony gently prised the fingers from his arm and held the trembling hand in his own. He studied compassionately the drawn face, sharp cheek-bones covered with grey stubble. The features were pinched and shrunk. Father Anthony had seen the approach of death many times and he read the signature clearly. He had known the elderly monk only briefly but had come to admire the strength of his simple faith. He saw that this wasted figure had been a robust man in his prime, strong and vital. He had come from peasant stock and would probably have been more at home tilling fields than praying in a cell. But he was devout and disciplined, inured to the rigours of monastic life although now, that energy and vigour was sapped away. Father Anthony looked up.

"Michael, call the doctor quickly. Officer, take your colleagues outside. I must hear this confession." The authoritative tone brooked no refusal. Just before they closed the door on the dying man and his confessor, they heard Gregor whisper, "It has begun again."

Brother Michael hurried towards the Abbott's office to reach the only telephone. Meier, Ruth and Tom stayed outside the infirmary door. It was not long before the monk returned with a portly gentleman in a dark suit carrying a case. Brother Michael knocked gently on the door, heard the Abbott's voice giving permission to enter and ushered the doctor through. Ten minutes later Father Anthony emerged, his face clouded in sadness.

"Gregor is dead. He was ready, at peace with himself and with God." He looked at Meier. "You want information, I know, but I cannot reveal the words of the confessional. But you were right, there are secrets in this church. The figure is the key." He sighed. "So many secrets. Christ meant us to live simply and full of love but that message has almost been lost. He would not recognize His own church. Sometimes I think we are still in the Dark Ages."

"Or earlier," put in Ruth.

"Indeed, or earlier," assented the Abbott. "If you wish to explore the wall where the figure is etched, you have my permission. Gregor wanted it. I must stay here for now and deal with matters of death. I will join you later in the church."

He went back into the infirmary and Ruth, Tom and Meier returned to the church. It was late afternoon. The mountain shadows were plunging the little town into a gloom which deepened by the minute. The church was empty of visitors. They went to face the wall.

It looked solid. The surface was darkened with years of candle and incense smoke. Tom beat his fist gently against the stone but there was no sense of hollowness.

"I wonder what the old monk said that made the Abbott take us seriously," Ruth whispered to Tom.

"It's strange," he replied, "but I recognized the old guy. I noticed him when I first visited. It's as if I knew we would meet again."

"He said something that disturbed the Abbott. What's Meier up to?" Ruth inquired.

He was studying the wall, laying his palms on the stone and feeling each block, working in wider and wider circles, running his finger-tips along the joints until he had covered an area as high as he could reach and down to the floor.

"Nothing," he said, undeterred. "This looks as solid as when it was built. Perhaps the Abbott misheard."

"I don't think so," said Tom. "He was confident. Are any stones misaligned?"

But there were none. The pattern was regular and unbroken. The only significant feature was the figure. Ruth stared at it.

"It has to be this," she said. "This is here for a purpose." She traced her fingers along the shallow grooves of its outline, around the head and down the arms. Tom watched her.

"It's the fingers," he said, quietly.

"What?"

"One five-fingered, the other four. The same detail on the figure on Spirstock. It's pointing."

Meier moved closer to the wall and traced a line extending from the extra digit. The he took a penknife from his tunic and began to scrape the joints between the stones which were on the line. At first his blade made no impact but then came a little trickle of sand.

"This is newer mortar," Meier muttered, suppressing his excitement. "Look."

Tom and Ruth peered closer. Where Meier was working looked no different to any other part of the wall except that his knife was prising loose little pieces of sand and mortar around one block, a block in direct line with the pointing finger. As he worked, the blade juddered against crystalline solidity, chipping and blunting, but gaps began to appear.

"We need better tools," he grunted as the little knife bent under pressure. "See what you can do with this while I find something stronger." He passed his penknife to Tom and went to find tools.

"How did we get involved in this?" Ruth whispered over Tom's shoulder as he continued scraping.

"Fate," said Tom, lightly, although he felt the weight of the word.

"Does this make you nervous?" she asked.

"A bit. You?"

"Yes. Excited, too. There is hidden history here."

"Damn!" hissed Tom as his fingers jarred. He withdrew the knife to find it had half a blade. "I can't go very deep," he said. "Less than the depth of this blade. It's odd. I would have thought these blocks were thicker than that. Good, here's Meier."

The policeman had a lump hammer and a cold chisel. "There are workshops by the outhouses," he explained. "You've made progress, I see," he said, smiling at the broken pen-knife. Tom returned it.

"I don't think this stone goes very deep," Tom said.

Meier set the chisel blade in the narrow gap and smacked it hard with the hammer. The stone grated in its setting. Crushed mortar fell to the floor. He wiggled the chisel out, replaced it in a new position and gave it another blow. The clank echoed around the church and the stone shifted again. Meier worked methodically until he could rock the loosened stone. When there was enough to grasp with the hands he worked it from side to side, slowly drawing it out from its setting. The shallow space it revealed showed more stonework but with one differ-ence. An iron ring. Meier looked at Ruth and Tom then grasped the cold metal and twisted. Nothing.

"Pull," suggested Ruth.

The handle moved outwards a fraction and there was a dim clunk.

"Something's happened," whispered Tom.

Meier heaved and they heard the pattering of fragments on the stone floor. Clearly revealed by the loose mortar was the shape of a door, the figure in its centre.

"This has been sealed, too," said Tom. "Give me the hammer and chisel."

He took the tools and quickly worked at the loose material. Chunks fell heavily and the hidden door could be seen clearly. He and Meier grasped the handle together and hauled. A section of wall slowly swung open, grating and grinding against the littered floor. They saw how the stone camouflaged the structure. Ruth thought of those doors covered by books in the libraries of stately homes. They peered into the blackness, breathing the stale, aged air.

"We need a light," said Ruth.

Meier produced a torch from his tunic and they ducked through the low opening into the chamber beyond.

Cold. Whitewashed walls and a low arched ceiling blackened with smoke. Placed centrally was a rectangular stone table on which was a carved, ivory casket banded with metal straps. Two pewter candlesticks were placed at either end. The dust of decades had silted everything to a soft outline. Meier flashed his torch around the room illuminating a soft bundle of rags in one corner and a niche in a wall barred by an iron grille. The dead air was oppressive. Meier's torchbeam had a dullish hue as if it gasped for oxygen. Ruth found breathing hard. There was evil here. This deadly space contained a reservoir of dark forces which she could feel. She put her hand to her forehead and felt the clammy chill of faintness. Her vision swam. Then she felt Tom's arms around her, his face full of love and concern.

"Are you all right?" he whispered.

Ruth's strength flooded back, her eyes cleared and the nausea which had been threatening to overwhelm her receded. Tom's simple compassion cut through the black activities of this place and shamed its secrets. She breathed freely again.

"Lack of air, I think. I'm fine." She squeezed his hand.

"This is a vile place," said Tom. "I think that whatever went on in here was not for all eyes. Meier can do the close inspection."

Meier was systematically searching the chamber, noting contents and positions. He crouched down to inspect the pile of material. When he lifted the top item dust motes danced in the torchlight. He was holding a ragged overcoat. Below, two more coats, also torn, one small, child-size. On the back of each was a dark mark. It was the original colour of the cloth contrasting against its faded surroundings in the shape of a five-pointed star. Meier showed them silently to Ruth and Tom.

"Star of David," breathed Ruth, and Meier nodded. He gently replaced the garments in their corner and turned his attention to the casket on the table. He blew at the dust which was covering the intricate carving in ivory. The table-top was patched with dark stains. He stared at it with professional interest before placing his hands gently on the arched lid of the box, opening it and peering in. Tom and Ruth heard him pause in his breathing, then he beckoned them to his side.

"What do you think?" he asked, shining his torch inside.

Two objects lay on a bed of black cloth. A crude knife, the blade short, the handle, bone, and a finger. The skin was like parchment, dry and stretched over traceable bones. The nail was a curved, black talon.

Ruth spoke first. "That's not real," she said.

Tom and Meier bent their heads to inspect more closely.

"It was made. It's not human. It's too big."

"And has five knuckles," murmured Tom.

Meier reached in and gingerly lifted out the grisly object. They could see that it had been created from a finger and thumb, the thumb crudely sewn on to create a large claw. On the underside were stitches where skin had been stretched around and sewn up. The talon, animal or bird, had been inserted. It had mummified. Meier offered it to Ruth for a closer look but she stepped back and shook her head.

"I've seen enough," she said.

Meier placed it back in its box and frowned. "Fräulein," he said. "Tell me again about the lederman."

Ruth bit her lip, her eyes drawn to the thing in the box. "I have tried to connect Brucke's story with my own research. Brucke claimed that the accidents and deaths on Spirstock are as a result of the work done there. Local legend says Spirstock protects the town and is not to be visited. There is a guardian, created to protect the mountain. If disturbed it exacts vengeance. Until recent times there was a practice of placating it. A brotherhood was formed to ensure peace for the town. It was active up to the Second World War. Brucke's father was one of the elect. I have researched into pre-Christian practices. Special places of power, often mountains, could have guardians conjured up to protect them. But the legend here says the guardian was made, not conjured. I thought at first I had misinterpreted. But if Mary Shelley visited Unteriberg before she wrote *Frankenstein* it adds to the possibility that a figure actually was constructed, basically humanoid but larger than life and more fierce. She probably heard of the legend here and borrowed it for her tale. I think what we're looking at is a piece of the ledermann but the question is, where is the rest? If this story is a powerful force in the town it is certain that others beside the Bruckes know of it. I think someone, obsessed by the legend and furious with the Spirstock development, has metamorphosed himself into the ledermann and has exacted punishment. Sacrifices placate an angry, supernatural power. The greater the sacrifice, the more effective. Officer Meier, my interest here is not just academic. I have a family connection with Unteriberg. My grandparents were Jewish refugees from Germany during the war. They crossed the Alps to Unteriberg with their two children. Apart from my mother, they all disappeared." She looked at the forlorn pile of clothes.

Meier was impressed by Ruth's seriousness. It seemed that this apparent dead-end was a passageway into a world of horror. But his hard-headed superior would only want to know the whereabouts of the figure seen last night. He took the knife from the box and turned it over in his fingers.

Tom meanwhile had halted by the aperture in the wall. He peered through the grille into a dark space beyond.

Ruth called. "What is it, Tom?"

"Can't really see. I need the torch."

Meier passed it over and Tom shone it inside. He recoiled, then looked back.

"What is it? What do you see?"

"Fingers. And these look real."

Meier joined him. Row upon row of shrivelled fingers, some with the flesh pulled away from the bone, blackened and dry with age. They lay in pitiful witness to the horrors of the chamber. The purpose of the knife was clear. The offerings looked to have had a long and bloody history.

"Here are your sacrifices," Meier said to Ruth.

Ruth looked and saw what she had dreaded. Three fingers at the front looked less aged than the others. One was small—a child's.

"It's the blood that is the power," she whispered. "They thought that by offering blood they could keep the power alive. But where are these people?"

"I think we know," said Tom. He held Ruth tightly. "Spirstock. Let's get out of this place." He led her out into the church and sat her down, holding her until she stopped shaking.

Meier followed. He was contemplating his next move when Father Anthony approached, face full of wonder at the open door.

"So it was there," he breathed.

Meier spoke briefly and urgently, then took him inside. When they emerged the Abbott was crossing himself fervently. Wonder had been replaced by horror.

"We will have to investigate further," Meier told him. "It may yet be a matter for the police. I must seal the area and call our forensic team. Keep the church closed. I will organize this immediately." He turned to Ruth and Tom, now all authority and decisiveness. "Come, we will go and speak with Inspector Beck. Herr Shepherd, help me close this door."

As it ground back into place, the air sighed as if glad to seal up its dark secrets. "Father Anthony, no-one must enter here until we have fully investigated. I suggest you station one of the brothers here to keep out the inquisitive. Do not speak to anyone about what is behind that door."

They left the young monk staring after them, thumbing his rosary beads as they headed for the clean air of the outside.

"So, Herr Shepherd," Meier said. "You think there are answers on the mountain?"

"I'm sure of it," Tom replied. "And I know where."

"We will speak to Inspector Beck. Nothing can be done about Spirstock until first-light. You will need to come with us."

It was black dark as they stood on the entrance steps. The cobbles gleamed in the lamplight. From everywhere came the sound of running water. It poured from the corners of roofs, chuckled down the gutters into drains, dripped from the fast-melting icicles in the fountain and fell softly from the night sky.

❋ CHAPTER FIFTEEN ❋

Abreeze made the red and white plastic tape flap. It cordoned off a section of mountainside, the word "Polizei" printed repeatedly along its length. Within it, a team of mountain police carefully removed items from the slush and mud and carefully placed them in plastic bags. The focus of operations was the upper station of Spirstock's new development and its black boulder. It was bitter in the wet wind although the dripping icicles on the girders told of a rise in temperature. The officers worked quickly, the risk of avalanche high. The ice spoke constantly in groans and crackles.

Tom had conducted them to this spot at first light. Beck had authorized Meier to lead the mountain team after he heard his report. The Inspector was not convinced that this historical stuff was connected to his murder but the English people clearly believed that something on Spirstock was a link. Herr Shepherd and Fräulein Francis had described their personal interests. Beck was thorough and as young Meier was blossoming with the responsibility, he was happy to see how far it would go. Meanwhile, another chat with Herr Brucke might produce a more flesh-and-blood suspect.

Tom took the team straight to the figure on the rock. Meier noted the missing finger, the dotted lines and its malevolent aura like its twin in the church. But here was a difference. The maimed hand was raised, pointing further up the hillside, and it was in that direction that they made the first discovery. A jumble of large rocks which had been hidden under ice and snow were exposed by the thaw and something yellow was showing. Meier and Tom scrambled up the semi-frozen debris. An arm protruded from the melting ice, an arm clad in a yellow ski-suit, a garment Tom knew well. He reached to remove the glove from the hand. Meier held out a restraining arm but Tom resolutely pushed it away, knelt, and eased off the glove. On the grey flesh of the third finger was the wedding ring he had chosen. His stony face broke. He pitched forward, the pain he had so grimly suppressed flooding his body in grief and release now that he saw this frozen shell that had waited for him for five years. Meier stayed at a respectful distance, keeping the other officers away. Ruth waited too, allowing Tom to pour away the poison of his loss. As he knelt, his forehead icily burning against the rock, he felt the wound begin to heal. He raised his head and Ruth rushed over to kneel by him, her arms around his shoulders. She pulled him to her and held his shuddering body to hers.

Meier stood over them. "Herr Shepherd," he said, gently, "I have to instruct my men to remove the body. Your wife?" Tom nodded. "You will have to make a formal identification later, you understand, but you need not stay here any longer. One of my men will take you down the mountain."

Tom glanced at the sad remnant waiting to be released from its icy tomb. "No," he said. "I want to stay. You must allow me that. I have a right. She was my wife." That was the first time he had thought of Anita in the past tense. She was gone. Here was the proof. Time to let go.

"Very well," said Meier. "Just allow my men to get on with what they have to do."

Ruth held on to Tom as the police approached the body. They had ice-picks, shovels, bags and a blow-heater capable of melting ice. They set to work systematically, carefully lifting loose debris and placing it to one side. Slowly, Anita was freed from the mountain's grip. Her body was well-preserved and appeared uninjured except for a neck wound. There would have to be a post-mortem but Meier's guess was a skiing accident, a broken neck and then some animal at the body before its interment under the ice. Gently, under the watchful eye of the forensic officer, Anita was lifted onto a plastic sheet and zipped into a body bag. The police conducted a close search around the body, picking up items and slipping them into evidence-bags. Meier watched with some satisfaction. He may not have solved a murder but a missing person's file could now be closed. He would be glad to get off this mountain. The mist was closing in, his finger-tips were numb and the roar from the blast-heater was giving him a headache.

"Sir!"

He looked to where a couple of his men were working a short distance away. They were beckoning.

"There's something else, sir."

Meier went over to inspect the new findings. The ice sheet was fragmenting. Cracks had appeared and there was dark cloth protruding. Meier called for the heater.

A hour later and there were three more bodies, two adults, one male, one female and a male child. This time there was more decomposition, the faces drawn, the shape of the skulls beneath the skin more noticeable. The clothes looked old-fashioned in style and material, the footwear rough leather boots. Like the Englishwoman, these people had throat wounds. Unlike her, their wounds looked to Meier more like cuts than tears. And there was something else which chilled Meier. They each had a missing finger. He left the team to bag the bodies and went to speak to Ruth and Tom who were sharing coffee from Ruth's flask.

"What's happening?" Tom asked. They had watched the flurry of activity and could see that something else was being removed from the ice.

"Fräulein," said Meier. "Tell me again what you found about your grandparents."

"I knew it," muttered Ruth to herself. She turned to Meier. "It's them, isn't it? You've found them, haven't you? This is where they died. And there's something else, isn't there? The fingers?"

Meier nodded.

"So it did continue," breathed Ruth.

"What, Fräulein?"

"I think you know, sergeant. You saw the chapel. This is where the final sacrifices happened. This is where the mountain is propitiated. The rock is an altar. I must see them."

She set off towards the row of black bags. Meier overtook her and reached his men first.

"This lady is to see the bodies," he said.

The bags were unzipped. The shrivelled figures were just ugly waste now, lips pulled back from teeth in a grimace, the wounded throats gaping. Ruth winced as she absorbed the truth of their dreadful demise. This was the fate her mother had escaped. This was why she was here today. So that her grandparents and her uncle would not disappear from history. Ruth felt her own roots dig fiercely into the past and it gave her strength and anger.

"Such cruelty," she thought. "Such barbaric ignorance." Her mind turned to Brucke and his blustering warnings and she was filled with loathing and contempt. History had taught her that no matter what advances there are in knowledge and ability, people will always be capable of breathtaking brutality when circumstances combine. Stupidity, ignorance, fear and barbarism had led to this mountain-top.

With a sense of déjà vu she felt Tom's arms around her. This was the only answer—love. They clung to each other like survivors in a storm.

"Sir!" came a voice.

Not again, thought Meier. "What?"

"Over here, sir!"

The heater had been clearing an area on the edge of the mountain's eternal glacier and the ice was giving up its secrets. This time the body clearly was extremely ancient. It had mummified over time, shrunk to the husk of a human being, blackened with age and frost. The head was bent back, hinged to the gaping throat but it was still recognizable for what it was as it emerged from its long entombment. Under it there was another.

"Turn off the heater! Now!" shouted Meier. The silence that descended was like a blow, to be succeeded by the sound of wind and trickling water. They had been on the mountain since dawn. Six hours in the cold on these unfriendly slopes. It looked like there was work for at least another six hours. Meier wanted to be off the mountain as did the rest. The succession of grisly finds was affecting even those used to dealing with violent death. Meier knew too that he was dealing now with ancient artefacts that needed expert handling by trained archaeologists, not by policemen.

Meier called a halt and addressed his team. "We stop for today, gentlemen. We need to get these body-bags down to base and to clear the site. Time is pressing and we will lose the light before long. These new finds will have to be excavated tomorrow by archaeological experts so for now I want you to cover these latest finds to protect them from animals and mark the site clearly in case of snowfall. And I would like a couple of volunteers to remain here to guard the site. We have alpine sleeping bags, a mountain tent, cooking gear, food and drink. There is shelter in the building site. Whoever stays will be on double pay."

He waited for a response. The men looked shiftily at each other, none liking the idea. The place was creepy enough, even in daylight. But they were professionals. There was a scattering of hands raised. Meier was about to select his men when Ruth stepped in front of him.

"I don't think this is a good idea," she murmured.

"Why not?"

"I don't know. I just feel it. I think they feel it, too. This is not a good place. I would get all your men off the mountain before dark."

Meier was unsure. He had felt the mountain's hostility but had a great reservoir of common sense.

"You think the ledermann will get them, do you?" he smiled.

Ruth smiled back, light-heartedness a relief after two days of gloom. Nevertheless she needed to persuade him.

"No, of course not. But I still feel there is danger here."

As if in confirmation there came a distant growl. Somewhere, insecure snow and ice had broken its grip and hurled itself down the mountain. It was enough for Meier.

"Right, men. Forget that. We're all going down tonight. Get this place tidied. Quick as you can."

Within the hour chairs were whining down on their cables packed with crates of equipment. There were also four large black bags. Meier took the last chair. As he dropped over the lip of the glacier he felt the back of his neck prickle and turned to look up. All he could see was swirling mist. He dismissed all thoughts of guardian creatures along with the other primitive detritus that lay in the deepest caverns of his mind. Above him, in its own deep cavern, a primitive mind was slowly stirring into life.

✱ CHAPTER SIXTEEN ✱

The post-mortems were brief. Anita's death was put down as misadventure. The records of five years earlier were re-examined but the outcome was the same—a skiing accident. The wounds to the throat were believed to be animal, as Meier had predicted. The elderly coroner, the same who conducted the first inquiry, hurried proceedings. He wanted the episode done with.

"As far as the three other bodies are concerned, the evidence of Fräulein Francis and Herr Schneider would appear to confirm that they are indeed those of a Jewish refugee family called Frank, Fräulein Francis's grandparents, in fact. The manner of their death suggests unlawful killing by person or persons unknown. The case will remain open but in view of the time that has elapsed, it seems unlikely that further evidence will be forthcoming. In this case, I record an open verdict. It is possible that the historical investigation into the ancient bodies also discovered at the site will shed some light. I authorize immediate release of the four most recent bodies for proper burial."

The Inspector had tried to glean more solid evidence but in his search for the Unteriberg killer it slid through his hands like melting ice. Meier reported the death of the old monk, Gregor, the last of the order who had been in Unteriberg during the war. The other, stronger link was Brucke and his father. As soon the bodies were brought off the mountain Beck had called at the Ledermann. All was confusion, an ambulance at the doors and Brucke silent and tearful. The old man had had a final stroke and was being taken away. Beck heard doors slamming shut on the past. Crime was turning into history.

A white-frocked priest intoned the sonorous Latin followed by a sable-clad rabbi in keening Yiddish. Their magpie look reflected the patchy snow freckling the black soil of Unteriberg's little cemetery, a tiny gated corner of Alpine meadow, uneven and rocky. The handful of mourners stood by the simple memorial stones as the caskets of ashes were reverently placed in the ground. Jakob, Sarah and Peter Frank were laid to rest alongside Anita Shepherd. Ruth helped Otto Schneider to his feet as he rose from placing the caskets with their eloquent five-pointed stars. Tom gently placed Anita's remains then returned to stand by her elderly father who had flown out from England the day before. They stood with bowed heads as snow gently began to soften the rawness of the memorials.

They had been granted a special dispensation for the service to be conducted for the two faiths simultaneously. Tom and Ruth wanted a symbol of reconciliation and hope. Although they had no religious beliefs themselves, Anita's family were devoutly Christian and her father wanted to see his daughter "decently buried" as he put it to Tom when he rang with the news. "Her mother would have wanted it too," he added. The fate of the Franks was so bound up with their faith that it seemed important it was properly celebrated in their funeral rites. At the same time, Tom and Ruth wanted the ritual to be a hope for the future. The appalling events of the past had, in time, brought about the meeting of two people who had found together the greatest power for good that we have.

Spirstock continued to disgorge its past. Research was to continue. Ten bodies emerged and many animal remains. It became apparent that they were from different eras, some reaching back to prehistoric times, others relatively recent. The archaeologists were tremendously excited by this telescope into the past where the ice had preserved clothing, flesh, and stomach contents as well as the evidence of fierce, sacrificial practices. The site was declared to be of major historical significance and hordes of academics from around the world descended on the little alpine town to pick the bones. Theories were put forward, papers written, reputations made and lost. A museum, dedicated solely to the Spirstock finds was set up in Unteriberg. The bodies were taken to the University of Zürich where they were carefully analysed, photographed, recorded and preserved. It was felt that public display was not appropriate. There was also a strong feeling that the site at Spirstock should remain undisturbed. When the ice returned it would be very difficult to continue to excavate. The archaeologists felt that they had extracted most of what was there, but wished to leave the area available to future historians who might have more advanced techniques at their disposal. All building work was halted.

Tom and Ruth sat in the departure lounge holding hands. They were the last of the winter tourists to leave, having stayed on for the investigations, post-mortems and burials. The hotel had been like a mausoleum for the final few weeks, the skiers gone and a hiatus before the summer visitors. Herr Brucke presided over it like a spectre, more morose than ever since his father's death. Ruth had witnessed Caroline's tearful farewells to Rudi, her promises to write, and her parents' tactful turning away as the youngsters indulged in a last kiss. She and Tom had been to dinner with Dot, Kath, Kristian and Geoffrey to say goodbye. They were not sure whether to go, neither being in the mood to be sociable but Kath had insisted with blunt, northern straightforwardness. It had turned out to be one of those nights that go on into the small hours because no-one wants to break it up. Kath and Dot's direct curiosity about Tom and Ruth had given them the opportunity to re-tell their stories, each recounting strengthening the bond between them. It had been a happy evening and, as wine progressed to liqueurs, it became clear that Kristian and Kath had spent more time together than anyone had been aware. Tom and Ruth slept late the next day and when they rose, the hotel was empty.

"Passengers for Flight BA45 to London, Heathrow now boarding at Gate 21," echoed the public address system, recalling to Tom the monks chanting in Unteriberg. He turned to Ruth, marvelling, as he constantly did, at the gift that had come his way, warm, glowing and filled with hope out of the depths of his hopelessness. The hollow space inside him was filled. He could let Anita go now and time would soften the edges of her tragedy. She could never disappear, her presence a bond, not a barrier, between him and Ruth. Ruth smiled at him as if she read his thoughts. She absorbed his love and her heart lurched at the mystery of it. It was the counterpoint to the quiet stillness that had enveloped her with the knowledge of her roots. Where it would take them, neither knew. They had not made plans. It was a measure of their relationship that they did not feel the need. They simply knew that their futures were entwined. They stood and kissed, an act, by now, familiar and yet still excitingly new. Then they walked hand in hand through the barrier and out into their lives.

❈ CHAPTER SEVENTEEN ❈

"These public meetings are always the same," thought Herr Kohl, chairman of Unteriberg's town council. "No-one listens to anyone else. Everyone has a personal agenda and they don't care about the bigger picture." He looked around the chamber. It was on the first floor of the old Rathaus. The walls were patched with paintings of Unteribergian worthies going back through time, bewhiskered, bemedalled and apparently befuddled judging by their expressions. "Which is probably the way I look," thought Kohl gloomily as another voice harangued the assembly with absolute certainty that its viewpoint was the only one worth considering.

The meeting had been called to consider the future of Spirstock in the light of the discovery of the sacrificial site. All interested parties had been invited and they now sat in the semi-circle of tiered benches and bleated at each other. Kohl had seen it happen before. No decision would be made, everyone would leave grumbling, and they would scowl at him as if it was all his fault. The leader of the local business organization was on his feet, a portly restaurateur wearing an expensively cut dark suit set off by a florid silk tie.

"Are you insane? Close the site? It's a goldmine. We can all benefit. Think of the number of people it has attracted already. And that is before it has been marketed properly. There will be countless sightseers wanting to view the most famous ancient site in the Alps. The infra-structure to get them there is already being built. They can be charged to view the site. That will enrich the town. They will stay in the hotels, eat in the restaurants, spend in the shops. It will help our summer season, and then people will see the ski-hotel and book for winter holidays too."

"I've already made enquiries about souvenirs," a voice belonging to a short, middle-aged man in an alpine jacket, cut in. "My shop always struggles in the summer season but now I've got postcards being designed with the little figure on them, ash-trays, pen-knives, key-rings with fingers, pens and pencils—"

There was a murmur of approval around him as he spoke. The commercial interests sat together for support, Marco Kreiz among them. But against this there came a rising grumble of voices across the chamber indicating incredulity and disagreement. A young woman clad in black stood quivering with indignation, her black look matching her outfit.

"Key-rings with fingers?" she shouted, appalled. "You have no idea what you have got here, have you? To you it's just an amusement from which to make money. I am Dr Stein from the Department of History and Anthropology of the University of Zürich. Overlooking your town you have not only a site of major, world-wide historic importance but a sacred site, too, one which requires treating with respect and dignity. Also, we do not know the full extent of the site. There is a likelihood of further finds. The terrain is difficult and dangerous. We cannot have tourists trampling all over the place. The university requests a complete halt to all development on Spirstock until a full, archaeological investigation is completed. This may take years. The site is impossible to work on for most of the winter months. After that, we recommend the area be protected from the elements and access allowed only to authorized people— academics who have a legitimate research reason to go there. It may be possible to have a few limited public openings in the summer months, carefully supervised. The museum in town is enough to cater for most people's curiosity. They can recreate the site in there as a full-scale model if they so wish. The site itself is not the place for gift shops and fast food. I would remind you all that people have died there over many thousands of years. It is not Disneyworld." She paused and let it sink in.

"Thank you, Dr Stein," Kohl offered, courteously. "We are pleased you could be with us today and grateful for your insight and knowledge on the historical aspect of the problem.

The commercial interests glowered. The sound of rustling banknotes which had filled their minds since the discovery, faded.

"Herr Riedler? Do you wish to say anything on behalf of the ski-school? I believe one of the reasons for the development of Spirstock was to expand the skiing area."

Dr Stein was vigorously shaking her head. She burst out, "You cannot have skiing there! This site is of world significance. It would be like... "(She paused to think.) "using the pyramids for skateboarding."

"Yes, thank you, doctor, we take your point," interrupted Kohl, "but I would still like to hear from Herr Riedler."

Franz Riedler stood up. His pale eyes in his wind-burned face looked as if they were focusing on far distances. It spoke eloquently of his mountain experience. He was not an Unteriberger but had been head of the ski-school long enough to have learned something of local feelings towards the mountain.

"If skiing were to go ahead," he said, "we would have to re-route all the runs and the access machinery to take account of the historical site. That would depend on the investors. It would be difficult and, I imagine, expensive. I also have doubts about the stability of the mountain. It is avalanche-prone. I am ultimately responsible for people skiing with our school. I think we should be very cautious about further development." He did not mention that his local instructors had already refused point-blank to work on Spirstock. "Personally, I agree with Dr Stein. I think the site should be protected and given limited access to those who can discover what there is to learn there."

The professor from Zürich looked surprised and gratified by this support from an unexpected quarter and smiled warmly at Franz. At which point Marco Kreiz stood up.

"Yes!" he said, angrily. "Shut it all down, that's right. Dismantle what's there. Chuck it all away. Easy for you to say. You lose nothing. But I have invested everything I have in Spirstock. No-one objected when I put my plans forward." He looked meaningfully at the town's business community seated all around him. "You all wanted a share of the wealth that would pour into Unteriberg once we could offer high-altitude skiing and had created a summer resort, too. Now, at the first sign of a problem, we abandon everything? The site may be prehistoric but we are not living in prehistoric times. We must progress or this town will die."

He glared at the presiding official as he sat down. Herr Kohl judiciously cleared his throat.

"Thank you, Herr Kreiz. We are well aware of how much this development is largely your inspiration and investment. However, I must inform this enquiry that, in the course of legal searches into the ownership of land on Spirstock following the discovery of the bodies, certain anomalies came to light regarding the planning application for the hotel and ski complex. There have been complaints in certain quarters that procedure was not properly followed. This is under investigation at present. In the light of this, I feel that unless anyone else wishes to add something at this juncture, we should suspend all work and allow time for enquiries to be completed. I also suggest that everyone with an interest in Spirstock, submits a written report presenting their concerns. These will be considered at a full council meeting to be held here in one month's time." He bundled his papers together. "The meeting is closed."

Marco chewed the ends of his moustache nervously. He had gone to his club after the meeting and was alone in its gloom. A third whiskey had not quieted the fears that were gnawing inside him. He had persuaded, cajoled, threatened and bribed his way towards his planning permission and now they were digging into this as well as into the mountain. He was overstretched and could not afford a new round of sweeteners (which would have to be substantial judging by the nervous looks of his friends on the council.) He drained his glass and reached for the bottle, his mind, like a rat in a maze, desperately seeking a way out. The project had to go ahead, otherwise he was bankrupt. It was miserable luck that the föhn had exhumed what should have remained buried for ever. The rain had been falling steadily all that day, slabs of loose snow thundering off rooftops into the streets. Icicles were breaking off gutters and dropping like javelins. As the whiskey softened the edges of Marco's reason, the germ of an idea began to stir.

He woke with his head on the bar, mouth parched and body aching in the stale air of the club. He recalled vaguely there had been a pounding on the locked door at some point and someone calling his name which he had ignored. It would have been his barman come to open the club. As he filled a tumbler of water, he remembered what he was going to do. He looked at his watch. Midnight. The right time for a dark and desperate deed. What should never have come to light would be re-buried. And he knew how to do it. Once the sacrificial site was back under tons of rock and ice it would be impossible to be reached again. They had removed all the visible finds, anyway, and further excavation might yield nothing. They would have to accept that the site was inaccessible for ever. And with that, there should be no reason for Marco's hotel not to go ahead. Avalanches happened. Only this one was going to get a little help.

He prepared carefully. Marco knew the risks he was taking but he had been among mountains all his life and was experienced and skilled. He packed a rucksack with all his usual survival kit—maps and compass, radio-beacon, first-aid, flashlight, flares, thermal sleeping bag—and added food, coffee and a flask of spirits. He strapped snow shovel, ice-axe and crampons to the outside. Then he dressed in his winter climbing gear. Tonight's work, apart from its climax, was to be done in silence. No sound of lifts to break the night's quiet. It must appear to have happened by nature. Faced with the prospect of hours of precipitous ice and snow, on foot, in the dark, he took a large swig from the whiskey bottle.

The potent fumes drove away the dullness of his afternoon's drinking and lit a fire inside him. He slipped out of the rear entrance of the club into a deserted alley, silent except for trickling water gurgling into drains and tapping on plastic refuse sacks. He was lucky. The sky was clearing and there would be a moon to guide his steps. The temperature was dropping once more. He headed for the monastery and the path across the fields which wound its way to the foot of Spirstock.

By the time he reached the construction site, the focus of his investment and ambition, the place which would make him rich, he was wearied to death. He had had four hours on Spirstock trudging upwards through heavy snow, scrambling among rocky gullies glistening with ice, startling chamois and roosting birds. Although he was sweating with effort, the cold had steadily increased and his eyebrows and moustache were crisply frosted. He leaned against the black rock, his centrepiece for the spectacular terrace which would be the most stunning mountain restaurant in the Alps. As his heartbeats calmed and his breathing steadied he looked around at his project bathed in greenish moonlight. It did not look like a building site in this light. The skeleton of girders, black against the snow, looked like a primitive temple. Or a large gibbet. Above was the ragged edge of the glacier, a scatter of rock, ice and rubble from where the bodies had emerged. There were poles, flags, trenches and spoil heaps. A hut had been constructed to allow field work to be done on site and as a place for finds to be temporarily housed. It would also give shelter to the workers in this inhospitable place. Marco stared up at it all. Such a little thing to stand in his way. He eyed the terrain judiciously. One small bang should do it.

Marco was not only an experienced mountain man. He was a trained soldier. He had done his National Service like all young Swiss men and he knew explosives. Where there were overhangs, steep valley sides and gullies, there would be unstable snow, and it was in these places around the building site that mortars had been placed and barriers built. When avalanches threatened they could be triggered, directed and dissipated under control. Marco had done this. He knew how it worked. All that was required was some repositioning.

It was heavy work for one man in the freezing darkness but Marco was in a frenzy. He took frequent pulls at his flask to keep out the cold and to numb awareness of the risks he was taking. Hauling the dead weight of a mortar to its new position and smashing the lock off the hut where the blank shells were stored, worked him into a froth of anger and energy. He growled imprecations against the town and its people, the visitors, the archaeologists and the mountain itself, almost losing sight of his purpose in the violence of his emotions.

He positioned the charge above the site of the dig where the reverberations would dislodge hanging snow, rock and ice from the glacier's edge. It should cascade over the site but miss the buildings. He stood with the remote contact in his gloved hands above the route of the fall and thought, "This will show them." He turned his head away, pulled his head-band closely over his ears and touched the button.

The sound was felt rather than heard, a solid crump which jarred his big frame, rattled his teeth and rang inside his head. There was a sense of something large shifting somewhere, great movements of something solid and he turned, expecting to see and hear a thunderous cascade of debris roaring across the site. But there was nothing. The markers, the poles, the trenches, the hut, they were still there. Nothing had moved. He worked his jaw, trying to clear his hearing. As the ringing faded it was replaced by distant echoes, then silence. Perhaps the charge had not been enough. He had been aware of the need for precision, not wanting to risk destroying the building work, but perhaps he had been too cautious. He would need a second charge.

It was when he approached the hut for another shell that he saw that something had, in fact, happened. The granite rock, his terrace centrepiece, was rent in two. The vibration from the explosion had split the stone. A huge fragment now lay in the snow. In the bouncing circles of his flashlight Marco could see that one of the shards contained the crudely carved face that had excited the archaeologists. What they had not seen, which no-one had seen for three thousand years, was the cave that had been concealed behind it and which now was admitting the beams of torchlight held in Marco's trembling hand. He was trembling because deep inside the cave he could see a figure encased in ice, like a corpse seen through water. So it was true. Marco had heard the stories and the theories, but, like most people, did not believe in the reality of a watcher of the mountain. Yet here it was, distorted and ghastly in its ice tomb where it had remained apparently undisturbed for eons. Marco knew that this was important. If the university people could see what he was seeing they would be in a frenzy. This must be unique. It was the Alps' own Tutankhamun. Who knew what else might be hidden in this cave? And with this thought came the realization that his own project was doomed. Even if nothing else was found at the dig, this pagan shrine—Marco guessed what it was—was historical gold-dust. He could say goodbye to all his plans.

Unless. Only he knew of this. He had set out tonight on a job of destruction. It only needed a little extension. Smash this thing then detonate another mortar and he could bury the lot. It was risky being so close to his buildings but insurance would cover him if he miscalculated. He decided to act before he thought too long about it.

His ice-axe bit into the frozen shroud with a thunk. Jagged splinters leapt out over his shoulders and stung his cheeks. He dragged his goggles over his eyes and chopped again, shards and chunks rattling to the floor of the cave. The translucence of the ice was now made opaque by the crunching and shattering and the shadowy outline was obscured. It made it easier for Marco for he had the atavistic feeling that, as he made his first swing, whatever the thing was, it was watching him. He closed his eyes and swung and swung again, piercing with the pick and chopping with the blade. He was waiting for the moment when the crisp sound of steel against ice was replaced by the softer thud of—well, whatever this thing was. But that moment never arrived. Instead, the point of his pick broke through the ice into a gap beyond and Marco realized that he was not breaking open a casing but smashing down a screen. He wrenched out his pick, peered through the gap and gasped. The thing was clearly a construct, a monster in the true sense of the word. Taller than Marco, it was a gruesome effigy, something that might be made to burn on a bonfire. It appeared to be an amalgam of human and animal body parts, made to look humanoid but bigger and fiercer. The leathery skin was skilfully stitched to create the huge limbs. Marco shone his torch through to illuminate the figure. He needed the fortification of his flask as he stared at the deathly face. It had the head a child might draw, quite round and with simple lines for features, two horizontal lines to represent closed eyes, a vertical line for the nose, another horizontal for the mouth. What a child would not have included, unless very disturbed, were the teeth that protruded from the mouth line. Animal teeth from a large carnivore. Fangs designed for tearing. Lots of them. He dragged his eyes away from the face and followed the arms down to the hands. Yellow claws completed the huge, black fingers, five on one, four on the other. The feet had black talons.

Marco stepped back, unscrewed the top of his flask and drained its contents. He needed all the help he could get if he were to dismember this thing, however old and dead it was. He placed his torch where the beam would illuminate the ice shield, hefted his ice pick once again and made to take aim. Then he stopped, frozen. A yellow eye, half-open, stared at him. Marco made an involuntary cry of surprise and shock and dropped the axe.

There was nothing else, just that one eye now half-open. Marco stood quite still, breathing deeply. He was many bad things—greedy, aggressive, corrupt,—but he also had a large share of natural courage and he was not to be made impotent by fear. He thought hard. Clearly the thing was made in more detail than it first appeared but there must be a reason for the alteration. As Marco considered it, he reasoned that the change must have been caused by himself. The thing had been sealed behind its ice curtain for thousands of years, he had now broken through and his own body heat was raising the temperature. It had been enough to unlock a frozen eyelid to reveal what looked like an animal eye underneath. He raised the axe and with four powerful blows destroyed the last of the ice wall to come face to face with the ledermann. It seemed to be winking sardonically at him. Were the teeth just a little more exposed? "Grin all you like," thought Marco. "You're about to be very smartly deconstructed into your separate bits and buried so deep you will not haunt anybody ever again." He giggled a little. "And we'll start with that sneering head, I think."

Marco's idea, if his muzzy thought could be called an idea, was to chop the head off first and put an end to the horrible feeling of being observed. But with the thing looming over him, he would not be able to swing his axe high enough to strike effectively. The creature would have to be brought low. He let his axe fall to the floor and pushed hard with his gloved hands against the leathery chest. He expected the feet to be frozen to the ground and so overestimated the power needed for the push. It fell easily. Marco almost fell on top of it as he pushed. He drew back sharply as the impact jarred open the second eye. And the jaw. Whoever had made this thing had paid attention to detail. This was no rudimentary suggestion of a being. This had all the workings. The gaping jaw had revealed teeth—a second fanged row. And a black tongue. Sweat broke out on Marco's brow. He took off his gloves and rubbed his face. He needed to finish it quickly before his nerve failed completely. He grabbed his axe, leaned over the fallen figure and eyed the spot where his first blow would fall. Whether it was his bare hands or whether his perspiration had frozen on the haft of the axe, as he swung upwards to deliver the decapitating blow, the handle slipped and the turning blade caught his forehead, gouging from eyebrow to crown. There was a pause as he registered the shock, then blood welled from the wound and dripped downwards, down into the waiting mouth below. The tongue moved first, slipping out between the fangs and back in again. Then before Marco could react, the arm that had lain quietly by its side whipped round Marco's hunched shoulders with the speed of a man-trap and pulled him downwards. Slowly, struggling wildly, Marco was drawn towards the waiting face as if he was being tenderly invited for a kiss. But the jaws gaped further like a snake's mouth. When it enclosed the whole of Marco's screaming face it shut suddenly with a soft crunch, efficiently removing the front of Marco's head. As his knees buckled, the clawed hand casually ripped off the remainder.

Spirstock had finished with Marco but had not yet vented the whole of its anger. Mountains are slow to move. They work on geological time. They will not be hurried. When Marco fired the charges he had been wrong in thinking nothing had happened. When the sacrificial rock had split, deep in the green heart of the glacier icy fissures had widened, frozen plates had slipped and cracked, slabs of rock had trembled in consort with the thunder of explosions, minute movements had begun which touched off other, larger movements which then heaved into massive shifts of the mountain itself. The floor of the ledermann's lair, black now with Marco's congealed blood, shook in anticipation. The creature waited impassively, ready for what was to come, its fierce heart prepared for thousands more years of waiting, guarding. Above, under the icy stars, the glacier split in two and the lower section slowly began its wild ride down the mountain. Like a giant ocean wave it engulfed all in its path, smashing, burying or sweeping it away. As it moved it gathered speed and size, adding to its bulk. Snowfields were ploughed up and propelled into the dark like breaking surf, trees were peeled off the mountainside, boulders picked up and flung like pebbles. All the while, the mountain raised its voice in a furious roar which began to be heard in the sleeping town below. Not content with flattening the impudent buildings on its flanks, the mountain hurled itself through the darkness like a vengeful fist. The little farmsteads on the lower slopes were the first to feel its anger, families hugging each other in terror before obliteration. The tiny buildings did nothing to slow the onslaught which hurtled onwards, its frontal crest a fifty foot moving wall of ice, snow, rock and debris. It smashed into the monastery at the top of Unteriberg, a thousand years of worship snuffed out in an instant, demolished and buried in one catastrophic blow. It slowed against the size of the building and the ground began to level out, but when it finally came to rest, the huge cloud of ice-crystals hung glittering over a town buried metres deep under its deadly onslaught. The air swirled and shook amid the mountain's fading growls, the moonlight sickly and ashen as it filtered down on the devastation. There were a few seconds of shocked silence before the screams began.

Like other places around the world where nature has exacted a terrible price for man's impudent trespassing, the name of Unteriberg would be forever associated with the worst avalanche disaster ever to occur in the Alps. People's voices would drop in memory of the appalling death-toll, the devastation, the horror. Unteriberg, like Pompeii, became the name for a tragedy, not a place. All else about it died on that night. A married couple in England would think about it often for the rest of their lives. And a dark figure resting deep under the ice and snow of the Spirstock glacier, waited.

Lightning Source UK Ltd.
Milton Keynes UK
UKOW03f1510180517

301502UK00001B/22/P

9 781782 011996